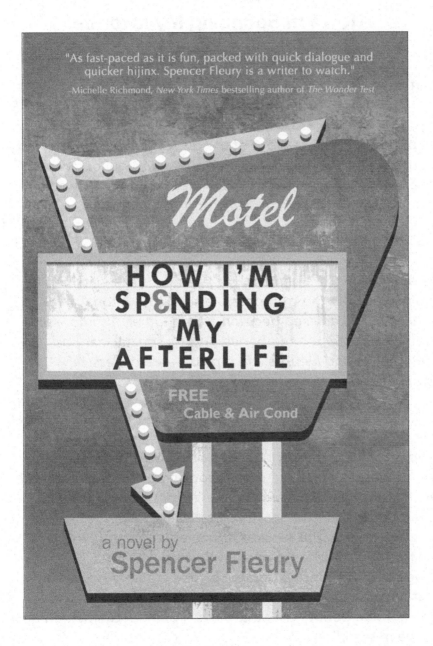

"As fast-paced as it is fun, packed with quick dialogue and quicker hijinx. Spencer Fleury is a writer to watch."

—Michelle Richmond, *New York Times* bestselling author of *The Wonder Test*

Motel

HOW I'M SPENDING MY AFTERLIFE

FREE
Cable & Air Cond

a novel by
Spencer Fleury

Woodhall Press
Norwalk, CT

Advance Praise for
How I'm Spending My Afterlife

"A breakneck dissection of truth, lies, and all the troubles in between."

—Stephanie Hayes, author of OBITCHUARY

"Spencer Fleury busts out of the gate in a frenzy with a dark, comic debut that will have you ripping through pages much like he wrote them: in a maniac's glee. You won't be able to put it down until the final, satisfying conclusion."

—Eryk Pruitt, author of
DIRTBAGS and WHAT WE RECKON

Reading How I'm Spending My Afterlife is like watching a train wreck—in the best possible sense. As Alton Carver makes one ill-advised decision after another, it's impossible not to keep turning the pages. Alton's spectacular bad judgment—and Fleury's sharp prose—are obsessively compelling.

—Janis Cooke Newman, author
of A MASTER PLAN FOR RESCUE

"Spencer Fleury's How I'm Spending My Afterlife starts out of the gate at an all-out sprint, hooking us by the end of the first paragraph and luring us relentlessly forward with his sharp, propulsive prose. His deft pacing raises the stakes and ratchets up the tension with every twist and turn, and his knack for balancing poignant reflection with dark, side-splitting humor is undeniably top-notch. Add to that an authentic, engaging narrative voice, and what you have is memorable debut novel that's a hell of a good time and not to be missed."

—William R. Soldan,
author of IN JUST THE RIGHT LIGHT

How I'm Spending My Afterlife

SPENCER FLEURY

Woodhall Press
Norwalk, CT

woodhall press

Woodhall Press, 81 Old Saugatuck Road, Norwalk, CT 06855
WoodhallPress.com

Cover design: Luke Murphy
Author photo: Ken Eldridge
Layout artist: Wendy Bowes

Library of Congress Cataloging-in-Publication Data available

ISBN 978-1-949116-93-9 (paper: alk paper)
ISBN 978-1-949116-94-6 (electronic)

First Edition

Distributed by Independent Publishers Group
(800) 888-4741

Printed in the United States of America

For my parents, who taught me to love books so much that I had to write them myself.

ONE

Alton

Beach Drive has always had the smoothest pavement in the city, because that's where the money lives. I remember how the steering wheel trembled in my hands that afternoon as I drove along the edge of North Shore Park, and I made a mental note to check the tire pressure in the morning. But then it occurred to me that in three or four hours I would be dead, and the Porsche would become someone else's problem.

I nudged the gas pedal, and the Boxster's engine responded, as if it had been anticipating the weight of my foot all along. I slipped past slower-moving Jaguar S-Types and Lexus SUVs piloted by retired hedge fund managers and solitary platinum-blond soccer moms. The late-afternoon sun hung in the sky, two or three hand widths above the horizon, winking through the gaps between the condo towers as I drove past. I couldn't beat the light at Twelfth Avenue, so I drummed my fingers on the steering wheel while I waited for green and tried to pretend I didn't notice the cars I'd just passed had already crept up to join me at the intersection.

Fuck it. Slow and steady might win the race, but it's certainly no way to live.

That day was cold for March. My hands felt raw on the steering wheel. It was probably somewhere in the forties that day, colder than usual for a March afternoon, and I hadn't thought to bring my gloves that morning. I probably could have blunted the chill a little by putting the top up, but I never did that unless it was raining. Driving a convertible with the top up seems pointless to me.

The cold worried me. The weather could scuttle everything I'd been planning for the last few weeks. There wasn't any room left on the calendar to push this back. All my arrangements were in place. All the external forces beyond my control were coming together in a vortex that would upend everything soon, possibly a matter of days. Maybe less. If I didn't go that day, I might not get another chance. How could I be sure that those gray-suited, humorless sons of bitches wouldn't show up at nine o'clock the next morning? Hell, they could be at the office right now, at this very moment, overturning filing cabinets and confiscating computers and bullying my staff. Could I be sure they weren't?

No. I couldn't. So it had to be that day, chill or no chill. Then the light turned green, and as usual I was first off the line.

It took a little less than fifteen minutes to make the drive from my office to the Eighth Avenue Marina. I rolled through the gap in the long chain-link fence and heard my front bumper bounce and scrape along the tricky little dip in the pavement, the one I always forgot about, right next to the tiny wooden guard shack, streaked in peeling blue and white paint. There was no guard that day. I don't know why I even bothered to look. In all the years I had kept my boat at Eighth Avenue, I'd never seen anyone in that shack.

There were only three or four other cars in the lot that day, typical for a weekday. That marina's been just barely hanging on for years now. The only reason I used it was the location. It was just a few minutes away from both the office and my house, so whenever I felt the urge to be on the water, I could drop whatever I was doing and be half a mile offshore in less than thirty minutes. I was surprised the place was still open at all, because every couple of years the Beach Drive Residents Association tries to convince the city council to shut it down. So far, the marina's won every time, but I've always thought the residents have a pretty good case. That marina is about as out of place as it could possibly be.

The Porsche glided through the lot almost on its own, past the small cluster of cars until the closest one was about ten spaces away. I parked across two spaces, at about a thirty-degree angle. I started parking that way after I had to spend twelve hundred dollars to get a tiny scuff mark buffed out of the side panel a couple years back. Body shops see you roll up in a Porsche and they will squeeze you for whatever they think you're good for. In my experience, people usually want to kidney-punch anyone who parks like I do, but there's plenty of parking anywhere you go in Florida, so it's not like I was ever really putting anyone out. I went around to the trunk, which was empty except for a couple of bottles of Scotch that I picked up at the ABC on the way over. I'd never heard of the brand before—I wasn't even sure I could pronounce it, to be honest—but it was expensive, and I knew nobody would believe I'd waste my last hour or two on Earth with the cheap stuff. Those are the details that sell the story.

I squinted and looked northward, toward the marina's squat, mango-colored office building. Its jalousie windows probably dated back to the 1950s and were coated with a thin film of dried sea salt residue and precipitate from marine diesel engine exhaust. With the glare of the setting sun reflecting from them, I couldn't tell if anyone was watching me from inside. I waited for a minute or two and then grabbed one of the bottles. The cork-bottomed cap twisted off easily, and I sat down on the pavement, leaning against the rear bumper with my legs splayed out in front of me.

I looked out past the empty slips, toward the open water, where it was nothing but whitecaps. From what I could tell, the largest swells were maybe two feet, which meant it would probably be worse offshore. That was both a good thing and a bad thing. Bad because it meant I'd have to work harder—maybe a lot harder—to make it back; good because it was another detail that would help sell the story. I closed my eyes and massaged the bridge of my nose for about thirty seconds. When I opened my eyes again I was looking at my wedding ring.

I took a swig from the bottle and instantly regretted it. The Scotch tasted like perfume and caramel and dirt, and it scorched my esophagus on the way down. I wondered why I hadn't just bought vodka instead, but then I remembered that I didn't actually have to drink any of it. It was just a prop.

Other than the handful of parked cars in the lot, there wasn't a hint of another person at that marina; still, I couldn't shake the feeling that someone was watching me. I did my best to look relaxed as I stood up and scanned the parking lot. A few scattered weeds poked through cracks in the pavement and bowed with each gust of wind. Nothing else moved.

I took a deep breath and tried to look casual as I strolled over to the nearest empty slip, where I dumped the bottle into the oil-slicked water below. Then I went back to the car, opened the other bottle, and let some of it glug out onto the pavement. I splashed the rest of the bottle's contents onto the passenger seat and into the foot well, and then tossed the bottles in after it. I hated to do it. But it was all part of the rich tapestry of bull-shit I was trying to weave together.

The quicker I left, the less chance someone would see me. I knew that. But I lingered, just for a moment or two, brushing my fingers on the door panel, back and forth. I'd wanted a Porsche since I was nine, and the day I bought it—a Thursday, with light rain in the morning that cleared up by lunchtime and a flawless afternoon for a top-down cruise up the beach—was one of the three or four happiest days of my life. I know how that sounds, but it's the truth. Yes, it was unreliable, and yes, it was an impractical way to get around, and yes, it had been the focal point of jokes, amateur psychoanalysis, and—occa-sionally—simmering resentment from Nicole. But none of that mattered, or at least, it mattered less than the fact that the car made me feel like the man I'd always thought I was supposed to

4

feel like, a man who was somehow above the world he floated through, always on his way to more important places. And now I was about to let it go.

Again, I know how that sounds, to talk about a car like that. It's just a car. I know that. But all I can say is that either you understand what I'm talking about or you don't, and if you don't, I feel sorry for you.

I stood there for a couple minutes, the key fob clenched in my fist, squeezing it hard enough to turn my fingers white, as if I was trying to turn it into a diamond. I slid the keys into my pocket, pushed the trunk lid down until I heard a quiet click, and then turned away from my baby for the last time and headed off toward my slip, number 34.

The dock leading out to my slip was tricky in spots. Once I tripped over a warped piece of decking. The planks were all split and weathered, sometimes with gaps an inch wide between them. They all should have been replaced years ago. I almost fell in the water, and even though I hadn't really been hurt, I threatened to sue the marina anyway. One of the advantages of people knowing you're a lawyer is that a threat like that packs a little more weight. The marina's facilities manager, this befuddled little man with a brushy mustache covering his entire mouth, nodded his head and promised to pour more money into facilities maintenance, but only if I agreed not to file suit. Which was fine with me, because suing them would have been more trouble than it was worth, and I don't do personal injury work anyway. I leave that to the correspondence-school lawyers. Anyway, they started by yanking out the offending plank and replacing it with a fresh one, nice and flat and sturdy. As it turned out, that's also where they stopped; in the two years since, nothing else had been fixed, not so much as a loose nail. They never even bothered to paint the new plank.

My boat was a twenty-six-foot Island Runner, yellow hulled and glorious, and that afternoon it bobbed in time with the slow three-quarter beat of the harbor chop. I hopped aboard, timing the waves so that I didn't even have to break my stride when my feet hit the deck. I couldn't quite shake the feeling that I'd forgotten something, but the backpack, kayak, and paddle were still lying along the starboard side of the console, right where I had left them the night before, so I just fired up the engines. They chuckled at me for a few seconds before settling into a nice throaty purr. I cast off the lines and dropped the props into the water, and then I was off, blasting into the open sea, the raw, elemental power of the machine surging up through my hands, the chill wind blasting into my cheeks. I smiled, knowing it was the smile of a free man, or of a damned one.

I'd been going full-bore for about half an hour before I figured I was far enough out, maybe five miles or so. At that distance nobody on shore would be able to get a good look at what I was doing, but it wasn't so far that I'd be unable to make it back without exhausting myself in the process. I cut the engines and sat down on the bench, looking west, into the setting sun. There was still too much light. Then I realized that I had no idea what time sunset actually was that day. I'd completely forgotten to look it up. From the color of the sky, I figured it was at least another twenty minutes off.

To pass the time, I tried to busy my mind, to fill my thoughts with the procedures and timetables and logistics of . . . well, whatever all of this was. Was it insurance fraud? From a legal standpoint, certainly, but that wasn't the point. The fraud was just incidental. I wasn't doing this for the money. This was what I had to do as a man, as a real man who loved his wife and daughter more than he loved himself, or anything else for that matter. The money was just . . . well, all right, I will concede that it would all be impossible without the money. I needed it if I was to have any chance at all of sparing them from the indignity and humiliation that—

—and then just like that, I was exactly where I didn't want to be. Thinking of Nicole and Clara, whom, assuming everything went the way it was supposed to, I would never see again.

I rested my forehead in my hand and rubbed my temples. My family was all that had ever mattered to me. More than career, more than material things. This is something you will have to understand if the rest of this story is going to make any sense to you. I missed them so much already, with this deep and insistent ache in the pit of my chest that I knew would only get worse. I had meant to snap one last picture of Clara this morning before she left for school—maybe at breakfast, that would have probably been the time—but I had forgotten. Well, not so much forgotten as run out of time. Just as well, really. My phone could never show up on land, could never be dialed, could never be switched on again. Disappearing meant disappearing, and something as simple and inconsequential as that phone could give everything away: the plan, the money, all of it. So instead I flipped through the photos I'd memorized long ago—Clara in the car seat, clutching her prized stuffed walrus and grinning in that innocent and slightly maniacal way only a small child can pull off; Clara sprawled on the orange-and-white polka-dot carpet of the children's section at the library, surrounded by stacks of picture books; Clara with her face buried in a piece of birthday cake (she refused to use a fork because it was her birthday and she didn't want to, simple as that) while Nicole hovered in the background with this mortified expression on her face, trying to pretend it didn't bother her—until I couldn't, just couldn't anymore. I snapped to my feet and heaved that phone into the wind with everything I had. It climbed, flipping end over end, and I was pretty impressed with the arc I'd gotten until a fresh gust of wind took hold of it, and then the phone dropped from the sky like a wounded pheasant.

By then the sun was almost gone. My escape kayak was wide and stubby, only about twelve feet or so and not built to stand up to the rigors of ocean use. The week before I had managed to fit an eighteen-footer in the boat, but I hadn't been able to get it to lie flat along the deck, where it would have been out of sight of anyone who happened to walk past slip 34. (As an aside, it's surprisingly difficult to return a kayak to a certain big-box sporting goods store that I won't name here, even if it's never touched the water. So consider yourself warned.) If I'd had the ocean kayak, I probably could have gone another couple miles without any problem. But I didn't, so five miles it was.

The waiting, the thinking, the goddamn pictures—it was all ratcheting up the tension, all of it increasing the pressure in my mind, giving power to my doubts. Blood coursed through my head with a rhythmic thrumming; I could actually hear my own pulse. Wasn't that a sign of an impending stroke? I thought I'd heard something like that once. In any case, I didn't think it could be a sign of anything good. Then, finally, the sun retired below the horizon, and it was time. I stuffed my jacket into the waterproof backpack, an all-black, heavily padded nylon thing I'd picked up at REI. Then I peeled off my shirt—a soft cotton olive-colored Oxford, a Father's Day gift from Clara—khakis, and shoes and crammed them inside, on top of the jacket. From the backpack's front pouch I removed a pair of water socks and neoprene gloves—both black—to match the sleek wetsuit I had been wearing under my clothes since I left the office, and I put them on.

I crouched to fasten the paddle to the kayak and then pitched it all over the side, steadying it with the boat hook to keep it close aboard. I tightened the straps on my backpack so it didn't slide, tugged down the sleeves of my wetsuit, and took a few quick, deep breaths. I was ready, or at least as ready as I was ever going to get.

TWO

Alton

Even with that overpriced wetsuit, I was freezing. The Gulf of Mexico was an ice bath. The cold air scratched my lungs. I was gulping down mouthfuls of it as I dragged that paddle through seawater that felt as thick as treacle, trying to force that kayak shoreward. But I was flailing already, and any forward progress I made was through sheer stubbornness alone. I kept trying to gain the entire five miles with each stroke, to put this entire ordeal behind me with a single thrust. But after maybe ten minutes or so, my arms were overstretched elastic, flaccid, and spent.

I was just about ready to start panicking—I know, panicking after only ten minutes, pathetic—when this feeling of deep calm just radiated outward from my core. Technique. That's what I needed to focus on, and I knew that because every single one of the kayaking how-to videos I'd watched on YouTube emphasized the importance of proper paddling technique. Especially in rough conditions like these. And proper paddling technique has just three steps: catch, rotate, and recover. It really is that simple. Do that and you'll maximize the power of each stroke while minimizing the effort required to make it. So I forced myself to throttle down on my panic, to slow my arms and unwind my torso with each stroke, to just dip the blade of the paddle instead of plunging the whole thing into the water. Before long I felt like I was—for the first time since ditching the Island Runner—in control of this overmatched piece of molded plastic. Even if I wasn't making much headway.

I was lucky to have made it off the Island Runner at all. But you can plan and plan for a thing like that and still not anticipate every potential breakdown. For one thing, there's nowhere to hide from the flames on a boat that small. I had known that perfectly well before I started the fire. But when I got to the rail, the kayak wasn't quite so close aboard anymore—it had drifted a few feet off, and now I wasn't sure I'd be able to make it in a simple leap like I had expected. It was still in range of the boat hook, but I'd left that on the other side of the boat, and I'd have to cross through the fire to get it.

So I gauged the distance to the kayak again. It looked far, impossibly far, much too far to jump. But then again, I was several feet higher than the kayak, so maybe I'd get a few extra feet out of the height difference alone. I wasn't sure I could make it, but it looked like I probably could. Barely. Maybe.

But by then it didn't matter, because the flames had spread more quickly than I'd expected, and now the only way back to shore was on that kayak. There wasn't a choice anymore. I climbed up onto the gunwale, took a deep breath, and sprung forward, reaching out with both arms and sort of kicking my right leg out in front of me as far as I could—

—and at that exact moment, a quiet little roller of a wave emerged from under the boat and bumped the kayak a little farther out.

Shit.

My arms came down hard across the kayak's stern, and my legs splashed down and dragged through the ocean behind me.

I'm in the water. Shit shit shit shit shit.

I reached forward, looking for purchase on the seat or the paddle or anything that would let me hold on to this empty plastic shell and keep it from sliding out from under me like a watermelon seed squeezed between thumb and forefinger. Then the backpack's left strap loosened, not enough to slide off completely but definitely enough to throw my balance out of whack. Just when I thought I was about to slip off the hull, my fingers finally found the cockpit coaming.

Got you, you bastard! I actually thought that. Like the kayak could read my mind.

At that point, the trick was going to be getting out of the water and into the kayak without capsizing it. I swung my left leg out of the water, trying to stretch far enough to reach the cockpit with my foot. Once I found it, I hooked my foot under the forward deck and, using that as leverage, somehow managed to roll myself on top of the kayak and slide into the seat.

I was in. I was in. Oh man.

My heart hammered away against my sternum. Thudududududup. Christ, that was close. But I couldn't dwell on that, not if I wanted to be sure I'd have the confidence to actually paddle through all this shit for five miles. So I tried not to think about anything as I unhooked the paddle from its thick rubber strap. My arms trembled the entire time.

It was finally dark now, really dark, the kind of dark that a man wearing a black wetsuit can get good and lost in. I could see lights in the distance, on shore somewhere, maybe from a low-rent beachfront motel parking lot, or some nondescript beach bar where a potbellied bald guy warbled an endless loop of Jimmy Buffett songs for tourists too drunk to know any better. Those lights looked impossibly far off. But my compass told me that's where I was going, so I hunched forward and dug into the water, pushing forward.

That was a strange night, weather-wise. I don't think I've ever seen the seas so confused. At some point over the previous couple hours, the wind had changed direction and was now blowing offshore, right into my face, giving me this ridiculous headwind to fight through. But the current felt like it was inbound. Waves bulged from the surface but didn't go anywhere, cresting and dissolving in exactly the same spot.

How do you paddle through that?

Eventually I settled on the tactic of just plowing through any wave that popped up in my path. After all, a straight line is the shortest distance between two points, right? This approach worked for the smaller waves, more or less, but I just couldn't muscle past the larger breakers. Every time

I tried, they just swept my kayak up and shoved it back a yard, maybe two. Like I said, that boat wasn't built for ocean service.

After a few minutes of that, it was obvious. This wasn't working. I'd never make it this way. So instead of going over or through the waves, I decided to just go around them. Any time I saw a wave forming, I dug that paddle into the sea and turned as sharply as I could. I was making almost as much sideways progress as I was going forward, but at least I wasn't going backward anymore.

That headwind was absolutely brutal, just a complete monster. It pushed back against my paddle blades whenever I lifted them out of the water. I cursed myself for not getting one of the paddles with the wind-resistant feathered blades. But there was no point in dwelling on that, then or now. All I could do was keep digging in, dragging myself toward shore, one foot at a time.

Which is exactly what I did. Catch, rotate, recover. Catch, rotate, recover. Again. And again. And again, for what seemed like hours but might have been just ten minutes for all I knew. But it was no good. I was starting to tire again, and while maintaining good paddling form did help keep my fatigue in check, the exhaustion I already felt made that good form much more difficult to keep in the first place. I was flagging. Come on, I told myself. Come on. Push. One more stroke. One more stroke. One. More. Stroke. Get there. Then my arms went limp—I can't explain it, I'd never felt anything like it before—and I just hung on to the paddle for balance. I couldn't do anything more with it. I was done. I knew I'd never make it. I fought to keep my eyes open, but they were just so heavy . . .

And then the kayak moved in a way I wasn't expecting, a motion that churned my stomach, skidding forward and spinning sideways at the same time. An inch of seawater, maybe more, sloshed around inside the cockpit. Had there been a wave? Had I passed out? For how long? I snapped awake, dropped one end of the paddle into the water. I had no idea how much water I'd taken on, but I could already feel a difference in stability. I couldn't even tell if I was going in the right direction—I couldn't find my compass, so I looked for the moon but I couldn't find that either. The stars told me nothing. All I could do was paddle, keep the kayak upright, fight through the confusion, the disorientation, the fog of fatigue—

—and suddenly there was a crack followed by a loud scraping sound, and I was jolted backward. The edge of the seat back dug into my lower spine. The kayak was no longer moving. I was at a dead stop, and the whole world seemed to be bathed in a sickly orange light. I looked behind me and saw that I was hard up against a concrete seawall. Behind it was what looked like some kind of forgotten graveyard for boats. The orange tint was coming from the sodium lights illuminating the property, and it gave the landscape of rusted trailers and scattered boat husks a surreal glow. The whole place looked radioactive.

I couldn't believe it. If I was where I thought I was, I had made landfall almost exactly where I'd originally planned to. I was two, maybe three, hundred yards off.

How the hell did that happen? But I didn't care, not really. Dry land. That's what I cared about. At that moment, that was all I cared about. Spent as I was, I somehow found the upper-body strength to hoist myself out of the cockpit and onto the seawall. I wanted nothing more than to just lie there for a while and let my arms re-inflate. But I was way too exposed out there. So I put every last bit of energy I could muster into pulling the kayak up after me. Then I staggered off toward the shadows, leaving the kayak between a pair of forgotten derelict day cruisers.

THREE
Nicole

Before we start, I think you should know that I am not the sort of person who opens up easily. This whole thing feels unnatural to me. So, yeah. Just putting that out there.

As bad as it is to hear the words that your husband is missing, as bad as you would imagine that to be—and it was bad, I mean of course it was, I'm not saying you'd think it wasn't—it honestly isn't the worst part. It's pretty bad, I guess. But I think I actually found that part to be kind of manageable, really. I think what I did was, I decided right away to treat it like just another piece of bad news, like finding out my car had been stolen or something.

It also wasn't the clueless teenage police officer, just a baby really, who broke the news—Um, we found your husband's boat on fire off Pass-a-Grille Beach this evening, but he wasn't on it and his car is in the Eighth Avenue Marina parking lot, but he's not in it and it's after midnight so, um, he wouldn't happen to be here, would he?—while standing on my front steps and holding a cup of coffee in his hand. A cup of coffee. Really. I know. He even took a sip while I was saying something, and he was obviously thinking about something else entirely. I wonder if he even realized he was doing it.

No, the worst part came later, once the police had gone. They left without answering any of my questions, but because of how they deflected everything, I really didn't notice that until much later. They left me sitting there on the very edge of the couch, all alone, to digest and process the life-changing information they'd stopped by to deliver. Like it was a pizza or something. They just dropped it all in my lap and left me alone with a four-year-old girl asleep upstairs, a girl who, when she woke up in a few hours, was going to want to know where her daddy was.

That's the worst part of it. Wondering how you'll tell your daughter.

I was all alone. Really alone. I mean, I'd been alone before, but this was different. This one time when I was eight or nine, my family took a vacation to Michigan's Upper Peninsula, and I got lost in the woods one afternoon. My dad found me about three hours later, which might not sound like much but is actually a long time to be wandering around the woods by yourself at that age. That was a terrifying experience. What I felt that night—early morning, really—was more of a trapped-on-an-ice-floe kind of alone, I think, like I was drifting off into the unknown, all by myself, and I couldn't do a damn thing about it. I don't know. Maybe that doesn't make any sense.

I knew I wouldn't get any sleep or answers right then. It was three twenty-six in the morning, and I kept thinking I should start making phone calls. But I was hesitant about calling everyone to break the news that my husband was missing. Is that even done?

Well of course it is. Don't be ridiculous.

But it was the middle of the night. I had literally no idea what the accepted etiquette was for that. Should I just start waking people up?

Yes. If I'm up, they can be too. It was time to make a list. Making lists is my most effective coping mechanism. I love lists. I've got notebooks full of nothing but lists that I've made over the years. Sometimes I will even make lists of the lists I've got going at any given moment. It kind of embarrasses me to admit that out loud. It sounds way OCD. And maybe it is, I don't know. It seems like it would be pretty common, though. I'm sure in your work you've talked to plenty of other people who do the same thing, probably as a way to bring order to the chaos of their lives or something. At least that's why I do it, I think.

I grabbed the Sharpie from the side table and an old ATM receipt that I was using as a bookmark in a novel I'd been reading for the last month; it wasn't really my thing, but I never have been able to abandon a book halfway through unless it's really horrible. Across the top I printed out "People to Call" as carefully as I could. I underlined it twice, because the title of the list should be set off from the body of the list. Then I underlined it a third time for emphasis.

So. List started. All right. Now who should I call?

Parents. That one seemed obvious. Let's start with parents. So I wrote it down and then thought, Aha, but whose parents—mine or his? Well, if I'm being honest with myself about it, I meant my parents. So I thought I'd better add his too. I printed out "Gail & Bob" next, just so I knew whose parents should be called in which order. Then I added "Alton" in parentheses, in case I forgot whose parents they were.

Oh, for the love of Christ.

Clearly, the list wasn't helping. Maybe it was too soon. I don't know. I could already feel things spinning out of control, all these thoughts in my mind running away from me almost before I could even understand what they were. It was all slipping away from me, and I had to be strong for Clara. Had to. She was going to need me so much. So I stood up, folded my arms, and picked a spot along the baseboards where I could focus my eyes. Deep breath. Another. You can do this. Be calm. Focus.

Missing. Missing. What a horrible word, the bland everyday-ness of it. How could that be right, missing? What the hell would he have been doing, taking the boat out on a cold and windy afternoon? And the Scotch—he didn't even drink Scotch. Did he? No. Why would there be two empty bottles of Scotch in the car? Could he even drink that much? Did someone else put those in there? Did they have something to do with this? Was he dead? Was he hurt? Goddamn it, where the hell was he?

I was walking laps around the couch without realizing I was doing it. My arms were still folded tight across my chest.

Work. I should probably call his office. So I picked up the receipt again and wrote it on the list: "Office (Alton)." Better add mine too; I had a lot of projects going on just then, but they'd have to get by without me for a day or two. Oh, and also Pineview School, not because I planned on keeping Clara home but because I wanted to make sure they knew what was going on, just in case. Clara would need structure; school would help with that. So I wrote "Pineview School (Clara)" at the bottom of the list. I guess I added her name in case I forgot which family member went to Pineview. So ridiculous. Then I crumpled the receipt and threw it to the floor as hard as I could, which was incredibly unsatisfying because you really want whatever you throw in a situation like that to have a little more heft to it. It just frustrated me more. So I flung the Sharpie down the hall and into the dining room, where I heard it skitter across the hardwood floor and ricochet off a stick of furniture. "Goddamn it." I said it out loud, to nobody, and that was when I felt my breath hitch, for just a second, but that was enough. With my very next breath I was sobbing, a quaking mass of uselessness, in a heap on the floor, leaning against the couch, face buried in my hands. To this day I'm so thankful there were no mirrors in that living room.

And then, the strangest thing. For a minute or so, I cried harder than I've ever cried, before or since. The sounds that were coming out of me—well, I can't imagine it was a good look for me. Let's just leave it at that. I don't think I had ever felt that exact combination of emotions before: angry, scared, cheated. There was some other stuff mixed in there too. It was probably the most intense feeling of helplessness I have ever experienced.

And then it just . . . stopped. I can't really explain it. I cried for less than two minutes and then it just switched off, as suddenly as it had started. It was almost as if I had somehow forgotten why I was crying in the first place.

17

Of course, I hadn't forgotten. It hadn't even been two minutes. But I couldn't feel it anymore. The emotion behind the expression just burned itself out. It all seemed less real for a moment, like it was happening to someone else.

Who am I really crying for?

What if . . . what if he was dead? What if all this was real, I mean really real? What if he actually had been on the boat that night and it caught fire and he fell overboard without a life vest because, of course, a man's man like Alton could never wear a life vest—and then he was just . . . gone? Would that really be so bad?

Of course it would. Of course. It would be horrible.

But you know, maybe not.

Maybe . . . maybe it really wouldn't be so bad after all.

There would be insurance. There had to be. Anyone who earned as much as Alton did—earned, he'd been missing for less than six hours and I was already thinking of him in the past tense; I know, I'm an awful person—would have to have insurance. I knew my paycheck alone wouldn't keep Clara and me in the house, but we had money saved, investments, because there was no way he could possibly have spent everything he made. Clara was safe. I had Clara. And I had—

I stopped myself right there. That wasn't good karma, thinking these things so soon after learning he was missing. First things first. Take care of Clara, which was going to involve telling a four-year-old girl that her daddy's never coming back. I know that technically he was only missing, not dead, but "probably never coming back" didn't sound any gentler to me. She loved Alton. She worshipped him. They had such a bond, those two, which I always found a little surprising because his work schedule didn't always leave much time for anyone else. This was going to crush her, and I really didn't want to have to be the one to deliver the blow.

I heard a noise on the stairs, and then I saw Clara, sitting there, watching me.

FOUR

Alton

I could feel the salt drying on my face, tightening my skin as I sat perfectly still at the foot of my bed. My wetsuit, peeled off and tossed aside, soaked a widening patch of low-pile maroon carpet in front of the closet door. Almost without thinking about it, I curled my toes upward from the floor. I wanted to minimize contact between my bare skin and the residue of dried bodily fluids and human desperation that were surely ground into that carpet.

It wasn't the kind of place I'd usually stay, a seedy hotel like that. The Royal Rest. That was the name of it. It seemed . . . optimistic. Aspirational. Delusional. I couldn't picture any kind of royalty staying there unless they'd just been overthrown, and it didn't feel especially restful either. A patina of anxiety and restlessness coated everything in it. The people who stayed in hotels like this one were more likely to need a place to shoot up or turn tricks than grab a good night's sleep. I was used to better. But it was by the water, it was out of the way, and it was cheap. More important than that, no one would think of looking for me there.

My attention was focused on an image on my TV screen, an image shot from high above, an image of a boat on fire in the middle of the ocean. Not just any boat, but a twenty-six-foot, yellow-hulled Island Runner. My boat. I made the eleven o'clock news. How about that. The segment started with a wide aerial shot. You could see a pair of Coast Guard boats circling at a distance, like they were afraid the thing might explode. That might explain why they seemed to have decided to just let the fire burn itself out instead of trying to extinguish it. There were no fire hoses, no grand arcs of water dousing the flames. I have to admit, I was disappointed. I guess I'd been hoping for a bit more spectacle. Now a close-up of one of the Coast Guard boats. A kid in a dark blue uniform and bright orange vest, kneeling on the bow and peering into the darkness. From behind him, a narrow spotlight swept the waters ahead. Now back to the wide shot. Another spotlight, most likely from the news helicopter, wobbled around the boat, sometimes sliding just far enough to one side that the boat itself winked out of view for maybe half a second. But you could see the flames the whole time.

And then it was over, just like that. Tonight's scores and tomorrow's temperatures are coming up right after these messages so don't go away.

That's it? That's all I get?

Evidently so.

But I wanted to see it again. I wanted to watch that burning boat over and over again on an endless loop, like O. J.'s white Bronco rolling across the LA freeways. I changed the channel, flipping through all the local stations and then back down the list again. Nobody else was showing it. Maybe they already had and had since moved on. Or maybe the news directors didn't think an abandoned boat on fire was as newsworthy as I did.

I was already exhausted—I had just kayaked five miles or so in the sloppiest seas I'd ever been in before, so I think I had a good excuse—and now I was just getting irritated. I knew I couldn't keep that up indefinitely, surfing from channel to channel, searching for news footage of my boat on fire and getting more and more annoyed by not finding it. So instead I turned off the TV, collapsed backward onto the bed, and fell asleep immediately. When I woke up, my feet were still touching that stained and threadbare carpet.

One morning, about three weeks before that first night at the Royal Rest, I had driven up to Highpoint, a faceless, anonymous suburb about ten miles from my house.

I picked Highpoint because I had never lived there, had never worked there, didn't drink there, and had no friends who lived there. I had no direct connection to the place whatsoever.

That day I stopped at the first Bank of America branch I found, which was just off Memorial Highway. I went inside and leased a safe deposit box, paying three years' worth of rent in advance. I'd been expecting some questions about that, so I had prepared this explanation about how I traveled internationally a lot and didn't want to accidentally miss any payments. I even rehearsed saying it in the car before I went in, so it would come out smoothly and casually. But nobody asked any questions. They just took my money. They were only too happy to do so, in fact.

Once I was alone with the box, I opened my leather satchel, the one my mother bought for me as a law school graduation gift—it's in perfect shape now, all beaten and cracked and worn—and started taking out wrapped stacks of hundred-dollar bills. I counted them out, three or four at a time, and when I was done I had thirty-three stacks wedged into that box. I remember because I wrote it down. Keeping accurate financial records is essential in situations like this. I ended up visiting four other banks that day, in four other forgettable suburbs you'd have no reason to know the first thing about, repeating the process until I'd stashed away a good chunk of the cash I'd been carrying around. All told, I left almost one and a half million dollars in those boxes that day.

You've probably figured out that the money was for Clara and Nicole to live on once I was gone. Not right away, though. That would look too suspicious. The plan was that I would send Nicole the keys in a couple of years, once the heat died down and everyone had forgotten all about me. I'd send a typewritten set of instructions on where to go, what to say, how much should be in each box. All the pertinents. I wouldn't sign it, of course. But she'd know it was from me. She'd recognize my writing style. And maybe she'd use the postmark to track me down, all the way to Costa Rica, and she'd bring Clara and the money down with her and we'd be reunited as a happy family, just like before. Only richer this time. A lot richer. Especially if Nicole still had some of the three million dollars she'd get from the insurance payout. I mean, I expected all this would be in two, maybe three years, so that didn't seem unreasonable to me. And even if none of that happened, I'd be just fine. I took care of myself too. I held back some of the money in that satchel. A little more than half, which would be more than enough to last me the rest of my life, as long as I spent it in Central America.

I barely slept at all that first night at the Royal Rest. I was worried about the money. I couldn't stop thinking about it. Just knowing it was there made it impossible to relax. I'd shoved the satchel toward the back of the closet, which was definitely not much of a hiding place. But the room didn't offer me any other options. I had just assumed I would hide it in the ductwork, like in this movie I saw once. But I will admit that I didn't exactly do my due diligence when I checked in. And what I mean by that is, I didn't actually go inside the room and look at it. I picked up the key, signed the guest register, and paid for a week in advance, but I didn't bother to look at the damn room. I just got back in the car and drove off. I would fire any assistant who made a mistake like that, so I have no one to blame but myself. In my defense, I was in a hurry, and making sure my hideout was secured and paid for was just one more checkbox on my to-do list for that day. But still. That's just an excuse, and excuses are for the weak and incompetent. It wasn't until I came back the next day that I saw the living conditions I'd be enjoying for the next week or so. That's also when I discovered that there was no ventilation ductwork;

the room had only a window-mounted air conditioner, with these dark streaks of mold spattered across the gray plastic vents. Naturally, there was no safe in the closet either—the Royal Rest was not the kind of place that would have a safe, which also never occurred to me, because what kind of hotel wouldn't have a safe?—so all I could really think to do was to shove the satchel as far back in the closet as I could get it. I leaned the ironing board on top of a garbage bag full of clean clothes in front of it, as camouflage. It was not a secure arrangement at all, even though I knew that nobody else knew I was there or what was in the satchel or that I even had a satchel in the first place. But my mind just couldn't stop picking at it. What if someone saw it when I checked in? What if the desk clerk has a habit of going through people's rooms when they're not around? What if someone breaks in? What if I'm being watched right now? Sunlight pounded against the flimsy white plastic window blinds in the morning; the whole room was bright enough to wake me up after just a couple hours of sleep. I rubbed my eyes and stood up too quickly; the room spun for a moment before snapping back into place. I had to remind myself: Nobody is watching me. Nobody knows I'm here. Nobody has any reason to even suspect that I'm here. Get ahold of yourself. Everyone is looking in the wrong place. If they're even looking at all.

Was anyone actually looking for me? At that point, I had no way of knowing. My head was pounding; if I don't have at least one cup of coffee by ten o'clock, I get these brutal caffeine withdrawal headaches. I desperately wanted to go get a coffee, but I didn't want to do that without knowing what the situation was. So I sat back down on the edge of the bed and switched on the television, poking at the remote until I found Bay News 9, the twenty-four-hour local news channel. One of the idiots running for governor had made a speech at the microprocessor plant on the north side of town. One of the local colleges had announced big tuition increases for next year. There was a shooting in a Ponderosa parking lot; the gunman was still at large. I cared about none of it. Then, finally, the footage I had seen the night before, my boat in flames. I turned up the volume; I didn't want to miss a word.

"A local attorney is missing after his boat was discovered abandoned and on fire off Pass-a-Grille Beach last night. Area Coast Guard units responded to the call at about eight thirty p.m., and after extinguishing the blaze, they found no trace of the boat's owner, Alton Carver," read the anchor. Then my grinning face suddenly filled the screen—it was my driver's license photo, for fuck's sake, they really couldn't do any better than that?—with the caption "Missing Lawyer" stretched across the bottom. Well, at least no one's going to worry about finding a missing lawyer, I thought. Then a jump cut to a car in a parking lot. It took me a second before I recognized it: my Porsche. "Carver's car was found this morning at the Eighth Avenue Marina, but it is not known if he was on the boat last night. A Coast Guard spokesperson tells us a search for Carver is under way." Then a teaser for a review of last night's Springsteen concert at the amphitheater.

The TV screen went black, and I tossed the remote onto the bed behind me. That was it: Four sentences was all I got. Four sentences that told me very little. The Coast Guard was actively looking for me, but they didn't know for sure if I'd even been on the boat in the first place? Did that make sense? What about the police—were they looking for me? The pleasantly vacant woman who read the news didn't say. And what was that "after extinguishing the blaze" crap? Anyone who watched the footage— the footage they were showing while she was saying the words—could see that they had done no such thing.

On the other hand, she didn't mention the investigation. Certainly she would have, if they'd known about it. It was a salacious little tidbit, just the thing an enterprising local news producer would latch on to as a way to give a go-nowhere story some legs. The fact that it wasn't in the report was encouraging.

Suddenly I was even more irritated than I had been the night before. I had no idea if I could take that news report at face value. Maybe I should just hide out for a few days. But I had no food in the room, so I wouldn't be able to do that for any length of time. I could always order pizza, but then I'd be risking being recognized by the delivery driver, who would then also have an address where the police could find that guy whose boat burned up the other night. No, I'd have to go out. I'd just have to roll the dice and risk being seen, or risk someone stealing the satchel filled with my entire future.

At least the maid wasn't likely to disturb anything. From the look of the place, I doubted she even had a key.

I dressed quickly, putting on a long-sleeved gray T-shirt and a pair of jeans. I remembered there was a convenience store about a half mile up the road from the Royal Rest. With any luck, their coffee would be somewhere on the drinkable side of charred toxic waste. I'd have to walk, though. As meticulously as I'd planned this whole operation—I have always been meticulous by nature, so this is almost painful to admit now—there was one thing I had somehow overlooked: transportation. I had no car. Picking up an old Caprice Classic or something for a few hundred bucks just had never occurred to me at any point during the planning phase. It's funny, but whenever I had imagined myself heading west to start my new life, I guess I always saw myself behind the wheel of the Porsche, top down in the bright sunshine. Why hadn't I caught that? I knew from the very beginning that I was going to have to abandon the Porsche at the marina. Usually in these visions I had a ball cap on too, the gunmetal-gray Manchester United cap I'd picked up in London a few years ago. Something else I'd forgotten to bring. Damn. That was supposed to be part of my disguise, too.

So I slid on a pair of cheap aviator-style sunglasses— the only element of a disguise I still had to work with at that point—and stepped outside, into the bright morning sun. The door to my room opened directly onto the parking lot, which was almost completely car-free that morning. Three or four doors to my left, a leathery old woman sat on a cheap folding chair, the kind made of hollow aluminum tubes and rough strips of fabric woven through each other. She drank from a blue thermos and watched the traffic pass. In another room somewhere, a man yelled in muffled Spanish at a crying child. I locked the door and walked past the woman in the chair. She didn't even notice me.

FIVE

Alton

The Coast Guard called off their search after less than four days. That surprised me. I had assumed it would take them longer than that to decide they'd never find me alive. But they found the charred remains of my life jacket on the boat, so that, along with the brutal currents from that night, is probably what convinced them to just put a bow on it and move on.

It was good news. I knew that as soon as I heard it. People were already starting to think of me as dead. I'd have more freedom to move around and then just float out of town when I was ready. Less reason to fear someone recognizing me. And if by some chance someone did recognize me, it would be easy to just write it off as a coincidence. Hmmm, that guy looks just like that dead lawyer I saw on the news—oh, check it out, Four Loko is on sale! Existing in the past tense would give me cover.

But still. There was something vaguely insulting to me about the short search. Four days? I was only worth four days of effort? Anyone can stay missing for four days. It's easy—hell, you could even do that by accident. I would have figured they'd have kept at it for at least a week. That seemed like a more appropriate length of time to search for someone like me.

The soporific pace of life at the Royal Rest was already getting to me. I slept in the daytime, or at least I tried to. The room was just too bright for that. The windows of room 18 faced south, so for the entire day sunlight leaked around the edges of those thin white blinds, seeping between them, illuminating them almost until they glowed. I'd already tried hanging towels and sheets in front of the window, but they

27

never stayed put for long. So the only thing I could do was try to sleep on my stomach—which I've always hated because I don't like how my rib cage feels when it pushes against the mattress; it always makes me aware of my ribs and my breathing, and once that happens it's all over, I can pretty much forget about falling asleep—with a pillow over my head.

When I was awake, there was nothing to do except watch TV. So I scoured the local newscasts for any new information on my case, any mention of my name, anything at all. That's how I found out the search had been called off. I got three sentences that time. I was getting less newsworthy by a few words every time they talked about me.

I'd also been killing time at night by going for walks along Cortez Boulevard, the six-lane highway that ran right past the Royal Rest, connecting the city with the swamps, the trailer parks, the wild countryside farther inland. It's a different Florida back in there, at least according to the stories I'd heard. But I'd never had any reason to see it for myself. The Royal Rest fit in well along Cortez, just part of a shabby collection of marginal businesses catering to marginal people. Gas station. Small-engine repair shop. Liquor store. Bait shop. Taco stand, closed long ago from the looks of it, held together by inertia and the long tendrils of overgrowth that crept up its sides. Weather-beaten strip malls, covered with cracked plaster and faded paint, fronted by weedy parking lots. There was no sidewalk along Cortez, which was just as well seeing how there was nothing around there worth walking to. But I was walking anyway, even without a destination, so I just kept to the shoulder. I hopped over drainage swales in front of darkened storefronts. I cut across parking lots and pushed through shaggy hedges, not caring where I was going as long as it was forward. And once I felt like I'd gone farther than far enough, I would turn around and go back. By the time I got to my room, the arches of my feet ached, my left ankle—always just the left—throbbed, and my shoes were full of sand.

But walking only killed so much time, and you can only walk the same stretch of road so many times before it starts to bore you right out of your goddamn mind. So one night, instead of going for another long walk, I crossed the highway and popped into the liquor store, where I bought a bottle of the cheapest vodka they had—a big plastic jug of something called Scottish Bob's—and some plastic cups. The clerk barely looked at me as he rang me up. I suddenly felt buoyed. Nobody's going to notice me, I thought. I'm completely invisible. I can just hide right out in the open.

The Royal Rest was dead silent when I got back a few minutes later, no lights shining through the blinds in any of the windows. The beach chair in front of room 15 was empty. A stray dog sniffed around the door to room 11 but ran away when it saw me coming. My original plan was to drink in my room until I passed out, but when I noticed the empty chair, I decided to call an audible. I walked past room 15, as calm as I could manage, very nonchalant. Just as I was about to pass the chair, I scooped it up and kept walking, past my room, past the ancient pay phone bolted to the wall and with half the handset missing, past the end of the building, and into the sickly orange glow of the sodium lights overhead. I headed down to Cortez and followed it inland for about half a mile until I came to a spit of land jutting out along the road and into a small bayou. I'd had no idea it was there, but it was the perfect spot. That was where I would be drinking that night.

It was a cool evening, not as cold as it had been the week before, but not nearly warm enough to have to worry about mosquitoes. My mind flashed for a moment onto alligators—I couldn't remember if they hibernate or not, but I thought they did, so I'd probably be okay—as I opened the beach chair and pushed it downward into the sand, getting it nice and level. The bayou splayed out in front of me and was completely still and silent. I twisted the cap off the vodka jug and poured myself a generous serving. Everything about the packaging told me to expect the liquor to burn my throat like stomach acid when I finally took a sip. In that regard, and that regard only, it did not disappoint.

No one was looking for me. I was presumed dead. It had fucking worked. So why couldn't I relax? I swallowed another mouthful of the vodka; it wasn't as rough the second time down. Maybe the problem was that I was still in town. Maybe I wouldn't really be able to relax until I left. Okay. I could take off in the morning. Buy a crappy used car, toss the satchel in the back, and head west, just like I'd planned. I could live like a king on the Costa Rican beach for the rest of my life with that money. Nicole and Clara could collect the insurance payout, and I'd mail them the safe deposit box keys in a couple years. I remember I had been thinking that maybe they could come join me then, but now I was starting to change my mind. The best plans are the simplest ones.

Maybe it was the fact that I had made a plan, or maybe it was the vodka, but it wasn't long before the tension in my shoulders dissipated and I was feeling almost calm. This was going to work out. I had done it. I had saved myself and protected my family. Nobody could touch me now, not where I was going, and Nicole didn't know anything anyway, not that that would stop those pricks from harassing her, at least until they were sure about whether she had anything to do with it, but—

You're doing it again.

It's true. I was.

This is exactly how you always lose control over a situation. How you let things slip away from you. How you push yourself into making bad decisions without even realizing what you're doing. Relax. Don't think. Breathe. Breathe. Breathe.

I had to admit, the voice in my head made a convincing argument. I took a deep breath and released it. Then another. Then another. Soon I was feeling mellower. My shoulders loosened, and I felt my pulse slow down. An eighteen-wheeler barreled along the highway, shattering the late-night stillness of the bayou for just a moment. But then the truck was gone, and all was quiet once again.

It was a little after five in the morning when I slid the chair back into its spot in front of room 15. I'd put away half that bottle over the course of the night. Even though it had been cool out there, I felt grimy, like I was covered with a thin film of grit and oil. I suddenly thought about my father and how he used to smell in the evenings, the ones where he'd been drinking since just after lunch, that vodka smell seeping out of his body through his pores. I couldn't help but wonder if I smelled like that right now.

Three minutes later I was in the shower, my head bobbing up and down in a sea of cheap vodka, and then a couple minutes after that the vodka decided not to bother with evaporating through my pores anymore. The entire night was suddenly right there in the bathtub with me, on me, that stinging vodka smell even sharper than when I'd first twisted off the cap. I vomited on myself twice more before I was reduced to coughing up yellow dribs of stomach acid. My throat was raw and my sinuses burned. My eyes watered.

Christ.

After I managed to get myself cleaned up and dressed, I propped open the front door to air out the odors of vodka, vomit, and mildew so I could maybe get a few hours of sleep. The old woman in room 15 was already in her chair. She turned and looked right at me; I couldn't quite tell if she was glaring at me or just squinting. It was not quite six in the morning. I closed the door and lurched toward the bed, where I slept without dreams for the entire day.

That night I took the old woman's chair back to the same spot where the highway crossed the bayou. I brought the bottle of vodka too, and over the course of the night drank half of what was left after the previous night's binge.

I was supposed to have left that day. I was supposed to be gone.

Sure, okay, I was hungover, really hungover, but that was just an excuse. I'd been worse. I'd closed huge deals, sometimes worth tens of millions of dollars, when I'd been hungover worse than that. From a logical point of view, that seemed like the perfect moment to go, to just pick up and leave town once and for all. Get on a bus or something. Whatever. And yet it still felt like I was forgetting something, like there was one more thing I needed to do before I could put the city in my rearview mirror and just leave it there.

I was out there the whole night, listening and thinking and drinking. Why am I still here? Why? When it was time to go back to the motel, I was no closer to answering that than I had been when I sat down. I carried the chair back to room 15 and placed it right where I'd found it and went back to my room. This time I did not vomit in the shower. I didn't even feel sick from the booze, not even a little.

When I woke up that evening, I thought I would go sit by the bayou again so I could finish the vodka and decide what to do next. But there was no beach chair outside room 15. The old woman had taken it inside.

So. No bayou drinking that night, which left me with the option of taking a walk instead. Fine. It had been a few nights. I could use the exercise. This time, I decided to walk along the highway across the bayou and into the swamps instead of heading back toward town. I had no idea what was out there, but it was probably my last chance to find out. And I have never been one to turn away from an opportunity to explore the unknown.

It only took me ten minutes or so to get to the bridge,

which I'd had no idea was even there before that very moment. There was a very narrow shoulder, not even wide enough to park a car without partially obstructing the right lane. I paused. It didn't look very safe. But it was also the middle of the night. There was never any traffic at that hour. So I stepped onto the bridge, walking in the shoulder on the left-hand side so I could see any oncoming cars a long way off.

After a while—could have been ten minutes, could have been thirty, I had no idea—I realized that I didn't have any idea how long this bridge was. A mile? Two miles? I couldn't see the other side of it in the darkness. All I knew for sure is that it was longer than half a mile, because that was the distance I felt like I'd already walked.

Then I saw a pinprick of light off in the distance, a single dot that quickly became two, as if by mitosis. Headlights. Coming this way. My instinct told me to crowd the concrete barrier along the outer edge of the shoulder, but then I thought better of it. The driver might not see me wedged up against the rail like that, so I moved back to the center of the shoulder.

The lights were closer now, and I could see they were unsteady. It looked like the vehicle was weaving from lane to lane. But I couldn't be sure. My night vision had never been great. A moment later I saw it was another eighteen-wheeler and that I was right—the driver was having trouble keeping the truck in a single lane.

I just froze. I had nowhere to go but into the water, and if I did that, I had no idea what was down there or how I'd get back onto the bridge—or if I could get back onto the bridge at all. The truck was closing the distance quickly, and then it suddenly veered in my direction. I threw my body against the concrete and pressed into it, hard, trying to burrow my way inside. The truck blew past me, maybe two feet from my head and right through the space where I had been standing just a moment before.

I didn't move, not even to breathe, for about twenty seconds. Once I allowed myself to exhale, my entire body started shaking, shivering, and not because of the temperature. I knelt down, then leaned forward on all fours, right there in the shoulder, and stayed like that until the shaking stopped and my nerves were under control.

The walk was over. I turned and started to jog, then run, back toward the Royal Rest.

The next morning I was surprised to hear my name on the morning newscast—surprised because I had assumed the Coast Guard's canceling the search marked the end of my fifteen minutes of fame, but also because I did not remember turning on the TV. I was lying on the bed, still a bit buzzed from the vodka. I wasn't sure how long I'd been awake; I'd been flitting between superficial sleep and semi-wakefulness for most of the night. I propped myself up on an elbow and watched the screen as my driver's license photo filled it again.

"Some new developments in the case of Alton Carver, the local attorney presumed lost at sea after his boat caught fire last week," the newscaster began. "Sources tell us that shortly before his disappearance, the FBI had opened an investigation into Carver's business dealings at Sloane Bryce McLaughlin, the law firm where Carver was a partner. Sources in law enforcement tell us they were investigating fraud allegations against him and are now considering suicide as a possible explanation for Carver's disappearance."

Well shit. So they knew about all that, did they?

Sources? Who the fuck are these sources?

My hand quivered, just barely but enough for me to notice, as I turned the TV off. Okay. It was fine. I'd known all that would come out eventually. I just hadn't expected it to happen so quickly, and certainly not before I had a chance to leave town.

Still. Let's not panic over this. They did say suicide, which meant they still thought I was dead. And they didn't say anything about the thing with the Securities and Exchange Commission, so maybe they didn't know about that. Either way though, this could complicate things for me, both in the short-term and further down the road. I swore at myself for being so careless—what the hell was I still doing there? Why was I still at the Royal Rest, living that way? That place was poison. It was starting to affect my thinking. I could have left, days ago, any time I wanted. What was keeping me there? I just couldn't see it, and more than anything else, that scared the hell out of me.

SIX

Nicole

That first week on my own was a complete blur. Okay, maybe not quite a complete blur. I can remember plenty of things from that week. I just can't quite put them in any kind of chronological order that makes sense to me.

I know I stopped going to work for a while. Which I'm sure is something they probably expected. Or at least should have expected. But I didn't notify anyone first, which I realize was very unprofessional of me, but what can I tell you, it is what it is. One day I just . . . didn't go in. And when nobody called to ask where I was or anything, I just stayed home the next day too. And the day after that. When I finally did go back to the office, which was something like two weeks later, nobody said anything to me about it. But I think some of them resented me for it. I remember getting looks from certain people, which in retrospect is completely fair. Yes, my husband was missing, probably dead. But I still could have called in. It's not like I'd suddenly forgotten how phones worked.

I think Clara held it together better than I did, as much as it embarrasses me to say that now. Especially early on. It was probably easier for her, though, because I don't think she really understood what was happening. For her entire life, Alton had always come home at night, had always been there to tuck her in or read her a story or tickle her until her head was as red as a beet. As far as she was concerned, he was one of the great constants of the universe. He was like gravity. He would always be there, because it was unthinkable that he could ever not.

There were a couple of times that week when I noticed her watching me, from her car seat or from her little perch on the stairs. Each time she had this expression on her face, this very grown-up expression of abstract concern. It reminded me of my father, when he would stare out over his brown lawn, wondering why it hadn't turned green yet. Or when he'd look up at the screen of departing flights at the airport, watching as flight after flight flipped from "on time" to "delayed" and wondering if we'd make our connection in St. Louis. Nothing like, Oh, my mommy is so sad and she's drinking wine all the time and my daddy is gone and I'm scared. It was all very clinical. I felt like I was under her microscope.

And yes, because I brought it up and before you ask, I was drinking a lot of wine that first week or so. A lot of wine. I would drive Clara to school in the morning, hungover, and then by the afternoon I was too tipsy again to get behind the wheel. The first time, I just walked down to the school to pick her up—maybe "staggered" would be more accurate—and then we walked home together. Clara loved it, of course. She loves to be outside. But then after that, for the next few days someone else brought her home for me. The first time I was mortified. I'd been drinking all afternoon and had completely forgotten to go get her. My god. What kind of awful mother was I? Staying home drunk while my daughter waited for me to come pick her up at school—that's not me, it's just not. That's the kind of thing that sends kids to therapy—no offense, of course, but you know. But then the second time, yeah, I kind of just let that one happen. It almost felt like I had permission. I knew someone would bring her if I didn't show up. After all, I was in mourning. They'd understand. And I was right.

The worst part is, I was never quite clear on who actually brought her home. And then later, once I had pulled myself together a bit, I was far too embarrassed to ask.

I remember neighbors stopping in to check on me. Most of the time, they didn't stay long. I couldn't blame them.

The conversation always ran dry quickly. I mean, it must be difficult to make small talk with a brand-new widow. But it's not as if I made it any easier on them, as numb and uncommunicative as I was. To be honest, I don't think I could bear to have people seeing me in the state I was in, all wrecked and crumpled and pitiful.

I was hearing strange noises all the time. Bumps and thuds. Creaks. Scraping sounds. I never found out where they were coming from, probably because I almost never got up to investigate them. I had these dreams, awful dreams, that would shake me awake, drenched in sweat and completely wrapped up in despair and fear. I don't remember any of them, though. I guess that's probably a good thing. In retrospect, maybe a two-minute cry hadn't been enough after all.

You know what? I don't think I want to talk about this anymore. Can we move on to something else for a while please?

SEVEN

Alton

I couldn't get back to sleep after hearing that news report. It rattled me, more than I would have expected. After a couple hours of tossing and turning, I just gave up on the whole idea.

At about ten o'clock I finally got out of bed, threw some clothes on, and pulled the satchel out of that dank closet. My laundry situation was becoming critical. It had started to smell of sulfur in there, that faint rotting-egg smell of the bayou. Maybe I would go find a Laundromat when I got back from car shopping.

I miss the classifieds. That's where I found my first used car, in the print of the Times-Picayune, back in my first year of law school. No IP addresses, no GPS triangulation, no invisible bread crumbs to give yourself away. You just had to be careful not to smear the ink with your thumbs. How much easier it must have been to fake your own death and slip out of town unnoticed back in the old days. But now the classifieds don't exist, or at least not in any form that's actually useful. Now you need an Internet connection, which of course I didn't have because I'd thrown mine into the ocean.

Jesus. I need to stop. I sound like my grandfather.

I knew there was a bus stop about a mile from the Royal Rest, and while I had no idea where it would take me—I don't think I'd ridden a city bus since law school, and that was in a completely different city—I figured I could get on whichever bus stopped there and just keep transferring until I wound up close to a library or something. I took some bills from one of the wrapped stacks of hundreds and slid the satchel back into its hiding place.

It took about an hour or so, but eventually the bus began to trawl through a part of town I recognized. I spotted the brown brick and glass façade of the East Lake branch library, an absolute jewel of a midcentury modern building that has always refused to blend with the standard-issue suburban blandness that surrounds it. It's a great building, the only indication that the neighborhood existed at all before, say, 1985 or so. I hopped off at the next stop and doubled back.

The chill of the library's air-conditioning smacked me in the face as soon as I pushed open the front door, a heavy, frosted-glass thing that lent the whole place an air of stately elegance. I headed directly to the small pod of eight computers, in the back just across from the reference desk. Six of them were already occupied. I sat down in front of one of the other two and surfed over to Craigslist. Before long, I'd collected the phone numbers for five promising leads, decided that was plenty, and got up to leave. Nobody paid me any attention at all.

I remember it was sunny that day, the sky a soft and pale blue. It felt good to be out of that motel room. I was enjoying the feeling of doing something, driving events, taking control of my own destiny again. I know, I know. It was just buying a car. People buy cars every day. It's no big deal. But in its own way, it actually was. It was the first concrete step toward leaving town that I'd taken since I landed at the Royal Rest. I didn't see a pay phone close by, so I started walking south, toward a cluster of big-box and strip-mall shopping centers.

Twenty minutes later, I was still looking. I'd spotted a phone in front of a gourmet pet treats store, but it turned out to be disconnected. I would've expected to find at least one in front of either CVS or Trader Joe's, but no such luck there either.

Then it hit me: What about one of those disposable phones? I was standing right in front of the CVS. They sell those here, right? They must. I mean, where else would they sell them? But I had no idea how those things worked. Do you need a credit card or can you pay cash? If I resisted using a credit card and tried to buy it with cash, would the clerk think that was suspicious? Would someone recognize me as that so-called missing lawyer they saw on TV?

Next time I stage my own death, I'm going to remember to set myself up with transportation first. And a disposable phone.

And suddenly, I was ready to give up. I was already tired of having to include a risk assessment as part of every single routine decision I made throughout the day. I hadn't anticipated that. It's actually quite stressful, an exhausting way to live, and I think that moment—right then—that was when the mental and physical demands of all of it finally caught up with me. I felt like every part of my body was starting to sag under the weight of this life that I had trapped myself in. My legs were about to go. I was about to collapse, right there in the CVS parking lot, mixed in with the scattered cigarette butts and crushed Diet Coke cans.

Hey, wait—that car has a For Sale sign in the window.

It was a Toyota Camry with a muted gold aftermarket paint job that was cracked and faded in spots, especially on the roof. The window-tint film had bubbled and split in at least a dozen places that I could see. The sign was taped to the rear window on the driver's side and said the car was a 1997 model—okay, sure, why not, I don't know anything about Toyotas—and that whoever was selling it wanted $3,800 for it, which to me seemed absurd for a car that was nearly twenty years old. But then again, was I really in any position to negotiate? I walked around to the front and leaned against the hood like I already owned the thing. I decided that when the owner came back, I'd give him an extra thousand if I could drive the car off right then and there, no paperwork, no questions asked.

Sixteen minutes later, I drove my very own 1997 Toyota Camry out of the CVS parking lot. The clutch was loose, and I could smell the faint aroma of burning motor oil. But I had a car, plus a pair of hundreds still folded in my pocket.

It felt like it had been years since I'd been home. But actually it had been only eight days. Possibly nine. Time had this way of doubling back around on itself and losing all meaning at the Royal Rest. As soon as I got the keys to that awful little car, I drove it straight to my house and parked it directly across the street. A powerful mixture of emotions—regret, longing, nostalgia, hopelessness, fear, and a few others I couldn't quite identify—filled my chest cavity nearly to bursting. It was a warm day, but I left the windows rolled up. My skin was sticking to the pleather seat covering, but I didn't want my neighbors to spot me, and even peeling window-tint film was better camouflage than nothing at all.

I lived in one of the city's oldest neighborhoods, which had a reputation for its Craftsman-style wood bungalows dating back to the 1910s. Large front porches, ceiling fans with blades the size of snowshoes, overlooked post-age-stamp front yards where not even a blade of grass was out of place, not a single desert rose wilting from neglect. Crape myrtles dotted the yards and shaded southern-ex-posed picture windows. It was peaceful, quiet, and polished, which is why I bought there in the first place.

My house was actually out of place on that block, but I had never noticed until that very moment. For one thing, it was neither wood nor a bungalow. It was a red-brick two-story—the only two-story on the block—and had no front porch, just a little awning over the front steps to keep the rain off the Jehovah's Witnesses who used to stop by every few weeks. I guess the reason I bought this one was because it reminded me of the neighborhood I grew up in, back in Baltimore. The yard guys—I didn't know anything about them, the yard was Nicole's passion—always kept the grounds in immaculate condition. I could tell they must have been out to the house since I disappeared. My mind flashed on Nicole writing them a check for the month, her hands trembling, trying to keep herself from crying. I don't know if I'd be able to handle the routine day-to-day tasks of running a household in her situation. I would probably have to hire someone to do just about everything.

I remember letting my eyes wander up the walk to the front door, thinking about Nicole's struggles, about the hole my absence must have put in her life and in Clara's life, about the years of happy family memories that still lived in that house for me. At least I didn't have to face that alone every day like she did. I remember thinking about how she had always been so completely devoted to me. I'd been her life for so long, and now I'd taken that from her. Even if it was only temporary, and even if I had made sure she was taken care of financially before I left, it was still a harsh adjustment for anyone to have to make.

I was thinking all of those things while I just sat there inside that stuffy car, but mostly I was wondering if she had moved the key.

It was a terrible idea, of course. I knew that as soon as I thought of it. Neighbors might spot me. The key could snap off in the lock. Nicole might come home from work early. Maybe Clara was at home sick with a babysitter. I might move something while I was inside and forget to put it back exactly how I found it. And what if Nicole had gotten a dog? She'd wanted one for years. Maybe she'd finally gotten one to help her cope with the loss.

But none of that mattered. I'd wanted to go inside from the moment I made that last left turn onto Reedmere Lane. It might well have been the only reason I went back there in the first place. I knew I was going to go inside that house, knew it as sure as I was sitting there, if only just to give myself a moment or two to say good-bye, properly say good-bye to my old life, and maybe, just maybe, give myself just

43

a small measure of closure on the mess I had made of my old life. The risks were at once significant and completely irrelevant.

Someone up the block was watching me.

I peered through the pollen-dusted windshield. It was Larry Combs. Of course it was. Who else would it be? I could see him through the sliver of space between his front curtains. Combs was a piece of work. He had retired from the school system years ago, made it as high as assistant principal or something like that, and now he never seemed to leave the house. He had run the neighborhood watch program for as long as I lived on Reedmere, right from that big picture window in his living room. Most of the neighbors who volunteered for neighborhood watch thought he was so insufferable that they quit in a matter of months. Knowing him the way I did, I assumed he was on the phone to the police already, reporting a suspicious vehicle on his street. I couldn't just drive off, because that would make it obvious that I didn't belong there. But on the other hand, I was probably far enough away that a decrepit old squinter like Combs wouldn't be able to read my license plate. So I started the car, made a quick U-turn and drove back down Reedmere, away from Larry Combs and his endless vigil.

Nine blocks due south, I parked the Toyota about a hundred feet from Westminster Presbyterian Church. From there I had a clear view of the playground, which was deserted.

It had been Nicole's idea to enroll Clara at Pineview, which was actually housed inside the church. Neither of us were religious, but she had met one of the preschool teachers at a Mommy and Me class—or whatever it was—last year and gotten along well with her, and the following week she decided to send Clara there based solely on that. Gut instinct. That was how Nicole made decisions, for better or worse. But Clara was happy there, doing well, always eager

to go to school and play with her friends, and she only rarely ever mentioned anything about Jesus. Like the time she
asked us, out of the blue, "You know who likes it when we
jump on the bed? The devil." And then she went right back to
her coloring. She seemed to consider the matter closed.

I didn't know if this street had its very own Larry Combs
or not, so I scanned the front windows of the nearby houses, looking for fluttering curtains or blinds suddenly lowered
most of the way down or anything else that suggested someone might be watching me. I didn't see anything.

Then the beige double doors separating the lunchroom
from the playground burst open, and a whirling mass of
about fifteen children spilled out. Was this Clara's class?
It might be. They were certainly short enough. But I didn't
see—Wait, wait a minute, there she is. There's my beautiful
daughter.

I watched as Clara bounced to the jungle gym—her yellow and white striped dress fluttering as she ran—where she
climbed up three bars and then jumped off, landing on her
feet. Then she kicked a soccer ball at a group of boys, who
claimed it for themselves until Clara ran over to them and
included herself in their passing drills. The rest of the kids in
the playground gradually fell away until I saw only Clara, her
bright pink sneakers stabbing and flailing at the ball every
time it rolled near her, her laughter the only sound I heard.

That was the first time I thought about just grabbing her
and taking her with me.

It would be so easy. She would go with me, no problem.
I could just wait until she was alone. But I knew almost as
soon as I thought it that it'd never work. Where would she
go to school in Costa Rica? Who would her friends be? What
kind of life would she have? And if I wanted to avoid unnecessary attention—which I did—maybe kidnapping small
children and taking them across state lines was something I
should reconsider.

But would it be kidnapping, really? She was my daughter. I had every right to see her, to take care of her, to raise her. Of course I did. I'm her father.

But Nicole needs her. And Nicole has suffered enough loss already.

I got out of the car before I knew what I was doing or why. This was an even worse idea than going into the house. There was no way to know how she'd react if she saw me. Would she yell? Would she be scared? I didn't think she'd be scared. We'd always had a great relationship; she loved me and almost certainly missed me terribly. But would she yell? Would she try to climb the fence and get out of the playground so she could run over to me?

She might. It was certainly possible.

But Clara wouldn't see me. She was too busy playing soccer with her friends. I watched her step into a kick that she missed completely. She spun around and fell, landing squarely on her butt. The boys all laughed at her, and all I wanted to do was rush in, scoop her up, and save her from those brutes, to tell her everything would be okay and to make her understand it, really understand what I was saying. So I started toward the playground—

—and then she was laughing too. Sitting in the mulch, legs splayed out at these impossible angles, laughing right along with the other kids, even louder than they were. I smiled. She was starting to become a person, a real person, her own person. And I got to see it, even if just for a moment, even if just for that one and only time. She picked herself up, using the ball for leverage, and then tried kicking it again. And this time she really nailed it, getting it right with her instep, just like I had taught her. I started coaching her early, but I'd always suspected she didn't quite understand what I was telling her when I tried to show her the finer points of the game. She was only four, after all. But now I knew she got it.

Then she looked up. Directly at me.

I froze. Shit. She sees me. I prepared myself for a scream, a shout, some kind of reaction. None came. She just grinned at me, a wide and toothy grin, and waved. I could see her teacher—she wasn't looking at me or at Clara, but was busy tending to a wailing fat boy who had fallen off the jungle gym. But Clara was still looking at me. She was waiting for me to wave back. So I raised my hand to about shoulder level and waved to her, pretty half-assed, I admit. I didn't want to move a whole lot for fear of attracting someone else's attention.

But that was apparently enough for her, because right away she turned back to her soccer game. I stood there for another minute, then two, just watching. I didn't really know what else to do, so I hurried back to the car and drove off.

EIGHT

Date: 26 March, 2014

From: Gardinier_Mari@pineviewpresbyterian.edu
To: principal@pineviewpresbyterian.edu

Subject: Clara Carver

Dr. Hagerty,

This morning I had a short conversation with one of the students in my class, Clara Carver. As you are no doubt aware, Clara recently lost her father to a tragic accident at sea. The conversation in question gives me cause for concern regarding her ability to adequately deal with recent events, and for the impact this may have on her development if neglected.

Today the children went out for their usual morning recess. I was with them, though much of my attention was monopolized by Donnie Fitzpatrick after he fell off the monkey bars, so I wasn't paying especially close attention to Clara during this time. However, whenever I did happen to notice her, she seemed to be playing happily with a group other children. Based on the behavior I observed, I would never have guessed that she'd recently suffered any sort of tragedy or trauma.

But when recess was over, Clara came over to me and said, "I saw Daddy."

As an aside, I know we have discussed my habit of showing skepticism when the children tell me things that appear to be obvious fabrications. I realize this is not always appropriate, and I have been working on this and continue to do so, but I fear I may not have succeeded this time.

"You saw your daddy?" I said. "Where did you see him, honey?"

"In front of the house," she said. "He was in the road. I waved to him."

I assumed she meant her own house, and asked her to confirm that. But she was not talking about her home.

"It was the green house outside," she said. "I was playing soccer with Markus and Andre and Alex and then I saw Daddy in the road. He was watching me."

"Honey, that wasn't your daddy," I told her. "That was just somebody who looked like him."

"No it wasn't." She was quite emphatic on this point.

"Honey, sometimes our minds play tricks on us," I explained. I thought that she might accept the truth more readily if she had an alternate explanation of what she had seen, or what she thought she had seen. "Sometimes, when we really want to see a person, our minds fool us into making us think that we do see them. But really it's not them at all."

At this point, Clara fell silent and looked at the floor for a good thirty seconds. I admit, I was at a loss on how to handle this. As you have reminded me on a number of occasions, I've only been a teacher a short while, and my training has not to this point included any instruction on handling children who have recently lost a parent. "Clara? Honey?" Her behavior was worrying me. "Are you all right?"

"That was my daddy. But my daddy's gone," she said. "He went on the boat and he fell off it and then the boat got on fire. He's under the water now." She then ran off, into the classroom.

I honestly do not know if this is something to be concerned about, or if it's just a normal part of the grieving process for a four-year-old. I will leave that determination to those with more experience in these matters. However, I felt I would be remiss if I didn't at least report it.

NINE

Nicole

Most people have a specific memory of the moment they met their one true love. The impact of that first spark of attraction, the first instant the possibility of a real connection is felt, whatever. At least, that's what I've been led to believe.

I actually don't remember specifically meeting Alton. I can remember not knowing him, and then there's a period where things are kind of blurry, and then after that I'm just kind of with him somehow. That was back when I was living in New Orleans; I remember that he was still in law school for the first year we were together. I think my friend Alicia might have introduced us because she wanted to get closer to a friend of Alton's. It might have been a Super Bowl party. Part of my mind seems to associate him with football for some reason, even though he never played.

No, wait a minute. I do remember. It was a Super Bowl party. I don't remember whose party it was, but it was in this tiny apartment somewhere in the French Quarter, which was a part of town I didn't spend a lot of time in, for various reasons. I remember I was getting some food when Alton sort of sidled up to me and asked who I wanted to win.

"I don't care," I told him. "I hate football. I don't even know who's playing."

"Then why are you at a Super Bowl party?"

"I love the Super Bowl," I said. "And drinking."

He laughed. "Hey, how about that. Already we have something in common." So we drank. And we drank some more. Then we went back to his apartment during halftime and just never came back. Christ, was Alicia pissed at me. For weeks.

Shit. I'd forgotten all of that.

Stop looking at me like that. I know what you're thinking. And you're wrong. You always read too much into things like this. There was a time when he and I were very much in love.

I remember we always found a way to have a great time in those early days, before there was any money, before there was Clara. Our time together was ours, and all we cared about was spending it together. We'd sometimes rent a sailboat and head up the coast for the day, up to Yankeetown and around there. That was a bit of a splurge back then, so it wasn't an every-weekend thing. Sometimes we'd drive down to Sarasota for the day and pretend we were old money. We'd drift through the art galleries and cafés, breathing in the same air as the people we hoped to become someday. Or we'd just go to the beach and drink all afternoon until the sun finally slipped below the shimmering horizon.

We both loved the water so much that we got married there, on the beach down in Key West. The singer we hired played "Into the Mystic" as we walked toward each other, taking those slow, deliberate steps toward the palm tree where we would meet and publicly declare our love for each other. It was all I could do not to break out into a run and leap into his arms, or tackle him on the sand. And now . . . well, to this day I can't hear that song without thinking about that moment. I heard it in the car just a couple days ago, actually. I had to pull off to the side of the road, my arms were shaking so hard. I could barely breathe. I sat there for probably ten minutes, just trying to get ahold of myself.

Jesus. I hope I never hear that fucking song again.

About a dozen of our friends came down for the wedding. We put them all up in a guesthouse that had a clothing-optional pool, which was Alton's idea of a joke because he didn't tell anyone about that part before they got there. They all found out the next morning, when they went out for breakfast only to find a pool area full of naked people, sunning themselves and reading the morning paper. And of course, they were exactly the kind of people you'd expect to find at a clothing-optional pool, which means, not the kind of people you'd really want to see naked. I remember wondering where he had gotten the money to pay for all that. I mean, we were just scraping by, and he had these huge student loan payments every month. But it was off-season, so maybe that was how he managed it.

He worked a lot, though. That's what new lawyers do. And older lawyers too, as it turns out.

He was so smart. Or at least, I thought he was. That's what attracted me to him originally. I do remember that, being so impressed with his mind. His brains actually intimidated me a little, you know? I mean, he'd been to law school. He'd read a lot more than I had. He knew . . . things. Lots of things. He had this vast collection of interesting little facts and notions or whatever, and he knew how to use them to make himself seem like the smartest guy in whichever room we were in. He was very practiced at dropping those nuggets into a conversation at precisely the right moment, and it never failed to impress at least somebody. They'd raise their eyebrows and say, "Really?" or "I had no idea," or something like that. It wasn't until years later that I saw all that for what it was, which was just a bunch of scattered bits of trivia he'd picked up over the years that were unconnected to anything else in his head. Normally when people talk the way Alton did back then, you kind of assume that what you're getting is just the tip of the iceberg, that there's more to them below the surface. But with him, there wasn't. That was pretty much it. And it took me a lot of years to figure that out.

TEN

Alton

I stopped at a Walgreens on my way back to the Royal Rest. I only needed a couple of things, but I scooped up a few other items—travel-size shampoo, aspirin, a bag of chips, some other stuff I don't remember—so as not to draw attention to myself. Someone might remember a man buying only an eyeliner pencil.

Once I was back in room 18, I headed straight for the bathroom sink. I took the pair of scissors and the eyeliner pencil I had just bought out of the bag and turned on the hot water. I looked at my reflection in the mirror. I remember thinking, Is this actually necessary? Would I just end up looking like a freak? Or worse yet, exactly the same as before but with no hair?

But the best disguise is one that you never actually have to put on. Before I could give myself another moment to talk myself out of it, I clipped off a thick clump of hair from just above my right ear. Then another, then another, and another. I cut as close to my scalp as I could get, but I think I could have done a better job with Clara's safety scissors. Once I was done, I soaked the washcloth in hot water and draped it atop my head. The cloth felt good, very alive and intense. I hadn't realized before how sensitive the scalp is to temperature.

I covered my scalp with shaving cream and slowly drew the razor back across the top of my head in a straight line, again and again. Each stripe through the shaving cream looked like a shovel's path through wet snow. The sink quickly filled with gobs of shaving cream and hair bristles. In just a few minutes, I was finished. And bald. I was definitely bald.

I cleaned myself up and took a look at myself in the mirror. I had expected to look like a cancer patient and was a little surprised that I didn't. It was the eyebrows. Cancer patients lose theirs. I still had mine.

The mustache was next. I'd grow a real one eventually, but I knew that would take a while. Facial hair has never come easy for me. In high school I was the last boy on the soccer team to start shaving. The eyeliner pencil was cheesy, but it was just a temporary fix. I started in the center, just outside the lip crevice, and drew a straight line out to the corner of my mouth. Then I did the same on the other side. The lines were straight enough, but something about it didn't look right to me. Maybe I was just so used to my own face that I saw right through the fake mustache. I don't know. But when I put on the sunglasses, everything just came together—the bald head, the sleazy mustache, the reflective aviator lenses. I didn't know who I was looking at in the mirror, but I knew it wasn't Alton Carver. Next time, Clara would not recognize me.

But would anyone else? People who knew me well enough might. They almost certainly would if they looked at me for more than a few seconds. But I wasn't worried about those people. I could duck them easily enough. They'd never get close enough to recognize me. I was more worried about complete strangers who watched the news and never forgot a face, the people I couldn't pick out of a crowd ahead of time and avoid. The disguise I had wasn't brilliant. But I was pretty confident that it would fool that lot for a few seconds at least. Those people wouldn't look at me twice.

Bullwinkle's Irish Pub was about a five-minute drive from the Royal Rest, in a strip mall next to a Vietnamese nail salon, a wig store, and a place with a plastic banner above the door that promised to turn broken gold into cold hard cash. From the outside, there was nothing especially Irish about Bullwinkle's. There was a leprechaun and a giant four-leaf clover painted on the window, but that was about it. A Coors Light neon sign perched directly above the leprechaun and buzzed. Coors Light. How many people in Ireland do you think have ever even tasted Coors Light? And of those, how many do you think would admit it? I pushed the door open and waited for my eyes to adjust.

The place was mostly empty. There was a cluster of five or six patrons throwing darts at the other end of the bar, three guys all sitting by themselves, and me. That was it. I pulled out a stool near the center of the bar, away from the other drinkers. The legs of the stool skidded along the cheap linoleum tiles with a loud scraping squeak.

"Get a vodka?" I said to the bartender. "One ice cube."

"Got a preference?"

"Well is fine," I said. If you only knew what kind of shit I've been drinking for the last few days.

The bartender shrugged and poured a stream of off-label vodka into a tumbler.

"Don't forget the cube," I reminded him. He gave me this pissy look as he used a clean glass to scoop an ice cube out of the ice machine and dump it into my glass. The man on my right snorted.

"You don't care what kind of shit he pours you, but yeah boy, don't forget the ice," he said without even looking at me.

"Warm vodka is like drinking rubbing alcohol," I said.

"So say on the rocks, then." The man turned to look at me now, was looking right at me. I felt my shoulders tense, my bowels tighten. My breathing shallowed out. The moment of truth—here it was. "Why's it gotta be, 'Oh, just a single ice cube, barkeep'?"

I waited a moment before answering. I looked closely at the man's face. Studied it. It was creased and rough textured, like 180-grit sandpaper. Was there even the slightest spark of recognition in those eyes? Was his brain trying to connect the face in front of it to some scrap of memory, buried somewhere under the accumulated flotsam from the last couple days of his own everyday life?

I saw nothing in there. I took a sip.

"Because I don't want rocks, plural. I want one rock," I said. "One cube is best because it chills the drink just enough, and also gets the liquor to the exact right viscosity when it melts." Fuck. I couldn't believe I'd just said viscosity.

The man laughed again. "Viscosity," he said. "You sound like a motor oil commercial."

"Heh, yeah," I said. I shrugged. "It's the only way I know how to describe it."

"You're probably better off drinking motor oil than that shit. That's some industrial-grade horse piss right there," he said. Then he grunted and went back to staring at the wall behind the bar. I downed most of my drink in a single swallow. My breathing was evening out again, my pulse back to normal; I could feel my confidence seeping back into me now. If the grunter did recognize me, he was hiding it well. I was ready for another drink.

"Can I get a Guinness?" I asked the bartender.

"We don't carry it," the bartender said.

"No Guinness." I shook my head. "You got NASCAR posters everywhere and basketball on the TVs, but no Guinness. Some Irish pub."

"That was all the last owner's idea," the bartender said.

"Thought it'd be a good way to get the yuppie crowd in here, I guess. Just haven't got around to changing it yet. You a yuppie?"

"I look like a yuppie to you?" I tried to sound dismissive and maybe a little offended by the question, but the truth is that I was very interested in his answer. I did not at all want to look like the yuppie I had been in my previous life. I wanted to ask him straight out: What do you see when you look at me?

"Not really," the bartender said. "But you never can tell

anymore. Especially with the whole 'one cube of ice' thing. That's a little fancier than we usually get in here."

"Fair enough," I said. "You can't really tell about most people."

"You want another of those instead?" he said, pointing to my empty glass.

"Yeah, that's fine."

I carried my drink over to the darts game at the far end of the bar. I stood back a bit, separate from the group. They all seemed to know each other. So I just sipped my vodka and watched them play. I tried to figure out the rules of the game—darts scoring never made any sense to me—but I gave up after a few minutes. Occasionally one of the players would look my way, and whenever that happened I tried to make and hold eye contact, maybe jog something loose in their memories. I was trying to push the boundaries now, to actively invite scrutiny instead of avoid it, to really test this disguise. But nobody paid me anything more than fleeting attention.

I finished my drink and left, dropping a trio of five-dollar bills on the bar as I walked out. I hadn't noticed how smoky the inside of Bullwinkle's was until I was standing outside in the parking lot, breathing in the clear night air. My eyes felt like they had sand in them. The cigarette smoke on my clothes, in my nostrils—that was the only thing I could smell. Normally that would have bothered me, but not that night. That night I didn't care about any of it. Because nobody had recognized me. Nobody had called the police to report a sighting of that lawyer who drowned last week. Nobody noticed me at all, really. This will work, I remember thinking, and at that moment I suddenly knew—with absolute, dead-on certainty—that I'd pull it off, that I'd fool everybody until long after it was too late for them to do anything to stop me. That night I slept soundly for the first time in ten days.

ELEVEN

Alton

I slipped the spare key into the lock and turned it, shoving my shoulder into the back door as I did. The doorjamb seemed to have swollen over the years and now the door would stick most of the time, especially on humid days. And that day was a humid day. I remember the springtime weather had returned to normal, which in that part of Florida means more or less just like summer. The cold snap that could easily have killed me the week before was now just a forgotten meteorological anomaly.

But the door popped right open. The security system squawked at me like it always did, and I reflexively punched my code into the alarm panel. Right away I felt a quick burst of panic—Oh shit, what if she's canceled it already?—but then the panel beeped twice and fell silent. For the first time in nearly two weeks, I was home.

I stood there in the kitchen and just took it all in for a moment. The room was awash in the reflected glow of the morning sunlight. Part of me had been expecting the place to be a disaster, a diorama of dirty dishes and empty frozen dinner boxes or something. But the pans all hung along the wall, right where they belonged. Bowls and plates, stacked neatly in the cupboards. No spilled food, no empty containers, not even any dust. The place was immaculate, not so much as a salad fork out of place.

Neighbors, I thought. Probably stopping by to check on her, help her out.

I opened the refrigerator, more out of habit than anything else, and then closed it. The fridge was covered with Clara's artwork, which now included several drawings I hadn't seen before. There was a line drawing of a frog, which she seemed

58

to have drawn in a single continuous stroke of blue crayon. There was a drawing of what looked like a Martian flower bed, which had apparently required all sixty-four of the crayons in her box. Then there was an abstract piece; I had no idea what that was supposed to be, or if it was even supposed to be anything at all. Finally there was a drawing of three stick figures—two large, one small—standing in front of a red house. The stick people were smiling. Happy little stick family. On the right side of the paper, she had drawn a sailboat, floating on a lake, with nobody aboard.

Things were already starting to change, and not just new drawings on the fridge. That was just the change I could see, staring me right in the face. But I could also feel that everything was somehow different now, that in just two weeks this house had changed in a very subtle, almost imperceptible way, but one I knew was almost certainly permanent.

What was I actually doing here? I asked myself that question as I drifted over to the butcher-block kitchen island. It was bare except for a tall stack of mail. I flipped through it. Something from the Neptune Society—that struck me as a particularly cruel joke, given the circumstances. Something from Our Lady Queen of Martyrs, Nicole's alma mater. Was it reunion time already? Or maybe they just wanted donations. Bills. Renew your subscription to the Atlantic. Fat envelopes with laser-printed return addresses but no company name.

Nothing from the insurance company, though.

I stacked the mail on the butcher block, exactly as I'd found it. It was time to leave. Whatever I had wanted from that visit, I knew I wasn't going to get it. This place wasn't my home anymore. There was nothing else there for me. I knew that now.

I spotted a legal pad on the counter, right next to the toaster. A pen rested on top of it. I could write a note, I thought. Just a short note. Tell them it'll be okay. They deserve to know.

It was a dangerous idea. But it was seductive too. Could I do that? Could I just pick up that pen and leave a note from beyond the grave? More to the point, should I? What would Nicole do with it? I honestly had no idea how she'd react to something like that. Would she take it to the police? Would she wait for me to come back and then hit me with something heavy or pointy for putting her through all this? Or would she fall into my arms, weeping with gratitude and happiness? Well, I guess we'll find out, I thought, and I clicked the pen and set myself to write . . . well, I didn't know, really. I'd just write whatever came out, just let it flow. But then I noticed there was already writing on the pad, and then I saw what it was.

It was a list. A list of people I knew. People from the office. People from the neighborhood. Relatives. Nicole's relatives. Some names I didn't recognize. Printed above the list, in Nicole's trademark neat handwriting, were the words "Alton's Wake," and a date. Just two days away.

A wake?

Already?

Seriously?

I'd only been missing for two weeks. And she already wanted to move on, to close the book on me, to announce to the entire world that she had given up hope of my ever coming back? She was right, I wasn't coming back, but she couldn't possibly know that. She had no idea. But already she was gathering all the people who knew me best to say their good-byes and celebrate my life—my complete and finished life? I get that funerals are for the people left behind, but this was ridiculous.

Wait. Wait a minute. Ah, I get it now.

It was for the insurance. She probably needed to prove to the insurance company that she truly and sincerely believed I was dead, since they'd never found a body. And the sooner she did that, the sooner she'd get paid.

But hang on. I forced myself to think this through. If she actually does believe I'm dead, that means she's not playing the insurance company. Wait, was that right? I couldn't focus on it, couldn't quite follow the train of logic, so I just stopped thinking about it. I made sure the back door was locked on my way out, and then I ducked into the alley behind the house and jogged back to the car.

TWELVE

Nicole

The wake was Lauren's idea. I think she was worried about me, about my drinking and what was happening to my mind in those early days of uncertainty and grief and all those other emotions I didn't understand quite well enough to name. A wake would be a way for me to gain closure, and then regain control, both for my sake and for my daughter's.

I'm sure that's what she thought.

But it was actually a very stressful thing for me to have to deal with. Not the planning of it, because Lauren promised she'd take care of most of that, which she did. She's the most reliable friend I've ever had, so I wasn't worried about that part at all. The stress was coming from someplace more basic. I couldn't shake the idea that I was giving up too soon, like maybe I was somehow betraying Alton in a way I couldn't really explain, even to myself. What if we had a wake and then the next week he walked right through the front door, all sunburned and soaking wet? "You'll never believe what happened," he'd say, and then he'd tell me where he'd been for the last few weeks. He'd give me some elaborate yarn, a tale of cosmically bad luck and narrow escapes. Something that could only happen to him. We'd laugh and hug and I'd pour us some wine and we'd go out to the patio and drink it. And then I'd have to tell him that all his friends thought he was dead because that's what I'd told them.

And then Clara. Oh my stars. How would her little mind process that? Daddy's gone and never coming back—oh, wait, my mistake, he's right over here. Never mind. Yeah, no, not doing that to her. This had been tough enough on her as it was.

But at the same time, if I was being honest with myself? If I was really being honest about my feelings, which as you know

62

isn't always easy for me, I'd have to admit that I wanted the wake. I wanted to move on. I wanted to put all of this behind me. I wanted my daughter to start healing. And I wanted him gone. Out of my head. I wanted to be happy again. So we had the damn wake.

What I couldn't figure out was whether that made me a horrible person or not.

THIRTEEN

Alton

On the day of my wake, I parked beneath the broad canopy of an ancient oak tree a quarter mile from the house. I didn't want Larry Combs spotting me again. Even if only half the people on Nicole's list showed up, Reedmere Lane would be choked with unfamiliar vehicles up and down the street. Combs had been pretty sharp, once upon a time, but I had to wonder if he'd recall the same dull gold Camry from earlier in the week. Still, I didn't want to take unnecessary chances, so I parked farther away and walked a few extra blocks.

You didn't think I would pass up the opportunity to see my own funeral, did you?

At first the whole idea of a wake had left me feeling shaken. It seemed rushed, like Nicole was just a little too eager to move on from our life together. I think . . . I think I took it as an insult. Of course, even after all these weeks of turning this story over in my mind, I've never been able to articulate exactly why I felt that way. Maybe part of me was afraid that it would be the last time anyone would think about me or miss me. I wasn't ready for that, especially if we're talking about Clara.

But then it occurred to me that I was being given a great gift here—or rather, I was being given the opportunity to give a great gift to my friends and family. The guests would be there to say good-bye to me, of course. That's the whole point. But those good-byes are never satisfying. There is always something hollow about an apology or a good-bye that goes unheard.

But I would be there to hear theirs. They wouldn't know it, but their words wouldn't just dissipate into the air. I would carry them with me, to Costa Rica, where I would listen to

64

them over and over in my mind, for the rest of my days.

Of course, they couldn't actually have known any of that at the time. So maybe the experience wasn't actually any more fulfilling for them after all. Maybe even less so in retrospect, now that they all know I'm not actually dead.

When I got to Reedmere I didn't break stride. I just crossed the road and ducked into the alley. Nobody sees you, I told myself. Nobody is paying any attention to you. People walk down this alley all the time. The six-foot privacy fences kept me out of sight. The stench of garbage baking in the enormous black plastic cans already hung in the air, thick and ripe, though it wasn't anywhere near as bad as it would be in a few weeks, when the scalding summer temperatures would make even the simple act of going outside unbearable for six months. God, I hate summer.

My house was on the right, fourth in from the street. I stood for a moment and looked at my—well, okay, Nicole's now—garbage can. I thought about opening it and rooting through it. But I didn't. Instead I unlatched the backyard gate for the house directly behind mine—Edgecomb's house—and slipped into the backyard. Edgecomb never locked his gate. I knew this because he never got tired of talking about finding another bum raiding his kid's vegetable garden or knocking on his back door in the hopes of doing some odd jobs to raise a quick ten bucks (which was always so said-homeless person could "buy a bus ticket back to Indianapolis because my sister is sick" or some such nonsense). I must have told him a thousand times that the easiest way to put a stop to that sort of thing was to just lock his gate. A thousand times at least. I lost count a long time ago. But for whatever reason, he never did it.

The sightline from his kids' tree house into my backyard was perfect, a straight shot. Not only could I see most of the yard, but I could even see directly into the house itself. Nicole had the French doors open so that the living room opened up directly into the yard. There was a long table—probably the folding table from up in the attic—with a white tablecloth draped over it. On top of that were bowls and trays heaped with food. The light inside the house wasn't quite good enough to make out exactly what Nicole had decided to serve. I remember thinking that whatever it was, it probably had too much dill in it—that's how it was with almost everything she ever cooked, too much dill—and just then she hurried into the living room and over to the table, where she set down another platter and whirled off again.

Nicole. That was the first glimpse of her I'd had in two weeks. She'd only given me a couple of seconds, but that was enough, more than enough, for right now. I closed my eyes and replayed that footage of her dropping off that tray, slowed it down in my head, pored over every frame, breathed in every last detail of how she looked, how she moved. I felt an ache deep in my chest, a tightness that radiated outward and worked its way into my shoulders and arms. Tears welled up in my eyes. Shit. I'd missed her more than I thought. I decided right then that I would send for her and Clara in a couple years after all. Yes. Bring them down to the estate I'd buy in Costa Rica. Be a rich and happy family, together again. How could I ever have even considered living apart from them? What the hell was I thinking? I wiped my eyes and watched the room. I fought the urge to blink, just in case she came back from the kitchen.

Instead I saw Clara amble out into the backyard and do a controlled collapse into a seated position on the steps. She squirmed in the crimson dress and white leggings Nicole had dressed her in. She looked more like she was attending a Christmas party than saying good-bye forever to her daddy, and she kicked at the ground without much enthusiasm for a minute or two before getting up and wandering around the back corner of the house. My first instinct was to call out her name, to spring out of that stupid tree house, go scoop her up, and bring her back. She knew she wasn't allowed to be by herself in the front of the house, which was obviously where she was headed; we'd told her that a thousand times. But I forced myself to be still, to just sit there and watch.

Nicole appeared in the doorway, looking around the backyard, craning her head left and then right before calling out my daughter's name. Clara stopped and looked over her shoulder, weighing the pros and cons of answering before committing to anything. Nicole stepped into the yard but turned the wrong way, still calling for Clara. This time she came back. I watched Nicole pick her up and carry her back in the house, closing the French doors behind her.

There was too much glare on the glass in the doors for me to see much of anything inside the house. Damn it. I needed an accurate head count, and I wouldn't get it if I couldn't see inside. I tried to tell myself it wasn't really that important a thing to know. But I had to know. Wasn't that the whole point? How could I come this far—to actually be sitting maybe a hundred feet from my own wake—only to be denied the answer to the question everyone asks at some point: If I died, who would come to my funeral? And how awful would they feel? Would someone break down weeping? Well of course someone would. It was just a matter of who. My money was on Ed Stanwyck. I'd seen the man cry over deodorant commercials. Or maybe Sheila Vilmure. She'd been in love with me since the moment we met. I thought maybe I could get closer, but I couldn't figure out how to do it without actually entering the backyard, which was out of the question. The tree house was the best vantage point I was going to get, so I stayed put there and waited. It was hot in that little plywood box, oppressively so, and after a few minutes I dozed off.

The slam of a car door woke me up, and for a brief panicked moment I thought the Edgecombs had come home. But it wasn't them. The sound came from farther away. I poked my head up to the window and saw someone on the sidewalk, just to the right of my house. But it was only a fraction of a second and then the person was out of view, obscured by the house itself. I had no idea who it was. Damn.

More guests arrived over the next ten minutes or so, and I cataloged them as they did. The Andersons. That Armenian guy from up the street with his skinny blond wife. Bob Sherman. A couple of people I couldn't name, because I either didn't see them clearly enough or didn't recognize them. Cass Tobin.

The French doors opened again, and Scott Ryerson, of all people—he was this advertising guy I knew from Kiwanis, skinny little prick with a perpetual smirk—stepped out and lit a cigarette. Ryerson and I had never been particularly close, and I was genuinely surprised to see him there. I doubt I'd go to your wake, Scott, I thought, and then smiled, because I had the perfect excuse to miss it now. I watched him smoke and give my backyard a critical once-over at the same time. Then he dropped the used-up butt onto the slate garden path and ground it out with his toe. What an asshole.

By then there were others in the backyard, holding small paper plates of food and bottles of beer, trying to eat with one hand without sitting down. I knew all of them. Jen Morgan— we used to work together until she got pregnant and took advantage of maternity leave to jump to a less toxic work environment—chatting with Amy Newman, whom I'd known since forever and almost had an affair with years ago but didn't, for reasons I can't quite remember now. Amy's husband Carl was smoking a cigar that I could smell all the way across the alley. Carl was deep in conversation with someone I was sure I knew but whose face refused to connect with a name. Tall guy. Red hair. Crabtree? No, that wasn't it. Next to them, Mike Ingram— who had gone to law school with me for a year before dropping out because he decided it was "total fucking bullshit, man"— also smoking, laughing, and blatantly hitting on two of Nicole's friends from Pilates class, but they didn't seem to be going for it. My parents. Nicole's parents. Nicole's sister.

People were cycling in and out at that point, looking for a place to smoke, somewhere to escape the awkward obligation of comforting a brand-new widow, even for just a few minutes. Soon food-smeared paper plates littered the grass, and plastic cups stood abandoned in the nooks and crannies of the back-yard landscaping, with only a swallow or two of dark liquid left at the bottom. Some had cigarette butts floating in them. I could hear music, at first some light jazz piano that took me a minute to recognize as one of my Bill Evans records, but then someone must have decided that it was too morose or cliché or something and instead put on some Bootsy Collins, which seemed like an odd choice for a wake. But it seemed to loosen people up, and once that record was over, the music kept going in that same vein for what must have been another hour and a half or so. And then whoever was deejaying put on one of my old Bill Monroe records, which I love but absolutely no one else does. That was about the time when the guests started saying their good-byes and floating off into the evening.

I slid back down onto the floor. So that was it. That was my send-off. Those were the people who thought enough of me to come and say good-bye. I started putting together a list in my head: Who'd been invited but hadn't come? But it was more than I could hold on to at once. There was too much rattling through my mind at that moment to focus. Maybe if I'd had something to write it all down with. I had gotten almost no grat-ification at all from the whole experience. I'd been just a little too far away to hear what people were saying about me. It was profoundly empty. I was empty.

I lifted my head up to the window, looking for any stray peo-ple cutting through the alley. Nicole was in the backyard again, arms crossed, drink in her hand, that familiar thousand-yard stare blanking out her face. She looked tired, so tired. Poor thing. You've had such a rough time of it. I wanted to reach out to her, to touch her skin, tell her that I was right there, I had always been there, and that everything would be all right soon enough and—

Oh, wait. Maybe it wasn't over yet.

A man—in his twenties, lots of hair, one of the guests I didn't recognize—walked through the French doors and into the backyard. He had a drink in his hand and walked up directly behind Nicole, who gave no sign she knew he was there until he was right behind her, against her, his left arm suddenly around her waist, his hand sliding across her belly.

What the fuck is this guy doing?

She reached back and touched his head without looking at him, letting her hand linger there for a moment before putting it on top of his left hand. Then she leaned her head back against his shoulder.

What. The. Fuck.

Seriously.

What

the

fuuuuuuuuuuu—

And suddenly I was soaking wet and cold, sprayed by a garden hose that Todd Edgecomb aimed at me from down on the ground.

"Goddamn it, how many times do I have to tell you?" he yelled. "Stay the hell out of my yard! My kids play up there, for Chrissakes! Get the hell out of here!"

I wanted to take that hose and shove it up his goofball ass. I wanted to choke him with it until his eyes bugged out of their sockets. Something was happening that I had to see. Something important, goddamn it. And he was fucking everything up.

But instead I scrambled to my feet and leaped from the tree house, bypassing the ladder altogether, and bolted through the back gate and into the alley. I sprinted the whole way back to the car and then past it, for blocks and blocks without stopping until my lungs burned and my heart felt as thin and as fragile as tracing paper.

FOURTEEN

Nicole

The doorbell rang just when I had my hands full with a tray of hot spring rolls.

"Clara, honey?" I called out. "Would you answer the door for Mommy? Please?"

"Okay, Mommy." Clara bounced her way to the front door, and I winced when I heard her say to whoever was there, "Hi! Welcome to the party!" The poor thing. She had no idea what was going on, what any of this was all about. I felt terrible for her. I dropped the tray off at the table on my way to the front door. It was just Lauren. Such a relief. I'd been afraid it would be my mother. And I wasn't up to dealing with my mother yet.

"How you holding up?" Lauren asked.

"Oh, I am so glad you're here." I sighed as we hugged. "I'm way behind."

"Whatever you need me to do," Lauren said. "You know that."

It's true, I was behind—I was expecting guests within half an hour or so—but I was already in a groove in the kitchen, so Lauren vacuumed and dusted and closed off the rooms where the guests had no business going. Lauren has been my closest friend for years; there was really nobody else I would even think of turning to in a crisis. I heard Clara screech and giggle as soon as Lauren turned on the vacuum. "Keep away from the vacuum" had always been one of Clara's favorite games to play with Alton.

I'd been working in the kitchen for a couple hours by then, and it had to be at least ten degrees warmer in there than the rest of the house. I felt like I needed to take a pause, so I pulled the bacon-wrapped stuffed jalapeños out of the

71

oven and set the pan on the counter. Then I stepped into the living room to cool down for just a minute or two.

Lauren blocked my path. "Um . . . got a minute?"

"What? What's the matter?"

"Oh, probably nothing," she said, then trailed off. "Okay, maybe not nothing. Does, um, does Clara know what all this"—and here she swept her arm through the air toward the buffet table and the cluster of pictures of Alton—"is for?"

"Why? What did she say?"

"Well, she asked when all the people were going to get here for the party, and I told her soon, really soon, baby. And then she, um . . ."

"She what?" But I already knew the answer.

"Then she asked when her daddy was going to get here."

"Goddamn it." I let out this heavy sigh. My body felt like a giant balloon deflating. "I've explained this to her."

"She's four. It probably just isn't processing, you know?"

"Yeah. So what did you tell her?"

"I, um, might have said that I didn't think he was coming?"

"Uh-huh," I said. I didn't know why that bothered me, but it did. For some reason, I wanted to be mad. I wanted to feel self-righteous because Lauren had somehow overstepped her bounds. But she hadn't, of course, not really. What else could she have done? I was just taking out my own guilt on her, which wasn't fair at all. "How did she take that bit of news?"

"Yeah, um, not great, no," Lauren said. "That's the only reason I told you in the first place, really. I'm sorry if I said something I shouldn't have. I honestly didn't know what else to do."

"You know what? It's fine. Of course you didn't do anything wrong. But I think I should go talk to her anyway. You mind watching the kitchen for a minute?"

"Of course not," Lauren said. "She's in her playroom now, I think."

Which is right where I found her, sitting on the floor, moving these oversize wooden cars of hers around on thick beige carpet. Her stuffed cow sat on its haunches in the center of everything, directing traffic.

"Clara, honey." I sat down next to her. "How are you?"

"Fine," she said. Her voice was thin. She didn't look up at me. Instead she focused on the task at hand, pushing her cars around in a circle.

"That's good, honey." I noticed my voice had taken on this obnoxious soothing tone I hate. That's a bad habit I have; I wasn't doing it on purpose. I've always thought I sound so fake when I take that tone, but for some reason I decided to just go with it. "Listen, Miss Lauren said you asked her something. Do you remember asking her a question?"

"I don't know."

"She told me you asked about Daddy. Do you remember asking her about Daddy?"

"I asked her when Daddy was going to get here for our party," she said.

"What did she say?"

"She said he's not coming."

"That's right, honey." I reached out and touched Clara's hair. She did not move. "He isn't coming to the party."

"But why? I want him to."

"I know you do. But he can't. We talked about this before, remember? Where is Daddy now?"

"He's under the water." Her voice went flat, this tiny little monotone, filled with defeat.

"That's right. He's under the water. And that's where he has to stay now. He can't come to our party because that's where he is. Do you understand?"

"I want to go outside now," Clara whined. "I want to play outside."

"Okay, baby." I wasn't sure she really understood, but on the other hand, I have to admit I was relieved to be done with that conversation. "Just be careful. You already have your pretty party dress on, and we wouldn't want it to get dirty, would we?"

"No," she said. She didn't take her eyes off the floor. I watched her for a few moments, waiting for her to get up and head outside. But she just sat there, staring at the floor and fiddling with one of her cars.

"Aren't you going outside?" I asked, and then she did get up and walk toward the back, saying nothing, head hanging and feet dragging, like playing outside was some kind of a punishment instead of her own idea. I thought about saying something, and maybe I should have. But I didn't, because just then the doorbell rang. I knew it was my mother, arriving early to help, which was almost never actually helpful, but you know how it can be with mothers sometimes. I took a deep breath and wished I'd had time for a drink before she got there. Then I went to let her in.

Before long, I was drunk. There was a house full of people and they ate like hyenas and there were cigarettes inside the house and food on the floor and Bob Sherman grabbed my ass twice and I was drunk enough to think, Well, why not, but then Mike and Crystal from next door pushed between us and told me how sorry they were and that Alton was a great guy and then I saw myself, what I must look like as the woman who lost her husband and—

—and then I was in the guest bathroom, on my knees, on the floor in front of the toilet, the inside of which now smelled like Chardonnay and bacon, but my head still felt thick and dumb and I knew I was still drunk—

—and then Lewis Pritchard was saying something, something about Alton, something about a trip to Atlanta and almost getting mugged and then something else about this bar where they did dwarf-tossing and I wondered, Was I on that trip? but I couldn't focus and Lewis's story was just so much word salad to me—

—and then I was sitting, on the couch, Lauren handing me a glass of water and a plate of cookies from Publix, and I swallowed huge gulps from the glass and scarfed a cookie in two bites before I noticed the people standing around me in a semicircle, just staring at me, and I wanted to yell at them, What are you looking at? Haven't you ever seen a woman whose husband is dead? but I didn't because I stuffed another cookie into my mouth instead—

—and I realized that someone must have gotten into Alton's record collection, because they were playing his goddamn disco records instead of the jazz Lauren had put on, and I remembered how much he had hated it when I called them disco and how he had always insisted they were funk, but I'm not an idiot, I know the difference, and then my mind cleared and the room snapped back into focus and then I suddenly didn't feel drunk anymore.

"I think it is time," I said to Lauren, "for these people to get out of my house."

"I know just the thing," she said. A minute later I heard bluegrass—loud intrusive tooth-rattling bluegrass, those trebly banjo notes just drilling their way into my temples—punching out of the speakers. Guests moved away from that side of the room, first toward the kitchen and then the front door.

I ask you, where would I be without her? Where would I be without a friend like Lauren?

"If you need anything—anything at all," Chad Blount was saying, "just call me or Debbie. I mean it." Debbie nodded energetically, which set her second chin to wobbling. And then it was Stacy Eldridge and Cass Tobin and Pete Fredericks and everyone else, one after the other in this surreal blur of flesh and perfume.

"We're right across the street," someone said.

"We'll cover for you at work Monday if you need it," someone told me.

75

"You're in our prayers," someone else told me. Actually, I think several people told me that.

"We all miss him. He was such a wonderful person," somebody else said, and I realized that it was all meaning-less, every word of it, all exactly the same, all completely ridiculous.

"Once the insurance check gets here, I'm sure you and Clara won't have anything to worry about." That one was from Kevin Cook—I remember that one, because the insur-ance money was already a sore spot for me just then.

"Yes, Alton took good care of us," I said. In fact, he took such good care of us that he fell off his stupid fucking boat and died and left me to raise our daughter, and he didn't even have the decency to leave his body where someone could find it, and now the insurance company is talking about not pay-ing because maybe it was a suicide or maybe he's not even dead, they can't say for sure because they don't have a body to poke and prod and cut open, I didn't add. I wish I had now. "Thank you so much for coming."

By then it was down to just a few stragglers. Lauren came downstairs from Clara's room; she had just put her to bed. "I can get started on the kitchen," Lauren said. "I mean, there are still a few people here but—"

"No no," I said. "You really don't have to. You've done enough. I think I'm just going to leave it all in the sink and do it tomorrow."

"Are you sure?"

"It'll give me something to occupy my Sunday." I shrugged. I already felt bad enough about monopolizing her time the way I had over the last couple of weeks.

"Okay. If you're sure." Lauren smiled. "To be honest, I'm completely wiped. If you're sure you don't need anything . . ."

"I'm sure. Go."

Then Lauren hugged me, pulling me in close. "You know where to find me," she said.

Finally it was over. I was out in the backyard, a drink—ginger ale, it calms my stomach—in my hand. Thank god all that was over with. My mother had asked why I was throwing a wake so soon—is that how you say it? Throwing a wake? I don't know—before anyone knew for sure if he was really . . . well, you know. Gone. I pointed out that the Coast Guard didn't think he could have survived, and that they probably knew a bit more about that sort of thing than either of us did.

"But Nicole," she said. "Miracles do happen, you know." I sighed loudly. "No, Mother, they don't. People like you think they do, but they don't. Waiting around for a miracle is the best way I can think of to just let your life slip away from you."

"I honestly don't know what I did," my mother said, "to raise such a disrespectful child."

"I am not actually a child anymore, Mother," I reminded her, and not for the first time. "Please do try to remember that."

Alton's parents, well, they hadn't come out and said anything, but I was positive I'd seen reproach in their eyes that afternoon, as if they resented me for forcing them to confront the possibility that their boy might actually be dead. It's like I was forcing them to say good-bye to him sooner than they would have liked, or pushing them into a closure they weren't ready for. Of course, it was also entirely possible that I might have just imagined all that. I had been pretty drunk.

But at the same time, now that it was over, I felt a little lost. Even with Lauren's help, putting that service together on short notice had given me something to focus on, a challenge, a way to distract myself from my feelings by concentrating on an organizational task instead. Not that I actually understood my feelings at that point. Not that I do now either, for that matter.

Now I could finally take some time and think about what should come next. I could start working, really working, on coming to grips with my feelings, whatever they were, about Alton's death and about Alton himself.

And you know what? The prospect absolutely terrified me.

I closed my eyes, just listening to the backyard at dusk, breathing in the evening air and holding it, savoring the quiet and the solitude. God, those people were exhausting. This . . . this was exactly what I needed after a day like that one.

Then I felt a hand slide across my belly, warm breath on my neck, and I knew that Davis was there with me. I leaned into him, grateful for the opportunity to shift my weight off my own feet and onto him for even a few moments.

"Hi," he said.

"Hi, yourself," I said back.

"You look pretty good for a woman who was throwing up a couple hours ago."

"Oh shut up." I swatted at his arm. "Don't remind me."

"I can help you . . . forget all about it." He began kissing my neck. "If you'll let me."

"Hmmmmm, be careful." It was risky. Clara might see. But to be honest, I wasn't sure I really wanted him to be careful, if you know what I mean.

"Maybe I don't want to be careful," he said, reading my mind.

"Uh-huh. Maybe I don't want Clara to wake up and look out her window and see us . . . like this."

"Oh, she knows," Davis said. "She's seen us kiss. She's cool with it."

"Oh my god, I hope not."

"Why not?"

"I just . . . I just don't want her confused. It's not about you, I promise. It's just too soon for her. Too much. That's all, I guess." I looked up at his face, just over my left shoulder. "Should we go in?"

"Yeah, probably, I guess," he said. "Jesus, what the hell was that?"

I heard Todd Edgecomb yelling from his yard, the sound of a garden hose and then his back gate banging against the fence. "Probably the neighbor. Spraying a bum with his hose. They're always getting in there."

"He should maybe try locking his gate," Davis said, and we went inside, his arm across my shoulder, my arm around his waist, and then the French doors were closed and locked for the evening.

FIFTEEN
Alton

I don't know how long I sat there in the front seat of the car. Call it two hours. It was hard to tell for sure—my mind was having trouble latching on to any of the usual temporal reference points just then. All I know is that I sat there long enough for my clothes to completely dry out, without the benefit of even a stiff breeze.

Two hours was a long time for him to be in there. Had he left during that brief interval between the moments Todd Edgecomb hosed me down like a stray dog and when I parked at the end of the block? That hadn't been very long. Not more than ten minutes, probably. Certainly long enough for this guy to say his good-byes—whatever those consisted of—and go slinking back to whatever bachelor-pad shithole he almost certainly lived in. Plenty long enough.

I'd planned to hit the road as soon as the wake was over. Had I stuck to that, I would have been just about to I-10 by then. Instead I spent those two hours trying to talk myself out of having seen what I had just seen. I'd almost succeeded, too. It was dusk. The light wasn't great. I was forty or fifty feet away and actively trying to stay hidden. They were probably at least a little drunk. Maybe she just kind of stumbled backward, and he happened to be there to catch her. Sure.

It was feasible.

It was also bullshit, and I knew it.

I may have been in shock, but I wasn't stupid. If he was the only guest still inside—after two solid hours—that could only mean one thing.

No. He's gone. Almost certainly gone. It's the only reasonable concl—

And then my front door popped open, and the guy bobbed down the front steps and into the yard. My heart withered. So. It was true. I had seen it after all.

I decided to name the guy Chas. He looked like a Chas to me.

Chas was in no particular hurry to leave, nor was he concerned with being seen. He handled the slightly too shallow front steps with ease. He didn't even trip on the loose brick in the walkway, and I suddenly realized that this was probably not his first time at the house.
My very next thought was to wonder when that had been, exactly.

Chas pressed a button on his key fob and a sleek BMW roadster flashed its lights. He had parked halfway between the house and where I was sitting, and even at that relatively close distance I couldn't tell if the car was navy blue or jet black. I followed four or five car lengths behind as Chas navigated through the neighborhood. He coasted slowly along the brick-paved streets, streets that routinely punished lead-footed hotshots in low-riding cars like the Beemer. But Chas apparently already knew better than to speed in Old Northeast.

Hmmm. I wonder how. Must have friends here.

A couple of left turns later and we were on the Crosstown Expressway. After three or four uneventful miles, Chas suddenly swerved out of the passing lane, hit the brakes and cut across the three empty lanes to his right to make for the exit ramp. Ah shit—he must have seen me. But I decided to play it cool; you never know, maybe he was just a terrible driver. I turned on my blinker, gave it several clicks in case there was a cop somewhere behind me, and guided the car down the exit ramp. I spotted the Beemer idling at the next light, three blocks up, waiting to turn left into a residential neighborhood.

This side of town was the beach side. Technically it was on the same side of the city as the Royal Rest, but that dump was seven or eight miles north of where we were and might as well have been in another county. Down there in Bayshore Gardens, the yards were small and neat, with crotons and birds of paradise shaded by the broad leaves of sea grape trees. Residents parked their cars on driveways of crushed seashell. The houses themselves were not large, mostly stucco with Spanish tile roofs, but I wasn't fooled by their modest appearances. These homes were much more expensive than they looked.

Now where the hell is Chas?

Oh, there he is. The Beemer rolled to a stop in front of a small, olive-green house on the next block. I parked about a block away and scanned the streetscape. No other cars moving in either direction. Nobody taking the dog for an evening stroll. No Larry Combs clones that I could see, peeping out their windows. It was never going to get any safer. I tried to look like I was supposed to be there as I got out of the car and strolled down to Chas's house.

The house was almost wall-to-wall windows. He switched on lights in every room, making it simple for someone outside to press nose to glass and take a quick inventory of the place. Aside from the out-of-proportion flat-screen TV on the wall—that thing had to be at least eighty inches—Chas seemed to be cultivating some kind of minimalist vibe. He hardly had any furniture, and what he did have didn't really match. It looked like it all came from consignment stores that specialized in pieces you'd see on *Brady Bunch* reruns. The bar next to the television was well stocked, as was the bookcase on the opposite end of the room. I was a little surprised by that. I wouldn't have pegged Chas for a reader.

Crouched there in the bushes just feet from the sidewalk, I could feel the muscles in my neck and shoulders tense up. I was too exposed, and I knew it. The gate to his backyard privacy fence was only about ten feet away from my hiding place. I gently lifted the latch and slipped inside.

I wonder if he has a dog.

Shit. I should have thought of that before.

I froze and waited for a cannonball of muscle and fur and fangs to launch itself out of the shadows at me. But nothing did. Then I heard the front door slam shut.

Was someone here? Was he, uh, entertaining? Was it Nicole? No—it couldn't be. Someone would have to be watching Clara. She'd never bring—

And just then I heard the deep throaty rumble of the BMW's engine.

Shit. He's going somewhere.

I thought about just staying put. I wasn't sure I could get inside, but at least I could snoop around without worrying about him seeing me. And if I did somehow manage to get inside, maybe I could find out who this guy was.

But I wanted to know where he went on his Saturday nights. And the house wasn't going anywhere. So I jogged back toward the car, trying for all the world to look like I belonged exactly where I was, like I'd never belonged anywhere else.

Ten minutes later, I was parked across the street from Brewfie's, an outpost of a regional chain of tap houses with all the depth and character of a Bennigan's on the New Jersey Turnpike. I don't know if you have those out here, but they all look exactly the same—red brick structure with large windows in the front, facing out onto a wooden deck that stretches all the way to the sidewalk—and they all cater to the same crowd, which is people who can't or won't accept the fact that they aged out of fraternity and sorority life five or ten years ago. It must be a very profitable formula.

I could see from the street that the place was packed, a squirming sweating mass of sunburned flesh and barely concealed desperation. I sat there for a few minutes and watched the deck, where Chas—who before leaving the house had put on a baseball cap with a golf club company logo stamped across it (he hadn't yet turned it around so the brim faced backward, but I knew it was only a matter of time)—sucked down a pint of dark beer and played something called "cornhole," which I recognized as the game we all called "beanbag toss" when I was in elementary school.

This guy. This was the guy Nicole was banging, just two weeks after I disappeared. Had been banging for who the hell knew how long.

This fucking guy.

It made no sense to me. At all. He was just some kind of overgrown frat boy. What could Nicole possibly want with him? What could he possibly do for her?

Well, besides the obvious. Obviously.

Chas used his shirt to wipe beer from his chin just as a skinny blond in black yoga pants rushed up to him and threw her arms around his neck. He grabbed her in a bear hug and lifted her off the deck just as two more Abercrombie & Fitch refugees—they looked like a couple to me; Chas high-fived the guy—joined the party.

I got out of the car and crossed the street. I hoped the place had a full liquor license. After the day I'd had, I needed a drink. A real drink, I mean.

"What can I get you?" the beefy, bearded bartender asked me before I had even begun to sort through the options. All those names, carefully scratched out in pale pastels on the enormous chalkboard directly above the tap wall. No vodka, of course. I could feel my face pinching into a sour squint.

"Give a guy a minute," I said. I almost had to shout just to be heard through the overamplified acoustic duo performing on the sad excuse for a stage, which wasn't much more than a riser back by the restrooms. "It's a bit overwhelming, you know?"

The bartender's brow furrowed. "What's that, brah?"

"All the options." I looked at the bartender, waiting for his expression to change. It didn't. He just tugged at his beard and stared back at me. "You know, the tyranny of choice? That sort of thing?"

"Uh-huh. We're doing a tap takeover for Railspike Brewing," the bartender said. He sounded unsure of himself, but he plunged forward regardless. I admired that. "Lotsa great stuff on tap tonight. The I'm Hard for Hops Imperial IPA is awesome." He drew out the last word, making it sound like he needed nine or ten Ws to spell it properly. "You wanna sample, brah?"

"Yeah, no thanks. Just give me whatever's dark."

The bartender's face lit up. "Yeah, cool, okay. Well, we've got the John Barleywine Must Die, the Imperial Kiwi Porter, or the Olde 909 Bilgewater Ale, then there's the Pineapple Marshmallow Stout or the—"

"Just gimme the Three Cups O' Joe Porter," I interrupted. It was the first one listed on the chalkboard that sounded even remotely drinkable.

"You got it, brah. Back in a sec."

I looked around the place, peering through the thicket of tanned bodies and cargo shorts and trucker hats and forty-dollar T-shirts with iron-ons from 1970s movies (I was positive that the chesty girl in the Close Encounters of the Third Kind shirt had never seen the movie itself; I would have been surprised if she'd even heard of it) to see out to the deck, where Chas and his light-beer-commercial friends were still tossing beanbags around. One of the girls squealed for some reason. She probably felt a thought forming. It can hurt if you're not used to it.

Then the bartender reappeared and set down a pint glass directly in front of me. A thick brown sludge with a thin layer of cream on the top crested over the edge of the glass. It looked positively chewy. "Hey, you interested in joining our Around the World in a Pint Glass rewards club?" he asked. "How it works is, once you drink a beer from every country on our map, you get a fifty-dollar tab on the house. And the points leader at the end of the year gets a party." He waved his thumb at a small chalkboard behind him. Beneath the words "Around the World Leader Board," someone had meticulously chalked in a list of ten names accompanied by a running points total for each. The top drinker on the board, someone who apparently preferred to be known only as "Sleethy McSleeth," had collected 765 points already. "It's fifteen bucks to join, and you also get a T-shirt."

"No thanks," I said. "I kinda doubt I'll be back here."

The bartender shrugged. "Suit yourself, brah," he said before busying himself with something at the other end of the bar.

I took a sip and my tongue immediately tried to crawl down my own throat. Ugh. This is why I don't drink this shit. But I had to look the part, so I forced myself to take another, and then a third. It tasted like a mixture of espresso and pancake syrup poured from a jar of potpourri.

I could see Chas but not hear him. And I needed to hear him. I needed to know the sound of his voice, the voice he used to whisper greasy, filthy things to my wife. In my own bed. Probably. I started to snake my way closer to him, pirouetting through the throng of bodies standing between me and the deck out front, between me and Chas and his entourage. Then the mass of flesh and Axe body spray dissipated, and I was outside, where the air was cooler and the music sounded far away. Somehow, I'd gotten there without even a drop of someone else's beer on my shirt.

"Spent the day on the Jet Skis, down at Pelican Pass," Chas's buddy said, lounging in a wire mesh chair like he owned the place. He looked like he'd been there his entire life, like he'd been born into that chair and then went to business school there. "Shoulda been there, brah. Perfect conditions for it. Grilled up some rib eyes after."

"Wyatt, tell him how you wiped out that one time," the brunette prodded, then turned to Chas. "He totally wiped out this one time. Just like—bam! And he's all like, what just happened? Ohmygod, it was ri-dic! Tell him, Wyatt!"

86

Wyatt pursed his lips and smiled. He didn't seem to find the incident all that funny. "Yeah, it was just like she said. I just pushed the piece-of-shit Jet Ski harder than it could handle, I guess. No biggie." He turned to the brunette, the one who was probably his girlfriend. "You sure do know how to tell a story, you know that?"

"You totally should have been there, Davis," she went on, ignoring Wyatt. "Totally."

Davis? This guy's name is Davis? Somehow that was even better than Chas.

"Sounds like it," Davis said. "I had some things going on today that I couldn't get out of." Sure, like banging my wife, you little shit.

Wyatt snapped his fingers. "Oh shit, yeah, that's right," he said. "That funeral thing, or whatever it was you were telling me about."

"Oh no, who died?" Yoga Pants asked. Her sympathetic tone sounded hollow and put on, as if she knew which emotion she was supposed to feel at that moment but didn't quite know how to pretend she actually felt it.

"Husband of a friend of mine," Davis said. "His boat caught fire a couple weeks ago while he was on it. They didn't find a body, but you know, after two weeks, everybody pretty much figures he's not coming back."

Well, at least I had that going for me.

"Yeah, I remember," Wyatt said. "Shit, sorry, man. I totally forgot that was today."

Davis shrugged. "It's totally cool. It wasn't your shit to worry about."

"Oh shit, wait a minute!" Brunette almost shouted. "I saw that on the news!"

"The news?" Wyatt laughed. "Since when do you watch the news?"

"It was on in the gym. And shut up." She punched him in the shoulder. "Yeah, the guy was a lawyer and he, like, killed himself because he stole a bunch of money? Or something? I don't know, it was hard to tell exactly. The sound was off."

"Yeah, well, I don't really know about any of that," Davis said. "But I've heard a lot of the same stuff, so who knows."

"How do you know a guy like that?" Yoga Pants asked.

"I didn't really know him at all, actually. I'm friends with his wife," Davis said, and when he saw the raised eyebrows and bemused expressions he added, "Yeah, well, what can I say. Cougars dig me." I wanted to go over there and smash him in his smug little mouth, maybe crack a couple of those perfectly bleached and straightened teeth of his.

"Wait, so you're sleeping with her?" Brunette asked. "But she's married!"

"Nice, brah," Wyatt said, completely ignoring her again. "So you gonna get to spend any of that sweet life insurance money?"

"Who knows. Like I said, I don't know anything about that stuff."

Okay. That was it. That was all I could take. If I didn't leave then, I knew I would be pounding his mostly empty skull against the pavement out front in less than ten minutes. I headed back inside, worked my way to the bar, and set my empty glass down. I turned to face the deck again, just in time to see Davis's buddy slalom his way past me and up to the stage, where he dropped a bill into the band's tip bucket. He said something to the singer before retreating to the deck, and a few moments later the guitarist strummed a couple of chords that sent a cheer reverberating through the entire room.

Christ. Not this fucking song.

I'd hated "Sweet Caroline" since I was a little kid, when my parents used to play Neil Diamond records on Dad's high-end (for the time, anyway) stereo system, the volume loud enough to shatter neighbors' windows and pulverize kidney stones. But this crowd, composed entirely of people who were years away from even being imagined back when

I'd had to endure this crap, this crowd ate it up, and they sang along tunelessly at the top of their lungs.

Yeah. It was time to go.

I dropped a ten on the bar and weaved through the throng toward the exit. As I crossed the street, I looked back over my shoulder to see Davis and his buddy scream the "Ba—ba—daaaaaaaaaaaa" part of the chorus directly into each other's faces. I got in my car and drove north, back toward the Royal Rest, my brain not even trying to process the day I'd just had. Instead it just let the images and contradictions flow across like a receding tide.

SIXTEEN
Nicole

I don't really want to talk about Davis, but I can't think of a way to tell this story without including him. Besides, you've told me more than once that the things we don't want to talk about but talk about anyway are the things we have to talk about. Or something like that. I'm sure you said it more eloquently than that. You always do.

Maybe it'll do me some good to share.

Nobody forced me into whatever it was that Davis and I had. I can admit that. It was my decision. I don't want you to think I'm trying to avoid taking responsibility for my own actions. I want to be very clear on that. Yes, I had my reasons, and some of those reasons did come from a place outside of myself. Alton wasn't trying anymore. He was never around. And even when he was at home, he wasn't really there, you know? Our marriage was . . . well, I don't know what it was, exactly. It might not have been anything at all by that point. If that makes any sense.

Alton and I used to have a standing Friday night date. We'd get a sitter for Clara and go out to dinner at Bella Brava, this not quite fancy but still elegant Italian place downtown. Not a checkered-tablecloth place or anything. More contemporary. Very open and airy, plenty of light, polished marble bar, lots of dark wood contrasting with lighter stone. Anyway, it's our favorite restaurant. Or was our favorite, I guess. He would come straight from the office and meet me there, usually halfway through my first glass of wine. Then it became halfway through my second glass. Then it was right about when I finished the bottle. Which then became the first bottle.

Then he just stopped showing up. And you know what? I didn't even say anything.

90

Because what was the point? By then it wasn't just forgotten dinner plans. There were all those Saturdays spent on the phone in his study. The awkward superficiality of the time we did spend together. I honestly don't remember the last conversation Alton and I had that went beyond recounting the events of the day. Well, if you don't count conversations about finances. Which I don't.

I needed more than that.

I know it's cliché, a wife having an affair because her husband is emotionally inaccessible and unavailable to her. But every cliché has a basis in truth. That's how they become clichés in the first place.

So yes. Alton pushed me away, closed himself off from me. And from Clara, which in my mind is so much worse. And I made the decision I made, which I'm not proud of, but honestly, given the circumstances, I think it's at least understandable.

We met at the big bookstore on Central Avenue. I was there to find a birthday gift for my friend Pam. She's a reader but not a really serious reader, so I was looking in the New Releases section for something she might like—not that I had any idea what that was, because Pam and I weren't as close as we once had been, but you never know where inspiration will strike you. I saw Davis, flipping through a Kafka novel and looking very focused about it. Then he looked up and saw me watching him. I looked away, and the next thing I knew he was standing next to me, trying to strike up a conversation. I liked him immediately, even though I couldn't quite put my finger on exactly why.

"I had this great line all ready to go when I came over here," he said. "But it's the funniest thing. Now that I'm standing here, I can't remember it." He smiled. He was handsome, there's no denying that. And he knew it. Oh, did he know it. "I wonder what could have made me forget it."

"I think you remembered your line just fine," I said. "In fact, I think I just heard it."

Pickup lines don't work on me. They never have. And that one didn't either. I'm not exactly sure why I kept talking to him, or why I let him talk me into meeting for coffee the next morning, or why that date ended with him on my couch and me on my knees in front of him. But it had nothing to do with that line.

I was attracted to him right away. No, more than that—I was drawn to him. He was hot, make no mistake about that, but I've met countless hot guys who did absolutely nothing for me. That smile of his—oh, there was something in that smile that stirred something in me, in a place I'd forgotten about long ago. I don't know if he was doing it on purpose or not, but somehow I felt worthwhile, desirable, important—all in the first two minutes I spent with him. Alton hadn't done any of that in two years. So really, it was pretty much a foregone conclusion at that point.

I know. That sounds horrible. And it was. It is. Maybe it makes me an awful person. It probably does, I guess. And it's hard to talk about that part. But there's no point in these sessions if I'm going to spend them lying to you or to myself. Lying to you won't help me move past any of this. So there you go. It is what it is, whatever that means.

I don't know why I let things go on for as long as they did with him. I've been in relationships like that before. The kind where there is plenty of physical attraction and I'm getting some much-needed attention, but that's pretty much it. Those relationships always burned themselves out fairly quickly. I don't know why this one didn't, and I don't think I have to know. It was different. It might not have been real, whatever that means, but in a lot of ways it was. So I take it back.

There are so many things I still don't know about him, even now. What was his favorite toy as a child? Who was his first love? What is his relationship like with his family? What is his biggest regret? But he learned all these things about me. All those things, plus a lot more. I was always very open with him, and in retrospect, maybe that's why I didn't notice that he never really shared much about himself. I was too busy sharing to listen; if I hadn't been, if I'd had just a little more situational awareness, maybe I would have noticed that there was nothing to hear.

SEVENTEEN

Alton

The morning sun glinted off the towering glass-and-chrome-fronted edifice of Crum Luxury Motorcars, which claimed to be the city's largest dealership for the BMW, Mercedes, Lexus, and Infiniti brands. I had been sitting there for nearly an hour, trying to decide what to do next.

This was where my morning surveillance had led me. I'd gotten up early that day so I could tail Davis and see where he worked. And now I knew.

So. Nicole had been getting it from a car salesman.

A car salesman. Let that sink in a moment.

A fucking frat-boy car salesman.

I ran that thought through my mind over and over again, hoping that with each repetition the sting of it would fade even a little. So far, no luck.

I had to admit, this would have been funny if it wasn't so . . . well, so not funny.

I should have seen this coming earlier. Because really, what other job would a frat-boy douchebag dude-bro who sleeps with married women have? What other job could he have?

I tried to see inside the dealership, but even with the sunglasses it was impossible. The piercing brightness of the windows left temporary imprints on the backs of my retinas. I could just imagine the sales staff, watching me through those enormous showroom windows, sipping scorched coffee out of their heavy ceramic mugs emblazoned with car company logos and asking each other how in the hell someone who drove something like that could possibly have found their way to this parking lot. Maybe Davis would recognize the car from before. And then everything would start to unravel, for real this time. I pressed my eyes shut for a few seconds and waited for my vision to clear. I took a few deep breaths to get my breathing under control. Then I got out of the car and walked across the parking lot.

I quickly counted three salesmen on the showroom floor. Two of them—including Davis—had customers, and the third hadn't noticed me yet. So I wandered around, ambling between the shiny new masterpieces of automotive engineering, my greedy eyes sliding up and along the sleek and perfect body panels.

Damn, did I miss my Porsche.

I reached out to brush my fingertips along the hood of the white Benz sedan in front of me. Frictionless, like touching a cloud. I have the money, I remember thinking. I could pay cash. I could just go back to the Royal Rest and get—

I felt three quick taps on my shoulder. I spun around to see the third salesman hovering behind me, standing a full head shorter than I did and grinning in that special way— benign and predatory at the same time—that only salespeople can really master.

"Hi," he said, extending a meaty, soft-looking palm. "Ed Hughey."

"Hi, Ed." I squeezed his hand and shook, two sharp up-and-down pumps. Ed's grip was casual, almost timid. I smiled. "Good to meet you. Frank Rizzo."

"Great," Ed said, looking past me. "Just great. So, Frank, what do you think?" He panned his gaze across the showroom, like a king surveying a newly conquered land from its highest hilltop, as if everything in the room were his. "There's a lot to like, huh?"

"Oh, no doubt, Ed. I've got a few questions about, um, this one," I said, pointing at the Benz. "But you know, that coffee is really going through me this morning, and I was hoping I could use the restroom before we got started."

"Of course," Ed said, pointing to the rear of the dealership. "It's just past the row of sales offices, but don't let that scare you—we're all out on the floor now anyway." And then he laughed at his own joke, a little too hard to really mean it. The row of nine sales offices had no walls, only windows. Any unsuspecting shopper who thought that ducking into the bathroom might buy them a few moments of refuge from the fast talk and high pressure of the sharks on the floor was in for an unpleasant surprise. They were all empty just then, at around ten-thirty on a Monday morning. But when the dealership was fully staffed, there would always be at least one salesperson in there to stare down the stragglers, to let them know there was no escape, and the only way out was to sign their way through a fat stack of incomprehensible paperwork and write a check.

The fourth one in was Davis's office. I knew I had the right one because of the framed picture of him—his full name was, according to a diploma from the University of Georgia that hung on his wall, Davis Randall Spaulding—on a sailboat, along with three other fit young dude-bros. Each of their faces was smeared with an identical entitled smirk.

Davis Randall Spaulding. Yeah, that sounds about right.

On the desk was a mug with Greek letters, Sigma Alpha Epsilon. Frat brother. I knew it. What it was they said about the SAEs when I was in college? Oh yeah: Somebody, Anybody, Everybody. Under the mug, a copy of *Men's Health*. I rifled through some of the loose papers on the desk and found a couple copies of FHM underneath.

SAE? Men's Health? FHM?

This made no sense. There is no way Nicole could possibly be . . . interested in this tool. None at all. This guy was just not her type.

"Can I help you?" Davis Spaulding asked from the doorway behind me.

Shit.

My body blocked Spaulding's view of the desk, so I dropped the papers back where I'd found them and hoped he wouldn't notice until I was long gone.

"Oh, hi," I said. "I was just looking for the bathroom. I guess I got turned around."

"Yeah, you sure did. The bathroom is back thataway," he said, pointing over his shoulder. "This is actually my office."

"Well then it's a good thing you got here when you did," I said. I could feel my pulse hammering away in my throat. "Otherwise there could have been a terrible mess."

"Huh. Yeah, exactly," Davis said. "That's funny." But he didn't laugh.

"Yeah, so, I'll just be moving along then. Sorry about the misunderstanding."

"It's fine. Hey, the bathroom is back that way," Davis called after me.

"Changed my mind," I called back. By that point I was almost race-walking toward the front door. "Thanks for your help." I brushed past Ed Hughey, his pasted-on grin now clouded with confusion.

"Hey, don't you wanna talk about—" And then I was outside again, the humidity suddenly weighing me down as I double-timed it across the parking lot. My hands shook so much as I tried to unlock the car that I jabbed the door with my key three separate times before getting the damn thing opened. And then—finally—I vanished into the anonymity of eight lanes of speeding traffic.

I could breathe again. I knew they'd watched me as I left, through those gigantic windows. I could imagine them talking, trying to figure out what that had all been about. Who that crazy bald guy in Spaulding's office was. Did anybody recognize him? Should they hire more security? Should they call the cops?

But I didn't care. They could do what they wanted. They'd never see me again.

EIGHTEEN
Alton

I could see the bartender—James, I think his name was James; I sort of remembered him from all the other times I'd been in there—eyeing me from the other end of the bar as he polished a few square centimeters of marble with a fraying dishrag. He watched me read for a minute or two before speaking up.

"You doing all right?" he called over to me.

"Just fine, thanks." I didn't look up from my book. I'd been just about the only customer in the place since four o'clock, and I'd been nursing the same vodka and tonic that entire time.

"Um, I don't know if you know it, but you're wearing sunglasses," he said. Yeah. James. That was his name. Loved Mississippi State football. We'd talked about our shared hatred for the LSU Tigers once or twice before. He didn't seem to recognize me, though. "Indoors, I mean."

"Migraines," I said. I fingered the hinge on the left side of my sunglasses.

"Oh. Right. Sorry. Wow, that must suck, huh?"

"It can."

"Okay. Well, you just . . . holler if you need anything."

"Great," I said, and just then the front door swung open and in streamed the after-work rush. I scanned the faces, tired and drained and needy, looking for ones I knew, hoping they wouldn't recognize the bald barfly with his nose in a book.

From the day it opened, the Rare Olive was an immediate favorite after-work spot for the lawyers at Sloane Bryce McLaughlin. The wood paneling and polished brass rails seemed to be reaching for an atmosphere of sophistication

98

and gravitas, but to me it always felt like a flimsy façade. A Potemkin bar. I'd spent plenty of evenings there myself over the last three or four years. I don't remember actively enjoying a single one of them.

Suddenly there were thirty or forty people in the place, all fresh from the office, drinking and bitching and talking shop. They talked over each other, stepping all over each other's sentences, everyone trying to top their coworkers' absurdist or humiliating or depersonalizing tales of the workplace. Nervous, high-pitched laughs. Quick glances around the bar to see who might have heard. Their work lives were all resentment and fear and frustration, and they couldn't even give themselves permission to escape it all after the workday was over.

The group I was interested in had clustered at a high-top farther down the bar, too far away for me to hear them. I watched them for a while, leaning in to hear each other over the din of the crowd, gesticulating and talking with their hands, nearly knocking over someone's drink with each point made or story told. Then another seat at the bar opened up closer to them, where I might be able to listen a bit, and I weaved through the other white-collar wage slaves to get to it.

"—and what was the deal with his wife? Were you at his wake the other day?"

"Oh jeez, that was—"

"She was a train wreck. A complete train wreck."

"You'd be one too if you'd been married to that guy for so long."

"Drank too much and puked in the bathroom. At her husband's wake."

"—then I had to spend half my day just doing their bidding. Every time I sat down, it was something else. Find this file, where's that document, fetch this phone bill. Jesus. I didn't get a goddamn thing done."

"They were in my office for forty minutes today asking about—get this—three emails. Three. Emails. Forty minutes. I dunno what the hell they think he did, but I can tell you, the emails they wanted? Didn't say shit about shit."

"Feds never say shit. Don't you watch movies? Everyone knows this."

"If he wasn't already dead, I'd kill him myself."

"Does anyone want to order appetizers or something? I'm starving."

"I'm so sick of talking about him. Can we talk about something else for once?"

"He fucked us over, Sandy. All of us. Hard. He's gonna be a topic for a while."

"She's right, it's all so boring now."

"Not to me it's not. I'm so fucking pissed. That fucking guy cost me my bonus this year. Yours too. Everybody's."

"What gets me is, I just don't know how he thought he'd get away with it."

"Get away with what, exactly? Nobody's said anything specific about what he did."

"Well I don't know, I guess that it just seems like if you try to . . . well, pull a fast one, I guess, if you try to do that anymore there are just so many ways that people can find out about it. So why try? Why risk it?"

"Wait, we aren't getting bonuses now? I hadn't heard anything about that."

"Yeah, me neither. Where are you getting this?"

"Um, do you actually remember the guy? The egomaniac you worked with for, what, four years?"

"Ha, yeah, I guess he did have a baselessly high opinion of himself."

"So did something like 80 percent of my class in law school."

"Touché."

"Where'd he go to law school anyway? Anyone remember?"

"Shit, I dunno. Alabama, maybe?"

"Who gives a fuck?"

"No, not Bama. I think it was Clemson."

"Clemson doesn't have a law school."

"Are you sure? Because I'm pretty sure that's it."

"They don't."

"Yeah, but it sounds right to me."

"It. Doesn't. Matter."

"Relax. We're just talking here."

"That greedy motherfucker."

"Everyone is greedy, Tony. Anyone who breathes wants more. It's the human condition."

"Such an optimist."

"So, what, he was stealing then?"

"What else would it be? Whatever it was, there is no doubt in my mind that it ended with a lot of dollars finding their way into his pockets that would otherwise not have gone there. The rest is all details."

"Here's what I'm wondering. How do you suppose he started a fire on his boat by accident?"

"I don't know. Smoking?"

"I don't think he smoked."

"He didn't."

"Not even cigars? He seems like he would've been the cigar type."

"A douchebag, in other words."

"Hahahaha. Bingo!"

"Hey, come on, my husband smokes cigars."

"Well, I don't know. I don't know anything about how boats work. All I know is you put them in the water, they're supposed to float. I don't know anything about engines or gas or explosives or anything."

"Who said anything about explosives? Nothing blew up."

"It does seem kinda weird, though, doesn't it?"

"Eh, not really. They aren't being straight with us about why the hell the feds are camping out in our offices. What makes you think they'd be straight with us about how he died?"

"It's all a conspiracy, is that it?"

"Who do you think's gonna get his office?"

"It better be me, goddamn it. I have been in that fucking broom closet for too long."

"Not until J. Edgar Fuckface Junior is outta there. And who knows when that'll be."

"People, focus. Appetizers. Come on now. Let's. Get. Some. Food."

"Hey, buddy, you okay?" It was James. Speaking to me. Just then, someone at the table made eye contact with me. It was Tina Stratton. She was new at the firm, and I didn't know her all that well, so I wasn't too worried about her recognizing me or anything.

But she didn't break her gaze. Even after the point where most people would probably feel awkward about eyeballing a stranger like that, she just held there. Oh shit. I could feel the panic start to well up inside me. Then I realized—she wasn't actually looking at me. She was looking above me, at the TV in the corner behind me. A rerun of The Big Bang Theory was on. That figures.

"Sure," I said. I felt like a deflated bicycle tire. "Just fine."

"Cool, just checking," he said. "Lemme know if you need something."

"Thanks," I said. I dropped a twenty on the bar and left. My head was swimming, my mind shooting back and forth too quickly for me to even finish a thought. Out in the parking lot, I lurched straight for the first familiar-looking car I saw and keyed a crooked gouge the length of the driver's side. It looked deep and rough and expensive.

NINETEEN
Tina Stratton

First of all, yes, I remember that night at the Rare Olive. I remember it mostly because that was the day I decided to quit Sloan Bryce and go find something else to do with my life. And yes, I remember seeing Alton. I did not recognize him at the time, though. That wasn't until much later, when everyone was piecing things together and trying to reassemble the whole story.

I do remember thinking the bald guy at the Rare Olive looked a bit like Alton. But I figured that was because we'd all been talking about him for most of the evening. You know how that happens. You have someone on your mind, and suddenly you start seeing them turn up everywhere? Right. That's what I assumed this was.

Anyway. I only spent about a year and a half at Sloan Bryce. I summered there before my third year in law school and went to work for them right after I finished at UF. It was fine, as far as it goes. I had the right background—they liked that I had a finance degree from Vanderbilt too—but it was only a few months before I realized I wasn't going to ever make partner there. That kind of work is so boring.

I never actually reported directly to Alton, thank God. But I had my run-ins with him. We all did. Some of the people there didn't have a problem with the way he was, but to me it was obnoxious and completely unnecessary. You don't have to treat people like dirt to get them to do what you want them to do.

I always found him to be incredibly condescending toward the junior associates, but especially the women. He would always talk down to us, explaining very basic concepts two or three times in this voice, like he was talking to a child. "Now, don't forget, Tina," he'd always say, and then wag his finger at me while he explained something that I invariably already knew. Uh, yeah, I've actually already been to law school, but thanks for the refresher.

And he would yell at associates for mistakes that were, frankly, his fault. I don't want to name names here, because some of these incidents could potentially be actionable. But let's just say that some of Sloan Bryce's clients might want to check the dates on some of their paperwork. That's it though. I always got the sense that the other partners weren't thrilled with him, but I never knew why. I mean, you hear rumors, of course. Law firms are all gossip vortexes, and Sloan Bryce was no different. I just tried to keep my head down, do my work, and wait for the right time to make my next move.

But yeah, I'd heard stories about certain accounts not balancing the way they should. Never any real details, though. It was just something that was sort of out there, just floating in the air. And we'd all heard about big deals that Alton may or may not have totally botched. More than one, trust me. But he always seemed to land on his feet, so I just assumed that's all they were. Just stories.

Like I said, I didn't recognize him at the Rare Olive, and I'm not the one who turned him in. If I had recognized him, though, I think I might've called the cops. Yeah, I think so. I don't owe him a damn thing.

TWENTY

Alton

The old woman was there, sitting in her chair and staring out beyond the passing traffic, when I returned to the Royal Rest. The buzz from my two vodka tonics had been slight to begin with, and in any event it had worn off a while ago. I was still trying to sort through what I'd heard, what it all meant, that these people I worked with for so long, who had been in my home, that these people would—could—talk about me like I'd just heard them doing for a full half hour.

Inside my room I stared into the bathroom mirror for two full minutes. But I felt like what I really wanted to do, needed to do, was look through the mirror, as if that would give me the unobstructed view inside myself that I needed.

How could I have misjudged those pricks for so long? How could I have been so completely wrong about them?

I'd spent the last hour driving around, making random turns every few blocks, and asking myself those questions over and over. I was no closer to answering them than I had been when I started. It was cruel, this little junior high game of theirs, pretending to like me to my face and then cutting me to ribbons when I wasn't around. When they thought I wasn't around in the most permanent way possible. I couldn't figure it out. Those people were my friends. Or at least I had thought they were. Some of them had even come to my house to pay their last respects on Saturday. My home. What did I ever do to them to deserve that kind of abuse, that venom?

That guy they were talking about at the Rare Olive? Whoever it was, it wasn't me. And they knew it. They had to know it.

I picked up two red plastic cups and the half-empty bottle of Scottish Bob's vodka and went outside, over to room 15. The old woman eyeballed me as I approached.

"You need somethin'?"

I held up the cups in one hand and the bottle in the other. "Interested?"

Her eyes narrowed. "Well, that all depends," she said.

" I don't want anything from you," I said. "Just someone to drink with."

"Gimme the cup that ain't got your finger in it, then," she said. I poured five or six glugs' worth into the cup and handed it to her, then sat on the parking block and poured a generous helping into my own cup.

"Here's to ya," I toasted.

"Mmmmm-hmmmm," she said, peering into her cup.

"How long you lived here?"

"Long enough," she said. "Long enough to know you can't trust none of the other scumbags in this dump, that's for damn sure." She took a long swallow.

"Yeah, I bet," I said, and after a pause I added: "You can trust me, though. I mean, you might not know it, but you can."

"Uh-huh."

"What?"

"You took my chair without asking." Oh shit. Busted. "What kind of a man does that? Steals an old woman's chair, I mean."

"You weren't using it."

"Not right then, maybe." She held up three fingers, little more than wrinkled stumps. "Three times. You stole my chair three times."

"Only twice. And I brought it back, didn't I?"

"That's why I had to take it inside at night. Had sand all over it. Made a hell of a mess in there."

"I could have just left it there, you know," I said. "Out by the bayou, where you'd never find it. Hell, I could have thrown it into the water, just to be an asshole. Or I could have kept it in my own room."

She laughed. "You want a cookie or something? For bein' such a good boy?"

"No, I don't want a cookie. Just . . . I don't know. Acknowledgment, I guess. Forget it. It doesn't mean anything. It's just a goddamn chair."

"Means something to me," she said. "It's my goddamn chair, goddamn it."

"I'm not a thief, you know." I took another swig but swallowed it too quickly. The liquid scalded my throat. "I like to think that I'm better than that."

"Everybody likes to think they're something they ain't," she said. "I don't know anything about you. Just what I see."

"You know what you see, huh?" Why am I getting angry? This is ridiculous. "You see who it was who brought you that booze you're drinking?"

"Yep. That was you."

"Yes. It was me. So I'm not so bad, am I?"

"No, I suppose you ain't."

"No one who gives out free vodka to strangers can be all that bad," I said. "Can they." It was more of a statement than a question.

"I guess it depends," she said with a shrug. "People are lots of things at the same time sometimes."

Suddenly I had had enough. Enough vodka, enough of this woman, enough of the Royal Rest. Enough.

"All right," I said, standing up. "That's it for me. I'm going back inside."

"What, happy hour's over already? Come on, leave the bottle at least."

"Guess I don't feel like company as much as I thought I did," I said, and I closed the door behind me without another word.

Hours later, when I cracked open the door and peeked out into the night, the chair was gone again.

TWENTY-ONE
Alton

My study was exactly as I remembered it, right down to the number of pens in my official Tulane University Law School mug. There were eleven of them.

Clemson. Ha. As if.

I sat in the small-backed leather club chair I'd bought at Pier 1 all those years ago and watched the sunlight wash in through the window. A fresh cup of coffee sat on the side table, a narrow and precarious thing that always reminded me of the mahogany telephone stand in Grandma's house, back when I was a kid. I was tired. Really tired. I felt it deep in my muscle tissue, a tingling weakness in my legs and hands that always meant I was either overtired or on the verge of getting sick. I let my eyes close. Just for a moment.

The house was quiet that morning. A delivery truck rumbled past and stopped farther up the block, its brakes gently squeaking. I knew I could fall asleep right there in that chair. Just drift off, and why not? I was home again, after all this time, home again, and where better than one's own study to indulge in a quick catnap and—

—and my head snapped up and I inhaled sharply and wondered for just a moment where I was. A moment later I realized I'd dozed off. That was dangerous. But it just felt like a natural thing to do. It was my house. My study. My chair.

I picked up the coffee and had a sip. Still hot, if you defined hot somewhat generously, but not so hot that I couldn't drink it quickly. I downed the entire mug in four or five greedy gulps and headed downstairs. If I was going to sleep, there were more comfortable places to do it than that chair.

As soon as I stepped into the bedroom—my old bedroom, our bedroom—I knew that something about it was off. But I couldn't quite figure it out. I dropped myself onto the bed, on top of the covers. I was on Nicole's side, and I'm not afraid to admit that it was because I hoped I would be able to catch a whiff of her scent. Even after everything I had seen, everything she had done to betray me, part of me still wanted to be near her. But the sheets had been washed recently; they only smelled like Tide. I closed my eyes and breathed deeply anyway. The familiar scent soothed me to sleep.

Twenty-four minutes later, the caffeine in my system finally kicked into gear. My eyelids snapped open like cheap motel window shades. I sat up on the bed and looked around. What was it that was bothering me? All the furniture—and there wasn't much, just the bed, a single dresser, two small nightstands, and a reading chair, all from Scandinavian Designs because Nicole loved that overpriced faux-modern stuff for some reason—was exactly how I remembered it. TV still mounted on the wall. Clothes spilling out of the hamper and the laundry baskets. (Nicole always put off doing the laundry for as long as she possibly could, though she'd gotten better about it after I accidentally shrank her favorite scoop-neck T-shirt a few months back. I was banned from doing laundry for that one, which was just fine by me.) Shoes.

Wait—whose shoes are those?

I bent down and picked them up. Men's, size nine, light brown. They looked like loafers on the top but had a thick rubber sole with deep ridges. The shoes converged into a point at the toe and then sort of pointed up, like something a court jester might wear. They sure as hell weren't mine—wrong size, not my style, and I loathe that particular shade of brown.

So what were they doing there?

You know what they're doing here. And whose they are. And suddenly I knew exactly what it was about the room that felt off. It had nothing to do with the shoes, and at the same time it had everything to do with them. It wasn't my bedroom anymore. Those shoes wouldn't have been there if it were. It was someplace else entirely now, someplace that looked familiar but wasn't.

I put the shoes back where I'd found them, smoothed out the sheets on the bed and went back upstairs.

I didn't have that same feeling standing in the doorway of Clara's room. It's funny. Nicole and I had expected Clara to turn out to be a princess, mostly because her mother had been one herself thirty-however-many years ago. So we decorated her room with pink and purple all over the walls to reflect that. And Clara certainly embraced princess culture. But she also refused to be limited by it. Her room was littered with Matchbox cars—some of the very same ones I had had as a kid, in fact—plastic dinosaurs and countless Lego pieces stuck together in one twisted architectural nightmare or another, or scattered across the floor, where they waited to embed themselves in the defenseless soles of some adult's bare feet in the middle of the night. Her soccer ball rested on her pillow, as if she had carefully placed it and instructed it to wait right there until school was over. It was all decidedly unprincesslike.

I wondered what they were telling her about me. Did they tell her I was dead? They must have—she was at the wake, after all. Then again, she was only four. So who knew how Nicole had decided to handle it.

I sat on the edge of her bed and picked up a book from the pile on her nightstand. Nicole really should get on her to clean this place up. The book was The Five Chinese Brothers, which had been one of my favorites as a kid. Nicole had given me a bit of static when I brought it home. She thought it was too dark and would give Clara nightmares. "She's too young for something like this," Nicole protested. "Jesus, Alton, the book starts with a little kid drowning. That's how it starts. How is that appropriate for a four-year-old?" But I knew she could handle it. She was the same age I'd been

110

when I first read it, or at least it seemed about right to me. Besides, it was important to me that I share the things from my own childhood that had stuck with me for so long. So the book stayed. I made sure of it.

I tossed the book back onto the pile, then reached over and picked up the nearest Matchbox car, a black and orange funny car. I rested it on my palm and let it roll over my hand, back and forth ever so slightly, crossing my lifeline again and again.

What the hell was I still doing there?

I'd seen my own funeral. I'd seen Clara playing in the schoolyard one last time. There was nothing else there that I needed. Why hadn't I lit out for Central America yet?

Because . . . because I still needed something. Obviously. I couldn't see what it was then. Sometimes I think I can see it now, looking back with the perspective that the passage of time gives you, but then it goes out of focus and shifts into something else, something irrelevant, something that actively distracts me from the answer. I could feel that it had something to do with Davis Spaulding, with all those assholes from the firm and their ignorant bar chatter, with Clara, with Nicole. Or at least I thought I could feel that. Because sometimes when I think about it now, none of those seem to quite fit.

I stood up and put the Matchbox car in my pocket and headed downstairs to the kitchen. The mail was in a neat pile on the breakfast nook table. I sat down on the bench seat, made myself comfortable, and started picking through the stack. Bank statements. Utility bills. Cable bill. March of Dimes solicitation. Something from Piedmont Insurance, which Nicole had already opened. Interesting. I slipped that letter out of the envelope and read it, something noncommittal about her claim being under review. The language was just vague enough to credibly sound threatening or benignly bureaucratic, depending on the reader's frame of mind.

Then I noticed Nicole's laptop on the kitchen table.

She had two, one for work and then this one, which was her personal machine. I flipped open the lid. It was still on, and after a second, the drive kicked in and it woke itself up from its hibernation. She had left several programs open, including the browser. I was just about to open a new tab and type my name into Google when I noticed that one of the open tabs was Nicole's Gmail.

I wondered if she was still logged in.

It wouldn't have surprised me. She was terrible about things like that: computer security, home security, even locking her car. Nicole had no situational awareness. It had taken me over a month to finally get her to put a password on her iPhone. What if she'd lost it? She never logged out of anything, so whoever found her phone would probably have easy access to our bank account, the credit cards, everything.

Email too.

But not this time. I guess my admonitions had finally sunk in. That, or it had just timed out and logged her off automatically.

Well, that was no problem. I could guess her password. I've known her for thirteen years.

I started with the easy ones. Birthday. Nope. My birthday. Uh-uh. Anniversary. Hmmm. My name. Clara's name. Clara's birthday. "Waylon," which was the name of the dog we used to have. Try the name of the street where she grew up, I thought, but I couldn't remember it, so I tried "Richmond," her hometown, instead.

Nothing.

I kept going, trying everything I could think of. Social Security numbers. Family member names. Favorite movie titles. Favorite foods. Nothing.

I slammed the laptop shut. I wanted to be proud of my wife at that moment, of her ability to thwart even me—

someone who knew her better than anyone else—in my attempts to crack her password. But all I felt was annoyed.

When I got back to the Royal Rest later that afternoon, I put Clara's Matchbox car on the dresser, in front of the TV. Maybe it would bring me luck.

TWENTY-TWO
Nicole

I could tell something was out of place the instant I walked through the back door and into the kitchen. I had just come home for lunch, which was unusual for me but I'd been looking forward to the leftover pad Thai from Nine Bangkok I had in the fridge all morning. You know how you get that feeling sometimes? Where you can just tell something isn't right? It literally stopped me in my tracks, that's how strong that feeling was.

But everything looked just like it had when I left for work that morning. So I set my purse on the counter, folded my arms across my chest, and just kind of let my eyes find their own way around the room, hoping that they'd lead me to whatever it was that was bothering me.

I was absolutely certain I hadn't left the kitchen like this. There were no open cabinet doors. No food left out. Breakfast dishes drying on the rack, just like I'd left them before taking Clara to school. Mail stacked by the saltshaker. Flowers in the window by the sink, light refracting through the crystal vase. Granite countertops sparkling.

I thought, This is silly. And maybe it was. I felt pretty ridiculous about the whole thing. But at the same time, I also wasn't really hungry anymore.

I looked down at the floor. I had no idea what I was expecting to find down there. Footprints? Microscopic fibers that didn't belong there? Maybe some suspicious dirt particles without a good alibi? There was nothing there—of course. Because I had just mopped the night before, and those tiles were still spotless.

I pulled a chair out from the kitchen table and sat down. I'd been skittish ever since the night those idiot cops woke me up to tell me about Alton. Now, I'm a suspicious person by nature—it's something I don't like about myself, but it is what it is, I suppose—and I just couldn't shake the idea that all this was some kind of a trick Alton cooked up for his own peculiar reasons, some ridiculous mind game he was playing with me, his firm, the government, the whole world. I think part of me expected to find him hiding in the bushes or something. I've been around enough to know that you should never trust anything that looks like fantastic dumb luck. There's always more to it. Always.

I mean, I finally had exactly what I wanted. And I wouldn't even let myself believe it.

Sometime in the weeks after Alton's disappearance, I'd had an epiphany—well, maybe it was more of an awakening than an epiphany—about the circumstances I found myself in just then. It's ironic—looking back on it now, it feels like I can almost pinpoint the first dawning of clarity to the very night he went missing, right down to the exact moment, just after those dumb cops had left me so shaken and alone. But I hadn't really noticed the seed taking root at the time.

It was when my tears just switched off, after exactly one minute and forty-three seconds of uncontrollable weeping. That's when it started. I'm sure of it.

This thing I figured out about Alton's disappearance was not the first life-changing revelation I'd experienced. And just like most of the others, this one hit me when I was in the shower. That's where I always do my best thinking, and it's where I finally realized something very important: The one thing that had always been standing in my way, getting between me and the life I actually wanted to live for myself, was Alton.

Alton kept me in Florida. Alton kept me chained to a drab and rote sex life. Alton kept me from pursuing my own interests and passions—okay, I didn't actually know what those were, exactly, but I was certain I'd had them, before I married Alton—and all so I could play the role of a law firm partner's wife. And it was Alton who had driven me into the arms of another man, saddling me with all the guilt and baggage that went along with that.

But I don't want to sound like I'm ducking responsibility for my own life choices. I'm not. I fully accept it. Just so we're still clear on that.

Now he was gone and I was free. Or I would be, just as soon as the insurance money came through. That moment in the shower, that epiphany—it knocked the breath right out of me. It knotted my stomach, sat on my chest and squeezed the air out of my lungs. I remember my legs went all wobbly and I almost lost my balance. I would have cracked my head open if I hadn't managed to grab on to the towel bar for support.

After my shower I went back into the kitchen. That leaky kitchen faucet. There was a certain way to adjust it—Alton had shown me a few months before—a way to adjust it that stopped the dripping, at least temporarily. But you had to get the positioning just right, and sometimes—

I stopped cold.

The coffeepot.

There was a quarter-inch of coffee in it.

That. That was it. That had been clean when I left.

Okay okay okay, don't freak. Maybe Davis came by before work. On second thought, no. He wouldn't have done that. It's too far out of his way, and he's never been one to go out of his way if he can avoid it.

Was I sure I had cleaned it? Was I sure I hadn't had coffee afterward?

Oh come on. Why the hell would I clean it and then make another pot?

Then who the fuck broke into my house and made coffee this morning? Why would anyone bother?

I touched the back of my hand against the glass pot. It was cold. So whoever had brewed themselves up a nice cup of my Tanzanian peaberry was long gone by now.

Probably. But not necessarily.

Very slowly I slid open the second drawer of the cabinet next to the stove and grabbed this heavy, two-pronged grill fork that had been just sitting in that drawer since the day we bought it. I'd thought all that grill equipment was a silly waste of money, because I knew we'd never actually grill anything, but I'll tell you, I was glad for the extravagance in that moment. I wrapped my fingers around the polished teak handle and took one shaky step, and then a second, toward the living room. My heart was in my throat. I don't think I was even breathing.

The living room was empty, which made sense because it was a pretty wide-open room, and it really didn't have any good hiding places. There were no doors to hide behind, and there was no way a full-size adult could slide under the couch. So I crept into the master bathroom and whipped open the shower curtain with a single swipe of my hand. No one was there. Under the bed either. So if anyone was there, they'd have to be upstairs, in Alton's study or in Clara's bedroom.

Of course, if anyone was in Clara's room, I'd never find him.

I felt so ridiculous, climbing the stairs with a grill fork thrust out in front of me like a talisman. Ridiculous or not, I wasn't about to lower it. The door to Clara's room was halfway open. The hinges groaned when I nudged the door open a bit further, and my eyes darted from one side of the room to the other and back again. I was ready to jump back into the hall at the first hint of danger.

Nothing.

I looked over toward the bed and saw that damn book, the one about the Chinese brothers who couldn't be killed or something. I hated that book, had always hated that book, but Alton had insisted she have it.

But Alton is gone now.

I lowered the grill fork and stepped over Clara's plastic chess set—she had been playing against the dinosaurs that morning before school, and losing—to reach the book. I was just about to pluck it from the pile of primary-colored plastic crap it was resting on, and then suddenly I took that grill fork and just speared that stupid book with it. I was surprised. Those prongs went right through it, without the slightest bit of resistance. I did feel a pang of guilt—But she loves this book—but it passed quickly enough.

She won't even notice it's gone.

That left the spare bedroom, the one Alton insisted I call his "study." And here was something strange. The night he disappeared, I'd closed the study door and hadn't opened it since. I remembered it very clearly. But now it was open, just a fraction of an inch.

Could have been Clara. That was certainly possible. Maybe she wanted to sit in Daddy's chair and pretend to read his books—Alton had always gotten a charge out of that, seeing her with a copy of the Code of Federal Regulations open in her lap, spinning her own story that had nothing to do with fiduciary obligations or CFPB compliance regulations or whatever the hell his stupid job was all about.

I pushed the door open. The room was exactly as I remembered it. Except—

That mug. It shouldn't be there.

There was Alton's beloved Baltimore Orioles mug, sitting on the end table. Had that been there when I closed up the room all those weeks ago? I couldn't say, honestly. I hadn't really—

Then I remembered. I'd used that mug for Clara's hot chocolate three or four nights earlier. In fact Clara had asked for it specifically. Not her Barney cup or her Dora cup, but Daddy's cup—just had to be Daddy's cup. And afterward I washed it and dried it and put it away, I was certain of it; I knew because I remembered wondering if I should maybe get rid of it soon, but then I decided not to, not just yet, in case Clara asked for it again.

Why was it up there now? How did it get up there?

There was still some coffee in it. I dipped a pinkie into the liquid—it was cold, just like the coffee in the pot downstairs. But it certainly didn't look like it had been sitting there for weeks. Wouldn't it have sprouted mold after a while? I was pretty sure it would. I remembered seeing mold grow inside the coffeepot after just a few days of not washing it, one time when I was trying to prove a point to Alton about the amount of effort it took to keep the house in the state he preferred, a point that he completely missed, conveniently enough for him. I picked it up. There was no mug-shaped gap in the thin layer of dust that covered the rest of the side table. It was even and uniform, like a new snowfall.

I carried the mug and Clara's book back downstairs and set them both next to the sink before I went outside. In the backyard, just outside and to the left of the door, I had a nice row of potted desert roses. In one of them there was this small wooden turtle, tucked away behind the plant's trunk. It wasn't exactly hidden, but it was easy to miss if you didn't already know it was there. I snatched it up and slid open the trapdoor on the turtle's wooden underbelly. That hollowed-out turtle was our secret hiding spot for the spare house key. I needed to know if it was still there.

And it was. Right where it was supposed to be.

I remember standing there a long while, trying to decide whether I should put the key back in the turtle or not. It had to be Davis, I thought, had to be. So I dropped the key back into its hiding place and set the turtle back down, next to the gentle bump of an exposed root.

Later that afternoon I tried calling Davis, who wasn't answering his phone. But that wasn't so unusual. Sometimes he left it on his desk while he was on the sales floor or whatever he called it. "A ringing phone gives a prospect a perfect excuse to end the conversation," he had told me once. He said it in a way that felt rehearsed. Probably something he'd memorized from some sales seminar or something.

I just couldn't concentrate on work that afternoon, no matter how hard I tried to force it. All I could think about was that coffee mug. But I still had to figure out catering arrangements for the economists' conference next month. The longer I waited on that, the harder it would be to get—

I picked up the phone and called Davis again. It was the fourth time I had tried since lunch. I don't think I'd called any guy that much since tenth grade. Voicemail—again. But this time, I left a message. "Hey, it's me. Um, when you get a minute, give me a call, okay? Thanks." I set my phone down next to my keyboard and tried, once again, to focus on work. My mind was racing. I needed to disengage from it, to ignore the tightness and churning I'd felt in my stomach since lunchtime.

Of course, I hadn't had any lunch that day, so maybe it was a blood sugar thing. I don't know.

When the workday was over, I still had not finalized the catering arrangements for the economists, and Davis still had not called me back.

That evening Davis came over, like he usually did after I put Clara down for the night. He didn't apologize for not returning my calls. Didn't even mention them. I found that irritating. I considered bringing them up myself, but I knew it wouldn't be worth the effort, not right now, when there were other things to talk about.

We sat on the long white couch, sharing a bottle of Tempranillo and watching *House of Cards*, which I love but I don't think Davis ever really got. But he watched it anyway, because that's what I was doing and he could be really sweet like that sometimes.

"Davis," I said after a while.

"Mmmmmm."

"You know I love having you here."

"Right."

Yeah. That's actually what he said. Right. I took a breath before continuing.

"But . . . look, I don't mind you coming by unannounced, like I said, you're always welcome here, but I'd prefer it if you didn't let yourself in when I'm not home. I mean, you can, if you want to I guess, but just leave me a note or something so I don't freak out when I come home and find things out of place."

"Um, okay," he said. "That seems reasonable enough, I guess."

"And it's not like I even expect you to leave the place spotless or anything. You can make yourself a cup of coffee, I totally don't mind at all. But this morning I was just so . . . well, I saw the coffee left in the pot and I knew I hadn't left it there, and then I found the mug upstairs and I knew I hadn't left that there either, and it was bothering me all day because it was just so, strange, you know? Which is why I kept calling you all day, sorry about that by the way."

"Yeah, I wondered what that was all about," he said. Then why the hell didn't you say anything about it when you got here? Jesus, this guy. "But, babe."

"Yeah?"

"What the hell are you talking about?"

I sighed. With Davis, sometimes you had to show him the stick before you threw it. "This morning when you stopped by and made coffee after I left for work. Like I said, it's fine, but you know, leave a note next time or something."

"Yeah, sure, okay, but I wasn't here this morning."

I sat up. The wine's pleasant fog, which had been slowly gathering around me for the entire evening, burned off in an instant. "You weren't?"

"No way," he said. "I mean, I'd love to swing by in the mornings, but I just can't get up that early. I was almost late to work again today, actually, which would have fucked some things up for me with Paul, but I made it with like ninety seconds to spare."

"Seriously? You weren't?"

"Babe, what's going on? Was someone in the house today or something?"

I set my wineglass down on the coffee table and sank back into the couch. I was suddenly wide awake, and maybe a little sick to my stomach. "I think so, yeah. I thought it was probably you. I figured you came over on your way to work or something and I had just missed you."

"I didn't," he said. "It wasn't me."

"Yeah, so you said," I kind of snapped at him, but if he noticed the tone in my voice, he didn't show it.

"Did they take anything? How do you know—"

"Whoever it was made coffee. And they didn't take anything, or at least nothing that I can tell."

"Okay, this makes no sense. Like, at all," he said. "Who the hell would break in and just make coffee? How'd they even get in? What about the alarm?"

"I don't know," I said. "I don't know, I don't know." Suddenly I couldn't get enough air into my lungs. Who the hell had been in my house? Were they coming back? Was I sure? Was I sure I was sure?

And then, instead of offering comfort or support or ideas or suggestions or even just keeping his damn mouth shut—any one of which would have worked better than what he actually said—he asked:

"Are you sure you didn't just imagine it?"

I said nothing, more out of astonishment than anything else. I guess he took that as an invitation to continue.

"Because honestly, when you think about it, the most probable explanation is that you did," he went on. "It's basic logic. It explains—"

"Stop," I interrupted. "Just . . . stop."

To his credit, he did shut up. I sat there next to him, arms folded, not moving or speaking, for what felt like five full minutes before I stood up and announced, "I'm going to bed."

"Um, okay," he said. I think he had more he wanted to add, but I was already closing the bedroom door behind me.

TWENTY-THREE

Alton

I was getting a little dirtier, a little grubbier with each night I spent at the Royal Rest, as if some of the desperation and despair left over from previous visitors had crystallized out of the air and settled on me and slowly crept into my pores. But at home that morning, the jets of hot water blasted away layer after layer of grime and sadness. All those weeks at the Royal Rest without even one single satisfying shower. I felt human again.

I let myself imagine settling into a comfortable routine there, sleeping in fleabag motels at night and then enjoying a more pleasant daytime existence, complete with all the upper-middle-class amenities, back at the house, my home for the last seven years. But that was impossible. My future wasn't in that house anymore. It was somewhere in Central America.

Rivulets of hot water coursed down my neck and back. I felt a stab of . . . something. Regret, maybe. But it didn't last. I thought of my satchel and what was in it and then imagined life in a ten-by-ten concrete box with metal bars on the windows. That chased away any ambivalence I might have been feeling about my situation.

I turned off the water and dried myself with the towel hanging from Nicole's towel bar. There was one hanging from the bar that had once been mine, but no way in hell was I going to share a bath towel with Davis Spaulding. I'd shared enough with the man already. When I was done I folded the towel and replaced it exactly as I had found it.

I went to the kitchen, made myself a single cup of coffee and washed out the pot when it was done. I carried my mug into the living room, over to my records. It wasn't a huge collection, only about two thousand titles or so, but it had taken me a lifetime to put it together. I couldn't even begin to count the hours I'd spent sifting through piles at record shops and collector shows and flea markets. I remember how after a while the dust from the old jackets would coat my fingertips, how it would poof out into the air when I dropped a stack of rejects back onto the pile, how it would find its way into my nostrils and make me sneeze. That's how I always knew it was time to quit. I had listened to each disc in my collection at least once. I was proud of that. A lot of collectors had more pieces than they would ever have time to listen to. I never saw the point of that. Then it's no longer a labor of love. It's just acquisition for acquisition's sake.

Now I'd have to leave the whole collection behind. I'd never be able to re-create it in Costa Rica. I wouldn't even be able to come close. Nicole had never liked my collection. Took up too much space, she said. But she tolerated it. I half-hoped she would just dump them in the alley behind the house, and then I could scavenge as many as would fit in the trunk. But she's no fool; she knew there was money in them, and she would probably sell off the whole collection as soon as she could. I was a little surprised she hadn't already.

I put Lou Donaldson's Midnight Creeper—one of my all-time favorites—on the turntable. I knew every pop, every hiss, every scrape of static. I always anticipated those sounds as if they were their own musical part. They were as crucial to the whole experience as George Benson's guitar tone or Blue Mitchell's horn. The needle dropped and the notes swirled around me, making me whole for just a few minutes.

The coffee was perfectly balanced, not too acidic or too watery. I breathed in its aroma and held it in my nostrils for few seconds before letting go. At least I'll be able to get good coffee in Costa Rica, I remember thinking. Right off the bush. I've never had coffee that fresh. Maybe I'll even grow it myself. Sure, why not? I can be a coffee farmer. Nobody would ever think to find me picking beans, or whatever it is coffee farmers do.

I took another sip and swirled the liquid around my mouth. This does taste pretty fresh, though.

But come on. I knew nothing about coffee farming—I didn't even know if it was properly called farming or growing or something else—or the industry, and to be honest, I had no real inclination to learn it. I did like the idea of spending my days coaxing coffee beans from the soil, living the simple and dignified life of a gentleman planter, with the added benefit of well over a million American dollars in cash to dip into whenever I needed it. It was an enticing idea, almost intoxicating.

I reached over to the coffee table and picked up the latest copy of *The Atlantic*, flipped through it for a minute, then tossed it aside. Despite the coffee, despite the music, despite the comforts of home, I was uneasy.

When the record was done, I put it away, in its usual spot on the second shelf.

Why are you still here? What is the point of all this?

Good question.

I went upstairs and pushed open the door to the study. Exactly as I'd left it. I sank into my club chair, cradling the warm mug in my hands. Nothing could have felt more normal, and at the same time more exotic, than this.

I shrugged. Maybe I'm not ready to leave yet. That's all. I'll go when I'm ready.

What are you waiting for, then?

To be honest, the fact that I didn't have a quick and convincing answer to that question at the ready was beginning to worry me. If I wasn't ready now, when would I be? What would have to happen before I was comfortable just driving away, leaving my home and family shrinking in the rearview mirror? Life had continued without me. I'd seen that already. It would keep going after I was gone. My old environment had already started to adapt to my absence. Soon the people who had once been closest to me wouldn't be able to quite remember how it all had been when I was alive, not really.

As sad as all that was, it wasn't the reason.

I didn't need to do any more reconnaissance, either. I knew where I stood by then. I knew who Davis Spaulding was. I knew what my coworkers really thought of me. And I knew what Nicole had been doing behind my back. How she'd betrayed me. Cuckolded me. Made a complete fool out of me.

Oh, I definitely knew where I stood with her all right.

And suddenly, I knew why I was still there.

And in that moment, it all seemed so stupid, so pointless, so counterproductive. I wasn't some petty little man who couldn't let go of a grudge. And Nicole, well, she was who she was. Nothing I could do now would change that. All it would do is make me feel a little better in the moment. But that moment would be fleeting, unfulfilling. I knew that from hard experience.

It just wasn't worth the risk.

So that was it. It was time. I would go tomorrow, first thing in the morning.

Why not tonight? Why not right this minute?

That . . . wasn't such a bad idea, actually. Drive over to the Royal Rest, get the satchel and be on the interstate ten minutes later. All of this would finally be behind me. And all I had to do was just . . . go.

And just like that, I felt ten feet tall. I was back in control, driving events instead of letting them drive me. I hadn't felt this way in weeks.

I stood up, swallowed the last of my coffee, strode into the hall, and heard the muted sound of keys jangling together, followed by the unmistakable rubbing-wood sound of someone shoving the back door open.

.

TWENTY-FOUR

Nicole

I've never understood what's so special about Wednesdays that Pineview couldn't keep the kids until the end of the workday, like they did the other four days of the week. It was always such a hassle, having to leave work at lunch and try to get work done from home. I know that sounds awful. I know I should relish every moment I get to spend with my daughter, because there are only so many of them that I'm going to get. But I've never found being a mom to be as clear-cut as all that.

I couldn't possibly be the only parent who wondered about this. I thought about bringing it up at the next Parents' Night, but I never did. I guess it's pretty much a moot point now.

Clara wasn't very happy about it either. She loved her school lunches and always seemed to resent eating lunch at home once a week instead, even if it was with Mommy. On the way home—the nine-block drive from the school to our house, mind you, nine blocks—she whined from the backseat about the juice box she was missing out on and the cookies that were rightfully hers but would now be eaten by someone else. She refused to get out of her car seat. She didn't want to go inside. She wanted to go back to school. And then, as we came in through the back door, she made that closed-mouthed moaning sound I hate whenever I suggested something for lunch.

"You can have peanut butter and jelly," I offered.

"Hmmmmmmmmmmm," whined Clara.

"Or I can make you some macaroni and cheese. How would you like that, huh?"

"Hmmmmmmmmmmm."

"Or you could haaaaaaaaave . . . nothing. Would you like that? A big bowl of nothing?"

"Hmmmmmmmmmmm."

There must be someplace that does twenty-four-hour daycare. And one day, I will find it.

"All right, I am going to make you a grilled cheese sandwich and cut up some strawberries for you and that's what lunch is going to be."

"I want cookies," Clara said. "And a juice box."

"You can have milk. And maybe cookies after, but only if you eat your sandwich and your berries."

"Chocolate milk."

"Deal." I smiled, and Clara grinned back at me. See? Easy-peasy.

"I'm going to get Brownie. Bye!" Clara ran out of the kitchen. Brownie was her stuffed walrus. It wasn't brown, though. It was gray, like most walruses. Alton and I never could figure out why Clara chose that particular name to go with that particular animal.

"Don't run up those stairs," I called after her. "You remember the last time you fell down?"

"I won't, Mommy." And then I heard a quick series of stomps that could only be the sound of a four-year-old running up a staircase.

TWENTY-FIVE

Alton

What the hell were they doing home already? It wasn't even one o'clock yet. I was sure Clara usually came home around four. Was something wrong? Was she sick?

Who the hell cares—just get out of this house. Get out get out get out GET OUT. You have to GO. Now.

Out a window. Wait, no—that way was too exposed, no ledges to stand on and no way to close it again once I was out. Down the stairs and out the door was out of the question. That left hiding somewhere in the house and sneaking out later. Hopefully before Nicole's . . . friend came over for a nightcap. I couldn't be held responsible for my actions if I had to listen to that. I mean, I'm a man like anyone else.

Hide.

Okay. Where?

Bathroom was too risky. I might be able to wait it out in the study—the door had been closed when I got there, so that's how Nicole would expect it to be when she got back, so maybe if I went in there and closed the door and locked it—was there a lock? How could I not know that? I thought there was, but then again I wasn't sure—and besides, she might never even try to get in there. She'd rarely gone in there when I had been alive.

But things were different now.

Maybe that's where she goes to think about me. Maybe she goes into the study and sits in my chair and looks at the books I've read or meant to read one of these days, and maybe that's where she feels something, where she thinks about the good times and cries a little because there won't be any more good times and—

"I won't, Mommy"—Oh shit, that's Clara, she's coming upstairs, shit shit shit shit. It was too late to open and close the

130

study door without her hearing me, or maybe even seeing me, which was something I could not allow to happen. Clara's closet. I could get there. I could make it. I turned and darted into her room just as she rested her hand on the bannister along the top step. I tried not to trample on or kick aside any of her toys as I scrambled into the closet and shut the door as gently as I could manage.

"Oh Browwwwwwwneeeeeeeeeee," Clara sang out. "Where arrrrrrrrrrrrrre you?"

Not in the closet. Don't look in the closet. I was trying to send her a telepathic transmission, trying to psychically will her away or something. Then I heard her leap onto her bed. The mattress springs cried out in strained surprise.

"BrowniebrowniebrowniebrownieBROWWWWneeeeee! Where! Are! You!" And I wished I could see her. I would have given just about anything to be able to watch her bouncing on her bed, grinning like a crazy person, happy in that way that only little kids can be. I noticed I was still holding the coffee mug, so I slid it onto the top shelf, the only empty horizontal space in the entire closet. Clara was humming to herself. I did not recognize the song.

"Clara? Honey? What are you doing up there?" Nicole's voice was clear and impossibly far away at the same time.

"I'm reading, Mommy," Clara hollered.

"Well come on down for lunch. It's ready."

"But I can't find Brownie."

"Did you look in the closet?"

Shit. No no no no no no. Don't look in here.

"Okay, Mommy! Just a sec!" And I heard my daughter launch herself off her bed and tromp through the Legos and dinosaurs and then the closet was suddenly filled with diffused afternoon sunlight and when I looked down, she was looking up at me, eyes wide, mouth open.

Not knowing what else to do, I held a finger to my lips and said, "Shhhhhhh."

131

TWENTY-SIX

Alton

"Daddy," Clara said in a stage whisper. "You're here!"

"Shhhhhhhhh," I said again. "Clara, honey, quiet."

"Mommy said you were gone," she said. "She said you were under the water."

"Yes, honey. That's where I was. Under the water. And I have to go back there."

"Daddy?"

"What is it, darling?"

"Are you a ghost?"

"A ghost?"

Holy shit. A ghost. A ghost.

I never would have thought of that. Especially at her age. "Yes. Yes I am. I'm a ghost. But don't tell your mother. She's afraid of ghosts."

"And ghosts live under the water."

I shrugged. "Okay, sure. That's where we live." I guess it could have been true. What did I know about ghosts?

"I saw you at school. Miss Mari said I didn't, but I did."

"Clara!" I could hear an edge to Nicole's voice, even from all the way downstairs. "Your sandwich is getting cold! Get down here—it's time to eat!"

"Go eat your lunch, baby." I bent down and kissed Clara on the forehead. "And don't tell Mommy you saw me. Remember, she's afraid of ghosts."

"Okay." She started to leave, then stopped. "Are you going to come back?"

I smiled. There was no way I would not be back. "Yes I am, Clara darling."

"Will you be here when I come back from lunch?"

"I don't know," I said. "I might be. Sometimes when you're

a ghost, you just disappear for no reason. But sooner or later, you always come back. So don't worry."

Clara nodded, a serious expression on her face. "I understand, Daddy," she said, and then ran out of the room, toward the stairs, and down to lunch.

TWENTY-SEVEN

Nicole

I think that was the same day all the ghost talk started.

"Mommy," Clara asked over lunch, as she picked a strawberry out of her tiny bowl, "where do ghosts live?"

"Ghosts don't live anywhere, honey."

"Yes they do," she said. "They live somewhere."

"For one thing, there's no such thing as ghosts. They aren't real. And even if they were, they wouldn't live anywhere, because they're not alive anymore. That's the point of ghosts. They're dead, and dead things can't live anywhere."

Yes. That was my life. Arguing semantics and metaphysics with a four-year-old. I flipped through the day's paper, utterly listless, looking for something to distract her.

"Maybe they live under the water," Clara offered.

"Uh-huh," I said, but I wasn't really listening. I know, that's awful, but I was reading about some meth-head, this woman who robbed a gas station completely naked, and when the cash register wouldn't open she grabbed as many Whatchamacallit bars as she could carry and just ran off. Security cameras had caught the whole thing. Not the usual kind of story I seek out in the paper, but it happened just a few blocks from the house.

"Maybe they live with Daddy," she continued. "Maybe Daddy is a ghost too."

That got my attention.

I looked up from the paper. "No, Clara," I told her. I sighed, maybe a little too loudly. But can you blame me? We'd talked about Alton being gone and how he wasn't coming back, and I knew it just wasn't getting through to her. But the ghost thing . . . that was new. I hadn't heard that before. Time to try again, I guess. So I leaned forward and hardened my voice. "Listen to me now. Daddy is not a ghost. He died. Okay? He died. He is under the water and is never coming back. He can't get out of where he is because he is not alive anymore. It's okay to miss him and dream about him and wish you could see him again, but that's not real either."

Clara said nothing and looked down at her plate. I went back to the newspaper. But then a minute or two later I looked up again. Clara was just picking at her sandwich, on the verge of tears.

"What's the matter, honey?" I asked. "Is something wrong with your sandwich?"

"I just don't want it anymore," Clara whined, and then I wanted to cry too.

"Tell you what," I said. "If you eat half the sandwich and all your berries, I will take you to the park for the afternoon. How's that?"

"Can I have cookies?"

"At the park. Deal?"

Clara's clouded face cleared in an instant. She grinned back at me. "Deal!" she nearly shouted, and she dug into her sandwich. I guess she forgot that she didn't want it anymore.

When she was done, I asked if she wanted to bring Brownie to the park with us.

"I can't find him," she said.

"Yeah, I bet you can't—your room is such a mess." I laughed. "Tell you what. Why don't I help you look for him? Then he can come with us and play at the park too."

"Okay!" she said, sprinting toward the stairs. "Come on!"

"Clara. Don't. Run," I said through clenched teeth, but it was hopeless. She was already scrambling up the steps, scuttling on all fours toward her room. That kid has only two speeds, and the other one is "off."

135

That's something Alton always used to say about her. Sorry. It just slipped out.

"Oh my goodness, Clara," I said in mock horror. "Just look at this mess."

"I know!" Clara said, giggling.

"However will we find Brownie? Where could he be?"

"I don't know, Mommy."

"Could he be . . . under the bed?" I dropped to my knees and shoved my face under the bed. "Browwwwwww-ww-neeeeeeeeee," I called out. "Are you down here?"

"No!" Clara cackled.

"No?" I stood up. The blood rushed to my head, and for a moment I struggled to get my balance. "Well then where could he be? Is he . . . on the ceiling?" I craned my neck around the room, searching for a stuffed walrus on the ceiling.

"He is not on the ceiling!"

"Hmmmm. This walrus really knows how to hide. Now, where would I hide if I were a stuffed walrus who didn't want to be found?" I snapped my fingers. "I got it—the closet!" I hopped over the pile of toys in the middle of the room and yanked open the closet door. "Ha—got you!" I reached down and pulled from the clothes lining the floor a slate-gray stuffed walrus, and then I held it over my head, like a prize.

"You found him!" Clara squealed. "You found Brownie!"

"He was just in the closet, honey. That's a place you should always look before saying you can't find something."

"Okay, Mommy."

"Are you ready to go to the park now?"

We spent almost two hours at the park. God, that was a wonderful afternoon. Maybe the last pure, unspoiled moment of fun I can remember having. Clara kicked her soccer ball, she scaled the monkey bars like a gecko, she leaped from the swing a dozen times, and ran circles around the huge oak tree in the center of the park. Someone's gonna sleep well tonight, I remember thinking. It was as close to a perfect afternoon as I had any right to expect.

That lasted exactly until we got home. As soon as I had the back door open, Clara ran straight up to her room, then started crying. Of course I followed her up there. I found her splayed out on her bed, lying on her back, sobbing.

"What's the matter, honey?"

"Daddy's not here," she wailed.

Damn it. I knew I shouldn't have been such a hard-ass earlier.

"Of course he's not." I tried to make up for my earlier mistake by using that cloying, faux-soothing voice I hated so much. "He's under the water, baby. That's where he'll always be. I wish he was here too"—do I?—"but there's nothing anyone can do to bring him back."

"But he said he would be here."

Huh. Well, this is new.

"Um, he did?"

"Yes. He promised."

"When did he promise that, Clara-bear?"

"When he was in there." She pointed to her closet. "Before we went to the park."

I sighed. How seriously should I take this? I really had no idea. Did four-year-olds actually hallucinate, or did they just have these very blurry lines between the imaginary and the real? I honestly didn't know, because Clara had never had trouble keeping the two separate before.

"Clara," I said. I hesitated for a moment, but I knew I had to finish my thought. I'm the parent. I owed her some parenting. "Daddy wasn't in your closet today."

"Yes he was. He said he would be there when I came back."

"Why would he be in your closet, honey? What was he doing there?"

"He was just standing there. And he said he'd wait right there."

"No, honey," I said. "I don't think he was. Maybe you dreamed it. Did you fall asleep when you were looking for Brownie?"

"No," Clara said. Her voice wavered, just a bit unsure.

"It's okay if you did," I said. "I promise, Mommy's not mad. When you miss someone a lot, it's normal to think you see them everywhere."

"But . . . he was there," Clara said, but even then I could tell that she didn't really know whether to believe it anymore.

"Well," I said. "If he was there, then maybe he'll come back tomorrow. Do you want to go downstairs and watch Caillou?"

"Okay," she said, sniffling. She reached out to me with both arms, and I lifted her off the bed and carried her downstairs.

So then Piedmont Insurance decided to deny my claim, which was all I needed. Just perfect timing. I mean, I had been half-expecting it, ever since I got that review letter in the mail a few weeks earlier. I guess the problem was that there was no death certificate and no compelling proof that Alton was actually dead, and therefore no reason for them to pay out. Or at least that's what they were telling me. I guess it could have been a stalling tactic or something, but I really had no way to know.

"This is the first I'm hearing about it," Marion told me when I called her. She'd been my insurance agent for something like eight years. "Honestly, I was never notified, which is highly irregular in situations like this. This is just awful, just awful. I know how you must have been counting on that money. Let me make a few calls and find out what I can and call you back, 'kay?"

"That's really not necessary, Marion, if we could just—"

"Won't take more than ten minutes, hon. Bye." And she hung up on me.

It took her two whole hours to call me back, which, I have to admit, bothered me. I mean, I understand that sometimes things take a while. If it's going to take two hours, just tell me that. Don't say ten minutes. "First of all, I am so sorry I was out of the loop on this," she said. "I still don't know quite how that happened, but I am gonna get to the bottom of it one way or another, let me tell you."

"It's fine." It wasn't fine. But whatever.

"Second of all, unfortunately I do have some bad news for you. But then I guess it's not exactly news to you, since you're the one who called me about—anyway, yes, I'm afraid the company has denied your claim. I am so sorry."

Well shit. "I have to admit, Marion, you really do sound sorry."

"Oh, I am, of course I am!"

I sighed. I had absolutely no energy left for any of this. "So, what next then?"

"Well. This was an unusual case, as you probably can imagine. We don't get a lot of claims without a, um, death certificate"—I'm positive she was about to say body instead but caught herself at the last second—"but every so often it does happen. As was stated in the letter—which I now have a copy of on my screen, so I'm all up to speed here—as was stated in the letter, there is just too much uncertainty around your husband's passing. The potential—and I'm sorry, I really am, I'm not saying that you're the kind of person who would do this, but you know, some people do try it—the possibility of fraud, well, it seems to have crossed their mind in this case."

"But it's only been a little more than a month," I said. "This letter, it seems so . . . so final. Like, that's it, case closed."

"Well, I hate to say this, but as far as Piedmont is concerned, the case is closed. At least until there are, you know, any new developments."

"They couldn't have just—I don't know, let it sit a while longer? Waited a little longer for my husband's remains to turn up somewhere? They had to deny the claim entirely?"

"I truly am sorry," Marion said. "But that's SOP these days."

"Well that's just great." I let out another sigh, this one a lot louder than the last. I'd been doing a lot of sighing lately. I was right at my limit. I could feel it, feel myself pressed hard against it. It was only a matter of time, really.

"Let me just take a quick look at the case notes here." I could hear Marion tapping out a lilting rhythm on her keyboard. "Um. Did you know your husband was under investigation by the FBI?"

"Of course I know that," I snapped. I didn't mention the fact that the first I had heard about any of it was on the news, a week or so after Alton died. That part was none of her business. "Everyone knows that. It was on the news. So what?"

"I'm sorry, I don't mean to make this difficult time any harder. I really don't. But to make a long story short, from what I can see, once those FBI agents told the Piedmont people about their investigation, well, I think they felt their hands were basically tied."

"Excuse me?"

"The timing of it," Marion said. "It just looked a bit . . . off, you know? He finds out he's a target of a federal investigation and then a month later he's dead in a freak boating accident?"

"A month?"

Wait a minute. He knew about this for a whole month? And never said a word?

"These days you can't blame them for being suspicious. Oh, I know you wouldn't even dream of doing anything illegal, but you know how some people are."

"Marion," I said. "You know Alton was a lawyer, right?"

There was a brief but noticeable pause on her end of the line. "Ummmm, yes, I think I did know that." I heard a few more rapid keystrokes on Marion's keyboard, more forceful this time. "Yes, here it is, listed under 'occupation.'"

"And you know who's friends with lawyers, right?"

"I . . . no. Who?"

"Lawyers. That's who's friends with lawyers. Because who else wants to be friends with a lawyer?"

"I . . . I'm afraid I'm not following you, hon."

"Here's my point, Marion. I was married to Alton for eleven years. I know a ton of lawyers. Some of them sue insurance companies just for kicks, and any of them would be more than happy to do so on behalf of the bereaved widow of a recently deceased friend and colleague."

"Well, hold on now—"

"So as soon as we are done, I'm gonna make some calls. I'm gonna go get Alton's Rolodex and start dialing." Actually, I had no idea where Alton's Rolodex was, or if he even had one. I think the last time I heard anyone mention having one was in the nineties. But it sounded good, and that was enough for me just then.

"If you'd just hold on a minute and listen." Exasperation crept into Marion's voice. "There is an appeals process here. Okay? So there's no need to go hiring any lawyers now. And there's definitely no reason to give any of 'em my name." Her laugh sounded forced, and that's the moment when I knew I had her.

"Actually, I think that's all the more reason to call a lawyer," I said. "Get someone in on this who knows what they're doing. Maybe that way people will start taking me seriously. Good-bye, Marion." I hung up without waiting for a reply and flung my phone into the couch cushions.

Goddamn it. Just one more fucking thing to deal with. And then I started to cry, very softly. I raised my hand to my face and pressed it against my eyes.

And when I looked up again, Clara was standing in front of me, watching me.

"Hi, honey," I said, trying to sound cheerful even though I could barely control my facial muscles. "I didn't hear you come in. Is—is everything okay?" I hated asking my four-year-old daughter the question I wished someone would ask me. If only there were someone around to do it.

"Yes," Clara said. "But you're crying."

"I know, baby. I . . . I bit my tongue. Have you ever done that?"

"Uh-huh."

"It hurts a lot, right?"

"Uh-huh."

"So . . . that's why I'm crying."

"Okay, Mommy."

I wiped my eyes, trying to dry them. You must look pathetic, I remember thinking, and then the tears welled up again. "Honey, are you done with your show already? Do you want to watch another one?"

"Power Rangers," she said.

"No, honey, that's too scary. But I'll tell you what—if you pick something else, I'll watch it with you, okay?"

"Super Why!"

"Okay, Clara-bear. We'll watch Super Why!" And we sat there on the couch, Clara completely wrapped up in her show, me staring straight through the TV, like it wasn't even there.

That evening, I decided to ignore Davis's calls and watch mindless television without him. I didn't have the energy to deal with him, and besides, The Real Housewives of Bangalore was on. I wasn't really paying any attention to it, which is fine, because you don't actually have to pay attention to those shows. By then I had already downed one glass of Riesling and was halfway through a second. Things are weird around the homestead, I remember thinking. I

142

watched the cold blue light from the TV fill the room as the daylight faded. There were no other lights on. Maybe more wine will help.

It would be nice if things were ever that easy.

TWENTY-EIGHT

Alton

As soon as Clara was back downstairs, I slipped out of the clos-et and padded down the hallway to the study, making sure the door was locked the second it was closed.

She thought I was a ghost. I couldn't have planned that any better. I still think only the mind of a child could have come up with that. Kids are open to possibilities in ways that adults are not, possibilities that apparently include finding the ghost of your father standing in your closet.

And because they are open, they're not afraid of things in the same way adults are. Which I guess is why she didn't scream.

But how does this change anything?

Well, I never said it did, did I?

You don't have to say it. You were all set to go. All ready to leave this place behind you and get on with your life, the one waiting for you in Costa Rica. You even said yourself that there was no longer any reason to stay. But now you're thinking of staying. Aren't you? You can't lie to me. I'm you, you know.

Maybe. Maybe I am. A little.

You should leave. Today. It's dangerous for you here. How does what happened today change any of that?

I don't know. But it does. Somehow. I don't have to say good-bye just yet. I can . . . I don't know, cushion the blow of it all, or something. Make the transition easier for her. Help her understand what death is, what it means.

So you're going to help her understand what death is and what it means by pretending to be a ghost. That's your plan. Do I understand this correctly?

Okay, fine. Point taken. But this gives us the chance to say good-bye to each other properly, without any of the "I wish

144

I'd said such-and-such" regrets that people always have when someone dies suddenly.

So that's who this delay is for. It's for Clara.

Of course. Clara is why I do everything I do.

You might not have to say good-bye just yet. You might be able to put it off for a while. But you will still have to say it. All this does is draw things out and add a little more risk with each passing day. Which is up to you, I suppose.

Yes. It's up to me to decide if my daughter is worth the risk.

Then I thought I heard Nicole say something about opening the closet, and for a moment I knew, just knew, that Clara would say something, forgetting her promise not to tell Mommy, but that's okay, she's only four and you can't expect kids to keep big news to themselves. But she didn't. She just shrieked for that damn walrus, and then bounded down the hallway, feet thumping right past the study door, as if she hadn't just seen her own daddy reappear from the dead and then vanish again. Just like a real ghost would do.

Of course, she's four. She lives in the moment.

Nicole followed her downstairs, and it was only then that I realized I'd been holding my breath. A few minutes later I heard the back door open and close, and then the Volvo's engine coughed and spat and finally growled softly as the car pulled out of the drive and crept away. I waited a few minutes in case they forgot something, and then I slipped out the back door and down the alley, vanishing just like a ghost might.

TWENTY-NINE

Nicole

I could tell something was wrong by the sound of my stream in the toilet.

Not wrong with me, exactly, but just . . . wrong. It didn't sound right, like there wasn't any water in the bowl. No, wait. Not that. It was more like the inside of the bowl was covered in some kind of cloth or fabric or something. I wasn't in the habit of inspecting the toilet before using it, so my first instinct was to assume there was some kind of leak somewhere. Things were always breaking around there, but that's how it is when you live in an older house. You get used to it after a while. I sighed. I really did not want to have to pay for a plumber's visit. I had enough to worry about as it was.

But when I stood up and took a look, I knew right away a plumber wouldn't be necessary. The bowl actually had plenty of water in it. It also had Davis's shoes jammed into the drain.

I'd been pissing on Davis's shoes. That's why it had sounded different.

What the hell are his shoes doing in the toilet?

I had no idea. I knew that I certainly didn't put them there, which left Davis or Clara. I couldn't imagine why Davis would do such a thing himself, though by that point I had found myself wondering more and more about why he did a lot of things. And it couldn't have been Clara, because she'd been at school all day. We'd just gotten home, in fact, and Clara bolted straight upstairs as soon as I had the back door open. Could she have done this that morning, before we'd left for school? I didn't think so, but our mornings were usually these frantic, whirling dervishes of breakfast and getting dressed and finding keys and locating backpacks and making sure teeth had been brushed and wiping up food off the

146

floor. So I guess I could have missed it. I really couldn't be sure.

But she's not even supposed to know about him yet, I remember thinking. Great. Because the last thing I wanted was for Clara to start thinking of Davis as a replacement for her father. I mean, I didn't even know if there was a role for him in my life at all, either right then or at some point in the future. I'd been reconsidering the whole arrangement by that point, which was the real reason I didn't want Clara to find out about him. That would just make things a thousand times knottier than they had to be when the inevitable happened.

"Clara!" I yelled up the stairs. "Come down here, please."

"Coming, Mommy!"

"Slowly, please," I said as soon as Clara appeared at the top step. "No running. You know that."

"I know, Mommy." Instead she took the stairs with exaggerated care, putting first one foot and then the other on each step, holding the handrail the whole way down.

"Clara, honey," I began, then stopped. Don't yell. Stay calm. Soothing voice. "Did you go into Mommy's bathroom before we went to school today?"

"No."

"Are you sure you didn't?"

"I didn't."

"Okay baby. How about after we came home?"

"Uh-uh. I went to my room to play," Clara said.

I looked at my daughter. She could have been lying, but if she was, she'd gotten really good at it in a very short time. She hadn't shown any talent for that sort of thing so far, or even an interest in it, so I was reasonably confident she was telling the truth.

"Mommy, I want to watch *Jake and the Never Land Pirates,*" Clara whined.

Ugh, that fucking show again. "That's fine, honey. Just not too loud, okay?"

"I won't, Mommy," she said, and she bounced off to the living room.

So. That left Davis. Which obviously made no sense at all. Yes, I had thought he was sneaking into the house before, and at that point maybe I still thought he had been the one who made coffee that morning while I was out. Our last conversation hadn't really resolved that issue one way or the other. But why would he stuff his own shoes into the toilet? I just didn't get that. Was he drunk? Was he trying to send me a message? Yes, fine, I'd made fun of those shoes before, plenty of times—and with good reason, too; if you could see them you'd totally agree with me. But if there was a message in those shoes, I wasn't receiving it.

Also, when would he have done it? It would have had to have been sometime between eight and four that day. But he'd had to work that day, and Davis's usual workday routine was sleeping until twenty past nine and then rushing straight to the lot.

I picked up the phone and dialed the dealership's main number.

"Crum Luxury Motorcars," chirped the receptionist.

"Davis Spaulding, please."

"One moment." I waited on hold for a few seconds. "I'm sorry, he's with a customer. Would you like his voice mail?"

"No, that's—wait, on second thought, yes, voice mail would be great."

"Great. Please hold." Then a click, a short burst of elevator music, and Davis's prerecorded voice.

"Davis, we talked about this before," I told his voice mail. "You cannot be coming in here when I'm not home, and you especially cannot be coming in here when I'm not home and not leaving a goddamn note. This is why I never

148

gave you a key in the first place, and I'm going to move the spare as soon as I hang up this phone. Good-bye."

Half an hour later, the phone rang.

"Um, yeah, I hope this doesn't come across as patronizing or rude or whatever, but what the hell?"

"So you're denying it, then?" I asked.

"Crazy stalker-girl voicemails at work are not what I signed up for," Davis said. "And denying what?"

"That you were here today. In the house. Like I told you not to be."

"Uh, well, since I've been at work all day, then yes. I am most def denying that."

Most def. Seriously? Jesus.

I sighed. "Listen, Davis, I need you to be totally honest here." I caught myself about to slip into the soothing voice I use with Clara. He probably wouldn't have even noticed. "Seriously, just be straight with me, and as long as you do that, we are cool. I just want to make sure I understand. You are saying you did not come into the house today, correct?"

"Yes, for Chrissake."

"Okay. I believe you. But I . . . I think someone was here today. While I was at work."

"Okay. Why?"

"Well, there were . . . things out of place. Again."

"Like the other day with the coffee."

"Yes, like that day with the coffee. Only . . . different."

"Okay, different how?" he asked. I was starting to regret initiating this conversation.

"Well, this time it was . . . something of yours that was moved. Your shoes."

"That's it?" he asked. "That could be nothing. Are you sure they were even moved? Because you know, shoes are the kind of thing that—"

"Yes, I am sure. They were in a place I would never put them. And I doubt you'd ever put them there either."

"Huh. Okay. Where were they?"

"In the, um, toilet."

There was a long pause before he said, "They were where?"

"They were in the toilet, Davis. The goddamn toilet."

"You fished 'em out though, right?" In my mind, I could see him leaping to his feet as he said this. He sounded like he was nearly shouting it into the phone.

"Oh yeah, I did," I said. "But I peed on them first. Sorry."

"You—what the fuck, Nicole? Why would you even use the damn toilet if it's got shoes in it?"

"I don't check the bowl before I sit down, Davis. I had to go, you know? And when I have to go, I go. So I went and I noticed it sounded different and when I was done I . . . well never mind, this is all very TMI, I think. The point is, that's when I saw them. I'm sorry. I know you really liked those shoes."

"So that's why you think someone broke in," he said. "To stuff my favorite shoes in your toilet. So you could piss on them."

"I don't know if they planned it out beforehand or what," I said. "But yes, that's why I think someone broke in. Because I found that. In there." Even though he couldn't see me doing it, I waved toward the bathroom to illustrate my point.

"You don't think there might just maybe be a simpler explanation? Like maybe your four-year-old daughter did it?"

"She never had the chance. I had at least one eye on her from the moment she woke up this morning."

"Oh, so it must have been me then," he sneered. "Because I can think of some other possibilities. Why not that weird dude who lives across the alley from you? The one who gets his kicks by spraying bums with a freaking garden hose? Nothing Freudian about that, right? Or that guy who was grabbing your ass at your own husband's wake for fuck's sake? Why not him?"

"Oh come on. Bob Sherman is a dirty old perv, but he's harmless."

"With you leaving that spare key out there, it could be anybody."

"Nobody knows it's there," I protested. "It's in a secret spot."

"Everyone knows what that fucking turtle is for, Nicole. They sell those things at Walmart. Everyone on Earth either has one or has seen them on the shelf and knows exactly what you're using it for."

"Well, like I told you, I'm getting rid of it as soon as we're off the phone. No more spare key in the turtle."

"Yeah, great, as long as whoever it is hasn't made his own copy already," he said. My stomach wrenched itself into a ball, and I felt a little chill on my neck.

"Shit. I never thought of that," I said. "Oh shit."

"Don't freak out. Just get the locks changed, like, tomorrow."

"Of course. I should have thought of that." I meant it, too. He was right. I really felt like an idiot just then.

"It's fine, you're spooked, I get it. And to be honest, it is some pretty weird shit. First the coffee, now my shoes. It's almost like your house is haunted or something."

"That would be a lot easier to deal with, I think," I said.

"You want me to come over tonight?"

"No, thanks but no, I think. It's been a long day."

"Okay, I guess," he said. I could almost hear the shrug. I think he thought the indifference made him sexy. "But y'know, if you change your mind, you got my digits."

"Yeah," I said, "I got 'em," and I hung up. I took a deep breath and held it for a moment. Keep it together, I told myself. Just . . . keep it together.

A few minutes later I was standing in the backyard, the wooden turtle resting in the palm of my hand. On an impulse I looked over my shoulder, toward the back fence. Across the alley, Todd Edgecomb was in his kids' tree house. He was looking at me—watching me? Now, there's a fine line—and he waved as soon as I made eye contact with him. I made a half-hearted effort at a wave back.

"Just cleaning the tree house," he called across the alley. "Kids. What can you do?"

I smiled and shrugged, then turned and went back into the house. I made sure to lock the dead bolt behind me.

THIRTY

Alton

Cramming those shoes into the toilet wasn't part of my plan for that day. It was an impulse, an involuntary reaction of the nervous system, a momentary inspiration that swirled together in my mind the moment I saw those shoes resting under the bed—my bed—again. I snatched them up and almost skipped across the room to the master bath, flipped up the toilet lid, and plunged those shoes as far into the drain as I could cram them. They were wedged together firmly, standing straight up on the points of the toes. I set the lid down, the way Nicole always left it.

It was a petty thing to do. Childish. But in my defense, those shoes were hideous. I wish you could have seen them. They looked just like a pair of size-eleven turds. They belonged in the toilet.

All that resolve I'd felt before Clara found me the last time I'd been there—to drive back to the Royal Rest, pick up my money, get out of town, and never look back—was completely gone, evaporated as if I'd never felt it at all. I was thinking of getting back into the house the moment I stepped into the alley. That would mean a really dangerous level of exposure, but I didn't care. Whenever I tried to visualize Costa Rica, the beachfront estate I would buy when I got there—or, on the other end of the spectrum, the cell I would be spending quite a bit of time in if I got caught—all I could see instead was Clara, standing in her closet doorway, looking up at me. She made me forget about the future, good or bad. That's the power my daughter's smile has over me.

I wanted to be able to get in the house whenever I needed to so I could see my daughter. So I could remind her of who I was. So she wouldn't forget me.

153

Until that point, I'd had no trouble getting in the house, because Nicole had never bothered to move the key. But after my little prank, I thought she might finally hide the spare key in a different spot, or get rid of it altogether. So on my way out that day, I took the key down to the Ace Hardware up the block and had a copy made. The original was safely back in its hiding place long before Nicole and Clara came home.

She might change the locks. I knew that was always a possibility. That's what I would do if I came home to find a pair of shoes shoved down the toilet. If she did that, I'd have to find another way in. But I figured I would burn that bridge when I got to it.

When I went back two days later, she had moved the spare key, just as I thought she might. But the copy I'd had made slid right in, even more smoothly than Nicole's spare had done. And just like that, I was back inside. Back home. So she moved the spare but didn't change the locks. After she knew that someone had been in her house who wasn't supposed to be there. She didn't know it was me. It could have been anyone. Does that seem smart to you? Does it seem like the work of a competent, attentive parent?

No. Of course it doesn't.

So yeah, I hadn't planned to put the shoes in the toilet; that was just a spur-of-the-moment impulse. But it had given me an idea. No, more than that. It inspired an idea. A mission. A work of performance art, intended for a very confused audience of one.

That's why I had come back that day.

The kitchen was immaculate as always, the faux-retro chrome appliances polished to perfection, the line of bamboo bowls dusted and precisely spaced along the counter. I closed my eyes and committed the entire scene to memory. It had to look exactly like this when I left, and I mean exactly.

Time to get to work.

I opened the cupboard closest to the back door and started pulling stuff out. Serving bowls. Colanders. Platters. This star-shaped thing that might have been for serving hors d'oeuvres—I wasn't sure because as far as I knew we'd never used it for anything. Dessert bowls. I took it all out and set each item out on the counter. The cupboard on the other side of the kitchen, by the living room entrance, held mostly coffee mugs. We had a lot of mugs. There were also a few dessert plates and plastic tumblers in there. I put all of it in the first cupboard, the one closest to the door that I'd just emptied. Then I put everything on the counter into the cupboard where the mugs were.

Then I kept going, doing the same thing with each remaining cupboard, swapping items between one and its opposite. But there was an odd number of them, so I had nowhere to move the items in the center cupboard. So instead I just put everything that had been on the bottom shelf up on the top, and vice versa.

Then I went over to the bookcase in the living room and flipped every single book upside down, so instead of tilting your head to your right to read the spines, you'd have to tilt to your left. I did the same for all the books in my study too. I stayed away for almost a week after that. I figured that should give her enough time to call a goddamn locksmith.

THIRTY-ONE >

Nicole

I don't even like to talk about it. That's how badly it shook me. Even now, knowing what I know—it's still too much, almost.

Someone had been getting into the house. Someone who wasn't Davis. I should have figured that out after the incident with the shoes. But I guess . . . I don't know. Maybe the whole idea, that someone was stalking me, trying to terrorize me, and using these creepy psych-out tactics to do it? Maybe it was just too much for me right then.

My problem—or one of my problems—is that I don't always step back and look at things logically when I should. Sometimes I would rather just assume the best and be a Pollyanna than be a realist. I know this about myself. I'm working on it.

It started in the car, on the way home from school. Clara was barely even fastened into her car seat before she asked about Alton.

"Mommy, when is Daddy coming to play with me?"

Great. This shit again. "Clara, we've been over this. Daddy's gone. He's not coming back. Ever."

"Maybe he will be in my closet when we get home."

"I don't think so, honey." I caught her eyes in the rearview mirror. "He's under the water now, just like I told you. Why would he be in your closet?"

"Because that's where he was last time," Clara explained to me like I was the four-year-old in the car. "He said he would come back. But he wasn't there today."

"Honey, it's okay to play make-believe and imagine your daddy is home, but you know that's not real. He's not coming here. He's gone and he's not coming back." I was starting to get exasperated by the whole topic. But I knew I was talking

156

to a small child who had lost her father and didn't seem to understand it all yet. Patience, Nicole. Be a parent. "Please. I really need for you to understand this. Daddy is gone. He died. Do you understand what that means?"

"I know," Clara said. "He's a ghost now."

I tensed a bit. Maybe this was the defense mechanism her brain had come up with to help her through the trauma of it all. I wasn't sure how I felt about that. "Oh, a ghost. So you know it's just pretend."

"It's not pretend." She pursed her lips and frowned, which is what she always did when she was frustrated with grown-ups doubting her.

"All right," I said. "I give up. When we get home, you can show me. Hell, maybe he's there now."

Clara's face lit up. "He is?"

"I said maybe," I told her as I pulled into the driveway. Crap. That was stupid. "Don't get your hopes up, kiddo." But Clara was already halfway up the stairs by the time I got inside.

I'd been planning to make chicken thighs and rice—one of Clara's favorites—for dinner, which takes about forty-five minutes or so to cook. So I headed straight into the kitchen instead of following her upstairs. I opened the cupboard to pull out my square Pyrex dish.

But it wasn't there.

I stared into the open cupboard. Something was wrong here. There were supposed to be baking pans in there. But that's not what I was looking at. I was looking at glassware. Wineglasses. Pint glasses. Highball glasses.

Then I felt like I didn't know why I was there, like I'd been looking for something and then forgotten what it was. Which I guess isn't too far from the truth, really.

A couple seconds later, the fog started to clear a little. Wait, what's going on here? Why are there glasses where the pans should be? Am I looking in the right place?

Somebody moved them. Somebody came in here today and moved stuff around. Somebody—but who—

Did I move them and then forget I did it? No. I'll admit I wasn't completely together at that point, but I wasn't so far gone that I could have been rearranging the kitchen without remembering having done it.

I took a deep breath. Then another. Then a third. Then I looked in the next cupboard.

It was all wrong too. They were all all wrong. And I knew, I knew in my heart that I hadn't done it and just forgotten about it. I knew.

I backed away from the cupboards like I would from an unchained, angry dog, very slowly, until I was in the living room. I think I almost fell backward over the couch. I can't quite remember—nothing made any sense to me just then. My mind started spitting out questions as fast as I could process them, which was much faster than I could actually answer them. Could Davis have done this? Why would he bother doing this? Is this some kind of message from someone? What if whoever did this is still here? How did they get in?

Then something else caught my eye, something so subtle it took me a few moments to articulate what my subconscious must have picked up right away.

The books. They're all upside down.

Every single book in my bookcase had been turned upside down, so the text on the spine ran up instead of down. They were all right where they were supposed to be—or at least, I thought they were, I didn't notice anything out of place. They were just . . . flipped.

"Mommy!" I heard Clara bellow from upstairs. "He's not here!"

Oh shit. Clara. What if—

"Mommy!"

"I'm coming, I'm coming," I called back, and I took the steps three at a time. Clara was waiting in the hallway, just in front of her open bedroom door, her balled fists planted on her hips.

"Mommy, I'm very upset with you," she said in her best adult voice. "You said that Daddy would be here. But he's not."

Okay. She's not scared. Let's not spook her needlessly, 'kay?

"I never said that, sweetheart," I said. "I said maybe."

"Well he isn't in there," Clara said. "I am very disappointed in him, Mommy."

I poked my head into the room. It was a mess, as usual. Toys and plastic crap everywhere. I remember thinking I'd need a snow shovel to clean that place up.

"Clara," I said. "What is that in your closet?"

"I don't know," she said. "Is it Daddy?"

I stepped closer. Alton's Baltimore Orioles coffee mug was on the closet's top shelf, far too high for Clara to reach.

I remember that my first reaction was very clinical, very detached. So that's why Clara thought Alton had been in her closet. She saw the mug up there and her mind built a whole narrative around it. Daddy's mug was in the closet. Therefore, Daddy had been in the closet too.

But let's step back a second here. There's a larger issue:

What the hell is THAT doing in here?

What the HELL is that DOING in THERE?

Somebody put it there. Somebody came into this house and rearranged the kitchen and flipped all the books and put that mug in this closet.

Maybe it was someone's idea of a joke. Maybe it was a threat. But what the fuck did it all mean?

I remember feeling relieved, because this meant that I wasn't going crazy. Somebody really was sneaking in and moving things around while we were out. I wasn't imagining it.

But that didn't last. Because someone was trying to send me a message—I assumed it was a threat, but I didn't know—through an act that felt like it had been designed not just to intimidate me, but to actually scare the hell out of me. And it was working.

"Clara," I said, with what I thought was a remarkably calm voice, considering the circumstances. "Um, when you saw Daddy in your closet, was he drinking coffee?"

"No," she said after thinking a moment. "He was just standing there."

"Okay, honey." Why the hell didn't I change those fucking locks? First thing in the morning, I told myself. Can I get a locksmith out here tonight? Because I won't sleep tonight if not. "That's what I thought. Thank you."

Maybe you should call the police. Maybe you should call Davis. Maybe you should just not be here tonight.

I wanted to call Davis, but Clara was right there. I didn't want her listening to me on the phone, but I also didn't want to leave her alone to go make the call. I wasn't about to let her out of my sight, not after this. I also didn't want to admit to him I'd forgotten to call a locksmith like he told me to. I mean, I had an alarm system. I guess I thought that should be enough. Obviously I was wrong about that.

"Ghosts don't drink coffee," Clara said, her face brightening.

The police, though. Yes. I was going to call the police. But first I was going to get my daughter the hell out of that house.

"Hey, I have a great idea," I said. "Why don't we go spend the night in a hotel? We can pretend we're on vacation. Would you like that? Wouldn't that be fun?"

"Can I jump on the bed?" she practically shouted.

"Of course you can," I said. "As long as you want. Until you get so tired from jumping, your legs fall off."

"Yayayay!" Clara cheered. "Hotel hotel hotel hotel hotel!"

160

She jumped up onto her own bed, like she was practicing for when we got to the hotel.

"Don't forget Brownie," I reminded her. She's got clean clothes in the dryer, I remember thinking. I'll grab her toothbrush and some books and—

The doorbell rang. I stifled a scream.

"Someone's here!" Clara shouted. She ran out of the room toward the stairs.

"Clara, don't you open that door!" I sprinted after her and managed to catch her by the wrist just at the bottom of the stairs. She turned around to look at me, and I might have grabbed her a bit harder than I had meant to. There was a look of utter incomprehension on her face.

"Don't open the door for people you don't know." I was almost growling at her, spacing and over-enunciating each word for effect. "Ever. We have talked about strangers before. Haven't we?"

"Yes." Clara looked like she was about to cry.

"Yes. That's right. So you know better." I think I actually poked her in the chest with each syllable. I hope I'm remembering that part wrong.

The doorbell rang again. I took a breath and felt calmed, somehow. I thought, If someone was trying to kill you, they probably wouldn't ring the bell. Especially if they had a key.

That's . . . well, that's a good point.

I snapped open the dead bolt and yanked open the door. Two men in ninety-dollar suits were standing on my porch.

"Mrs. Carver?" the shorter one asked.

"That's right," I said. "Who are you?"

"I'm Detective Crandall, this is Detective Mills," he said, jerking a thumb at the other guy. "Do you have time to speak with us?"

"What about?"

"Probably nothing," Mills said. "We just need to ask you a few questions about your husband."

THIRTY-TWO
Nicole

At first the detectives were sympathetic. Or at least they acted like they wanted me to think they were. They sat on my couch and listened politely while I told them—as calmly and clearly as I could manage—about the coffee mug, the books, and the kitchen cabinets. I did leave out the thing with Davis's shoes; I'd taken the precaution of sending Clara to the other room to play while I talked to them, but she might still have been able to hear us. She liked listening to grown-up conversations.

They asked plenty of questions.

"All the books were upside down when you came home?"

"When did this happen?"

"Can you think of anyone who could have gotten into the house?"

"And you're sure the mug wasn't there the whole time?" The whole time, I thought. What whole time? What does that even mean?

Also, they weren't taking any notes, which struck me as odd. I was telling them about a crime. Shouldn't they have been taking notes?

"I can't help but notice that you aren't writing any of this down," I pointed out.

The detectives looked at each other. "Well—"

"I know it sounds strange," I said. "But listen. My daughter is terrified. She and I would both feel a lot better if we thought the police were taking our concerns seriously."

"We understand that," one of them—Crandall, I think, not that it matters—said. "And we'll be happy to send a patrol officer over here to take a statement once we're done. But that's not what we wanted to talk to you about."

"We need to talk about your husband, Mrs. Carver," Mills said.

"Yeah, you mentioned that," I said. "Okay. What do you want to talk about? Because it's kind of a sore subject right now. As you can probably imagine."

"I can understand that."

"Because, you know, he's dead. He's dead, and the insurance company—the one he chose—won't pay my claim. I don't have a whole lot more to say about it right at the moment."

"Two-million-dollar policy," Mills said. "Isn't that right?"

"Yes. Two million dollars. Not that it's doing me any good, since my claim was denied." I could feel a headache coming on. "Which I just told you. You can check with Piedmont Insurance."

"If you don't mind me asking, how are you planning on paying your mortgage?" Mills asked. "Since you don't have that insurance money, I mean. Because this place"—and he gestured toward the rest of the living room—"does not look cheap."

What the hell is going on here? Then it dawned on me.

"You guys think I did something," I said. "You guys think this is all a big scheme. Insurance fraud or something."

"Nobody said that," Mills said. "Yet."

"Oh my stars," I said. "So ridiculous. Look. Even if there was anything to be in on, and even assuming I was in on it, how could I have committed insurance fraud? I never got any money. There was no check. So nobody was defrauded."

Mills snorted. "It doesn't work that way."

"It's all in the attempt," Crandall said. "That's where the crime is. The possibility that you might be incompetent at it wouldn't make you innocent."

"Daughter in private school," Mills said. "I know how that is. I have three of my own, all of them at Academy of Holy Names. Those bills add up fast."

"Must be tough, on a cop's salary," I said back. His eyes narrowed. Fuck you, I thought.

"How are you planning to manage it?" Crandall asked.

I had no idea how I was going to manage it. I was in a very tight spot just then, with plenty of expenses and a four-year-old daughter to support on my own and not nearly enough money to do it all. But I'd be damned if I was going to tell them that.

"Get a subpoena," I said, "and I will be happy to tell you all about it. Until then, mind your own goddamn business."

Being married to a lawyer does have its advantages sometimes.

The room was silent. We stared at each other for what felt like five minutes.

"Do you know how much money your husband stole?" Crandall asked me.

"I don't concede that he stole anything. I don't know the first thing about any of it."

"Nearly three million dollars," Mills said. "Enough for you to pay off the mortgage and set yourself up for life. More than enough."

"You wouldn't happen to know where we could find that money, would you, Mrs. Carver?" Crandall asked. And he smiled, this oily, insincere smile. His face looked like it was made of putty. It made me shudder just to look at him.

"Three million dollars isn't as much money as you seem to think it is," I said. "But it doesn't matter, because I don't know anything about it anyway."

"How can we be sure of that?"

"Well, I guess you could wait until the bank takes the house for nonpayment," I said. "Maybe when my daughter and I are living at a shelter, maybe then you'd be convinced."

"Mrs. Carver." Crandall leaned in. "Do you think it's possible that your husband isn't dead, that maybe he survived his boating accident?"

164

"They never did find his body, you know," Mills added.

"You don't say," I said.

"Is it possible that maybe he survived and is trying to get his hands on all that money he stole?"

"Oh, I doubt that," I said with a laugh. "His survival instinct has never been all that sharp."

"Has he been in contact with you, Mrs. Carver?"

"Of course not. He's dead. And I have to say, this is beginning to upset me."

"We apologize for that, but we have to ask," Crandall said. "So you're saying your husband hasn't been in contact with you since he disappeared, is that correct?"

"Yes."

"Do you think your husband could have planned this? You know, faked his own death as part of an insurance fraud scheme?"

That was, without a doubt, the most ridiculous idea I had ever heard. And I told them so.

"If Alton ever tried to fake his own death, he'd probably end up accidentally killing himself in the process," I said. "But even if he did, and even if he has all this money, what makes you think he'd share any of it with me?"

"Because you're his wife," Crandall said. "Because you have his daughter. He must love his daughter, at least."

"Anyone who gave a shit about any of that," I said, "wouldn't leave his family and fake his own death for a lousy three million dollars."

"He might," Crandall said, "if he knew his only alternative was prison time."

"He doesn't strike me as the kind of guy who could handle a long stretch in prison," Mills added.

I shrugged. "Maybe you're right. I don't know. But then the Alton I know wouldn't fake his own death and abandon his family in the first place, so I'm probably in no position to judge."

The two cops looked at each other, then back at me. Their eyes moved almost in unison, like they were two halves of the same creature.

"That's a pretty strange thing for a wife to say," Mills said.

"Or maybe it's not. Is it my imagination," Crandall said, "or are you being evasive?"

"I think she's hiding something," Mills said. "You got something to hide? You'll feel a lot better getting it off your chest. I promise."

"We think your husband is still alive," Crandall said. "He's been spotted. Walking around town. Showing up in bars. We think he's around, and we think he's hanging around for a reason. What we don't know is how much you know about it. But we will find out."

"I don't know anything about it. All I know is, either he's alive and he has this money, or he's dead and he doesn't. Either way, I haven't seen a dime of it and I don't expect to. And if he is still alive and I ever see him again, I will kill him myself for putting my daughter and me through this hell. He should hope you find him before I do." I stood up and folded my arms across my chest. The conversation was over. "Now please, feel free to get the hell out of my house."

The detectives stood up. "We'll get someone over here to take a look around for you," Crandall said, and then they were gone.

The hotel we stayed in that night was a Holiday Inn Express or something like that. Bland. Anonymous. But comfortable enough, I suppose. Clara was thrilled with the adventure of it all. She bounced right up onto the bed and started jumping on it before I even had the door closed.

"Be careful," I said. "If you fall, you'll hurt yourself."

"I will, Mommy," she said. Then I went into the bathroom, turned on the faucet, knelt by the toilet, and threw up. "I don't know these channels, Mommy," Clara said when I came out. She was sitting on the edge of the bed, grasping the remote with both hands. She seemed not to have heard me in there. "Where is Nick Jr.?"

"I don't know, baby. They might not have it."

"But I want it," Clara whined.

"Just . . . just watch something else, okay?" The full weight of the day's events pressed down on the backs of my eye sockets. I rubbed my eyes. It didn't help. "There are plenty of channels. I'm sure at least one of them has cartoons on."

"I guess."

"Watch whatever you want. Just no cop shows, okay?"

"Okay, Mommy."

THIRTY-THREE

Alton

My key didn't work the next time I went to the house. I tried it in the back door first, but I couldn't get it more than three-quarters of the way into the slot. So I went around to the French doors and tried it there. Same result.

Okay then.

And for just a moment, this intense burst of anger flashed through my mind, anger that Nicole would take such chances with her child's—my child's—safety. True, Clara was never actually in danger, but Nicole couldn't have known that.

Unless she did know.

But how would she have figured it out? And if she had, why hadn't she done anything about it? Not speaking up was not in character for her.

Maybe she did do something. You can't possibly know for sure. You don't even live here anymore. How could you know what goes on?

No way. The passive-aggressive approach just wasn't her style. She'd have been more likely to confront me directly, wait for me to come home again and then ambush me. Maybe she was waiting for me inside that very minute. Holding one of the kitchen knives, her fingers squeezing and relaxing on the handle, standing ready to drive that blade into my neck as far as it would go, the moment I stepped inside the house.

I pulled my Leatherman tool from my pocket. It took about thirty seconds of poking, jimmying, and swearing, but then the lock popped and the doors swung open. I closed them behind me, hustled over to the alarm panel, and punched in my code.

Beeeeeeeeeeeeeeeeeeeeeeeep. Invalid code. Did she cancel my code too? What's her code again? I struggled to remember.

I thought maybe it was her sister's birthday, which in turn took me another couple seconds to remember. I stabbed my index finger into the keypad and held my breath.

Beeeep beeeep beeeep. Code accepted. Canceling your dead husband's alarm code. I couldn't remember which of the seven stages of grief that was.

Once I was inside, the first thing I noticed was that someone had fixed all the books. I checked the kitchen cabinets. All the cups, bowls, plates, pans, measuring spoons, and god knows what else were back in their original places.

I guess she'd noticed.

The clock on the microwave read a quarter to three. I had plenty of time, but I didn't want another surprise, so I went upstairs to Clara's closet and sat down inside it, cross-legged and silent.

They arrived right on time, a little after four. I could hear their voices but not their words as they talked downstairs, probably about what to eat for dinner or what show Clara wanted to watch. I remember wishing she'd come upstairs to play with her Legos or Matchbox cars or plastic dinosaurs or whatever else she had up there. I could wait, though. It wasn't long before I heard the deep clangs of pots and pans bonking together. Dinner would be ready soon.

It also wasn't long before my legs fell asleep. I was sort of expecting that to happen. I've never been able to sit like that for more than a few minutes at a time. All I had to do was stretch them out and get the blood flowing again, and I'd be fine. I just had to be careful not to make any noise.

I tried to stand upright inside that cramped closet, and my legs immediately buckled. They weren't ready to support my weight—they were asleep, after all—and now I was falling. I reached out for support, anything I could get a finger to, but all I found was the flimsy wire shelving behind me. I grabbed hold and felt it start to pull out of the wall, so I let go of it and just let myself clatter into a pile of—well, I didn't know what it was, exactly. I just know it was loud.

Christ, I hope they didn't hear that.

Maybe the closed closet door muffled the sound of the crash. Or maybe not. I drew my knees up to my chest and waited to be discovered.

After a while—I don't know how long—I heard Clara's singsong voice and the thump of her feet on the stairs. I held my breath as she hopped into the room and bounced herself off the bed, shouting, "Boinnnnnng!" as she shot upward from the mattress.

"Clara," I stage-whispered. "In here. The closet."

I heard the sound of a small child scrambling across the floor. Then she flung the door open and there she was again, mouth agape, eyes wide. "Daddy!" she cried out.

"Shhhhhhhhh!" I said. "We have to be quiet, remember? Mommy is afraid of ghosts. Whisper. Like I'm doing."

"Okay, Daddy," she whispered. "You came back."

"I did." I smiled. God, I love her. "I said I would come back, didn't I?"

"Yes. Daddy, how do you breathe under the water?"

"I . . . don't know, honey, I just do it. Why?"

"Miss Mari said that fish can live underwater because they can breathe in water, but people can't breathe in the water. Only fish."

"Well, Miss Mari is wrong," I said. "What about whales and dolphins?"

"Those are fish."

"No, not really. They have to breathe air too. So they come up to the surface and take a really deep breath, and then they hold it so they can swim for a while. Then they come back up and get more air later."

"Oh," she said. I could tell she didn't really understand. Which was fine. That just meant I didn't have to work as hard at keeping my story straight.

"It works the same way for ghosts like me," I continued. "I can stay under the water a long time because I just take a deep breath and hold it. Ghosts can hold their breath a lot longer than people can, you know."

"Do it now," she said. "I wanna see."

"Oh, I don't know," I said. "Maybe I don't want to."

"Pleeeeeeease?" she asked.

"Well, all right. Since you said 'please.'" I took a deep breath and puffed out my cheeks, pretending to hold my breath but still breathing through my nose, but so slowly that she wouldn't notice the rise and fall of my chest. I bugged my eyes out and crossed them. She laughed. I kept that up for two full minutes before pretending I just couldn't hold it in anymore.

"See? That was a long time," I said.

"No it wasn't," Clara said, laughing.

"Sure it was. It was like an hour."

"No."

"Well it was pretty long, anyway."

"Daddy," she said, turning suddenly serious. "Did you move all the dishes around and turn the books upside down?"

Oh. Shit. I hadn't expected to get called out by my four-year-old, especially this quickly.

"I did, honey." I kissed her forehead. "I hope it didn't scare you."

"Mommy was scared," she said. "And then I got scared. But I knew it was you."

"You did? Did you tell Mommy?"

"No," she said, "because you said she was afraid of ghosts, even you when you're a ghost. But she was scared."

That's my girl. "She was, huh? Just a little scared, or a really lot scared?"

"A really lot scared," she said. "The police came and talked to Mommy. Then they went away. The policeman had a gun."

Well, at least she still had sense enough to do that much.

"I'm sorry I scared Mommy," I said. "I didn't mean to. I was just playing a game. With you."

"What kind of game?"

"It was the kind where I was saying hello to you by moving things around because I knew you'd guess that I did it," I said, which I know is complete gibberish, just the first thing I could think of to say. But it seemed to make perfect sense to Clara, who nodded and pursed her lips. For half a moment she looked just like her mother. "So you were scared, huh?"

"A little," she admitted. Then her face brightened. "Mommy says we might have to get a new house. Will you come too?"

Wait, what?

"A new house? Because I moved the books around?"

"I heard her say it on the phone."

"Oh, wow. A new house sounds like such fun. Do you know who Mommy was talking to?"

"No," she said. "Maybe Miss Lauren. Mommy talks to her a lot."

Moving?

No. She just—couldn't. Keeping her and Clara in the house, in this house, was part of the reason I'd arranged things the way I did, why I'd gone to all this trouble in the first place. That was Clara's home, the only one she'd ever known. She had just lost her father. She needed stability. She needed . . . she needed her home, goddamn it. Enabling them to stay in the house was the whole fucking point of it. And now, less than two months after I was gone, Nicole was talking about throwing it all away.

But she'd always loved that house. All she had to do was wait for the insurance check and she'd be fine. What was the rush? Too many memories? Maybe with me gone, it was just too painful for her to live there anymore, when every room triggered a flood of—

172

Or maybe she's getting a new place with him.

My heart tightened. I tried to settle my suddenly shaking muscles.

That's it, isn't it? She was going to start over. Start over with a backward–ball cap–wearing dude-bro car salesman. Erase every last trace of me from her life, from Clara's life. She's only four, I remember thinking. She won't remember me in a few years. I'll be just some vague shadow in her past that she will sort of understand was her father, but she won't remember me at all.

"Well I'm sure it will be a great house, baby," I said. I tried to keep my voice from cracking. I'm pretty certain I failed. "Honey, do you know if Mommy has any new friends? Does she have friends over to the house?"

"Miss Lauren comes over sometimes," Clara said. "She plays with me. She likes my dinosaurs. She likes allosaurus, but I like triceratops best. Do you want to play dinosaurs with me?"

"Of course I do, baby," I said, and we played together quietly for almost an hour, in the closet, where it was dark and she couldn't see my tears.

THIRTY-FOUR

Alton

I've always been the kind of person who throws himself into new interests. Headlong. Without restraint. When I took up cycling, I spent seven thousand dollars on a new Cannondale, and probably another two thousand on spandex and shoes and helmets and other assorted nonsense before I even rode a single mile. When I decided to learn to play guitar, I bought a beautiful sunburst Fender Stratocaster—an American-made one, the frets don't fit right on the Mexi-Strats—and paired it with a 1962 Fender Bluesman amplifier, just so I could get exactly the right sound. And then when I decided it would be fun to restore a vintage roadster, I scoured the Internet for months until I found the perfect classic 1970 Jaguar E-Type—in British racing green, of course—which I bought on eBay from some old tight-ass in Pennsylvania.

But the Cannondale didn't end up covering many miles beyond that first one. I put the Strat down once I started getting calluses on my fingertips, and I just never picked it back up again. And the Jag—well, I passed that on to some college kid who I hoped had a better feel for mechanical projects and a longer attention span than I do.

I get bored quickly. That has always been my problem. The only time in my entire life that it wasn't was law school. But even so, I had still expected to get a lot more mileage out of the poltergeist idea. It was the perfect way for me to fuck with Nicole's mind a little, which perhaps I shouldn't have enjoyed as much as I did, but which—let's be honest here—she clearly deserved. She deserved worse than that, a lot worse, but lucky for her I'm not really an eye-for-an-eye kind of person.

How I'm Spending My Afterlife

After just two turns as a poltergeist, the whole enterprise had lost its appeal. I didn't have any more ideas, or at least none that would be easy to deploy, easy to execute, and pack a psychological wallop at the same time. Simplicity was important. I couldn't risk spending the entire day in the house, building some towering Rube Goldberg–type prank. Even if it scared Nicole enough to get her Baker Acted, the potential return just wasn't worth the risk.

I'd spent most of the afternoon drinking cheap vodka in my hotel room and wondering what the hell I was doing with my afterlife. The booze had helped bring me to a place where I could really focus on this, really consider my situation, and see myself and my position relative to the entire fucking mess I'd helped bring about. I wouldn't be able to stop Nicole from selling the house and moving on with her life. I wouldn't be able to keep Davis Spaulding out of my daughter's life, if her mother wanted him to be in it. I understood—finally—that through my own decisions and my own actions, no matter how selfless they were, I had forfeited my right to be involved. Actually, I think I'd probably understood this already. I just hadn't given myself permission to think about it, not at a conscious level anyway.

The hard truth was that giving them up forever was part of the bargain I'd struck. You don't own a thing unless it costs you something. I heard that in a movie once, I think. Seems to fit here.

I decided right then that I would say good-bye—probably good-bye forever—to Clara the next day. Then I would leave town, leave Florida, just get myself gone and never come back. I hadn't decided if I would approach Nicole about relocating to Costa Rica in a few years or not, but at least I knew I had plenty of time to think it over and get the answer right. I would still send her the safe deposit box keys. Clara was still my daughter, and no matter what her mother deserved, Clara would be taken care of. I would see to it.

When my red plastic cup was empty for the fifth or sixth time that afternoon, I looked across the room at the empty jug of Scottish Bob's on the table. Felt like a good time for a refill. There were two more empties on the floor. Jesus. I can't believe I've been here so long. I rolled off the bed, rounded up all the empty jugs, carried them out the door with me, and tossed them into the rusted-out Dumpster in the parking lot. I listened to them rattling around in there for a few seconds, and then I headed across the street to Vegas Liquors. That was really the whole reason I'd gotten up from the bed in the first place.

The clerks in Vegas Liquors never gave any sign that they recognized me as a repeat customer. And I was probably the only person who ever bought this terrible vodka—nobody can keep drinking that stuff and live very long—which you might expect would be a reason for someone to remember me. I didn't know if they were discreet, bored, or just stupid, but it made me feel a lot more comfortable. Even after all these weeks—and even though I wasn't always as careful about it as I should have been, I admit—I was just as paranoid as ever about being recognized. I slid my eleven singles and a couple of quarters across the counter and walked toward the door, my vodka in a plain black plastic bag. The clerk never even looked up from his smartphone, not even to count my money. Good thing I didn't need any change, I guess.

I felt the season's first telltale signs of higher humidity the moment I stepped outside. Must be May already. It occurred to me that, now that winter was good and over with, I may have already seen my last sixty-degree day. Does Central America ever really cool off? I didn't know. Possibly in the mountains, but I wasn't going to the mountains. I was headed for the coast, not far from Puerto Limón. But coastlines mean low elevations, so unless there was a hell of a breeze coming off the gulf, Puerto Limón would probably be broiling and muggy most of the time.

Small price to pay, really.

My mind was light-years away and on a million other scattered things as I crossed the highway. But when I got to the parking lot, I stopped cold.

There was a police car parked in front of the office at the Royal Rest.

That car, and the cop who drove it there, were there for me. I knew this. I'd been living in that hopeless purgatory for something like six weeks now, and in all that time I hadn't seen a single cop out there until that very minute. The place was a dump, but it was a quiet dump that the rest of the world was happy to pretend didn't exist. And so far that had served me well.

My instincts told me to run. Bolt back across the highway to the liquor store. Just get the hell out of there and not give them any reason whatsoever to go into my room, and whatever you do don't look in that fucking closet. But I didn't. I might have done it if I'd had just another fraction of a second. But then the office door swung open and the thick-waisted cop moseyed on out into the parking lot. If I ran, or if I went back to the liquor store already carrying a bottle of vodka, he was sure to notice me.

So I ducked behind the Dumpster. And I leaned out just far enough to watch him.

The cop started at room 11 and went from door to door, knocking on each one in turn. Nobody answered, which didn't seem to surprise him. It didn't surprise me either. The Royal Rest was not a friendly place, even to the people who actually did belong there. The old woman in room 15 sat outside in her chair, same as every other day. I watched the cop say something to her; they were too far away for me to hear anything. The woman shook her head and looked past him, her arms folded. You are wasting my time, asshole—even I could read that body language. The cop shrugged and handed her a sheet of paper, and I suddenly had a deep need to see what was on it. Was it about me? A composite sketch? Surveillance photo? Did they even know who they were looking for? Were they even looking for anyone in particular?

The cop tried rooms 16 and 17 next. Same result. But when he got to room 18, he didn't knock right away. Instead he cupped his hands to the window and tried to look into the room first. Fuck, he knows. This place is blown.

Then he knocked. It sounded louder, more forceful than the one he used for the other rooms. He also seemed to be waiting longer for a response this time, but that might have been my imagination. Then just as I was almost—almost—convinced that I was in fact imagining these things, the cop knocked a second time. He hadn't done that with any of the other rooms. He obviously had a special interest in room 18. And I sure as hell wouldn't be sticking around to find out what it was.

Whatever it was, it didn't merit a third knock, and the cop moved on to rooms 19 and 20, and then back across the parking lot. When he got to my car he stopped, as if he knew exactly whose car it was. Well, why wouldn't he—it is parked right in front of your room, genius. He leaned forward and peered through the passenger window. There's nothing of interest to you in there, officer. Plain sight or otherwise. Sorry. Then he circled the car, made a few cursory notations in his pad, and ambled back over to his cruiser.

Maybe I was making too much of this. Maybe he was just angling for some overtime.

I watched the cop drive off and then looked toward the motel. From across the parking lot, the old woman from room 15 was staring right at me.

Three minutes. I figured that's all it would take to load up the car, wipe down the room, and disappear forever. I had never had to pack up and run before, but I was traveling light and highly motivated. Three minutes seemed eminently reasonable.

I started with the clothes. I dug all my clothes out of the closet and stuffed them into a large trash bag, clean mixing with dirty, which is something I have always hated. Clean clothes become dirty themselves simply by touching dirty clothes. Ordinarily I wouldn't have allowed that to happen, but it couldn't be helped. I made a mental note to rewash everything the first chance I got, and I shoved the bag into the trunk of the car.

Next, the garbage. There wasn't a lot—other than the vodka jugs, I didn't really let it pile up—but what there was, I sure as hell wasn't going to leave behind. You'd be amazed what someone can learn about you from what you throw away. I emptied the two trash cans into the bag I'd brought my vodka in just a few minutes earlier, tied the handles together, and tossed it on top of the bag of clothes. I suddenly wished I hadn't thrown those empty vodka bottles into the dumpster earlier. The cops could easily search in there without a warrant. The real question was whether or not they'd bother. Or whether it would even occur to them at all.

I snatched a clean washcloth from the bathroom and wiped down every single surface I might have touched. Yes, I knew this was probably overkill. I doubted the room had ever been cleaned thoroughly enough to remove fingerprints from a week, a month, a year before I checked in. But I'd been there about six weeks by then. I wasn't taking any chances. I started with the bathroom. The toilet tank, the countertop, the mirror, under the sink, the towel bars—if I could wipe it with the washcloth, that's exactly what I did, whether I specifically remembered touching it or not.

It took me a full five minutes to finish the entire room. When I was done, I grabbed the satchel and cracked the front door, using the washcloth as a barrier between my fingertips and the doorknob. The weight of the bag felt good in my hand, heavy and solid enough to see me through all this. I scanned the parking lot. No sign of cops anywhere. I left the door unlocked and drove off. I had no idea where I was go-ing, and I didn't care much, as long as it wasn't the Royal Rest.

A few minutes later I parked in a strip mall parking lot next to a Checkers, a sack of fast food on the front seat beside me. I slurped on a root beer and watched a young family—blond mom, golf-shirt-wearing dad, two small kids who both kind of looked like boys but you never can tell with kids that young—sitting at one of the red-painted metal-grille picnic tables in front of the walk-up window. I couldn't imagine why anyone would want to sit there. The tables abutted both drive-through lanes, where the parade of cars farted toxic metals and chlorofluorocarbons and carbon monoxide into the air right next to them. All that invisible poison fell on their faces and fingers and burgers. Kids probably thought it was cool. Dad seemed to be tak-ing it in stride, but Mom snapped at the kids and only had two or three bites of her burger. Whether she was unhappy about the seating arrangements or something else entire-ly, it was impossible to say. Family fights are almost never about what they appear to be about.

I had no idea where I was going to sleep that night. I could have just picked another hotel, but if the cops had managed to track me to the Royal Rest, they could track me to another random shithole just as easily. With my luck, whichever dump I picked would have a copy of that flyer with my face drawn on it, tucked right under the front desk telephone. I'd have to figure something else out. I poked a couple more fries into my mouth. This was going to take some thinking.

Just beyond the restaurant, maybe thirty yards away, a police cruiser crept through the parking lot.

I sat and watched it pass, moving only to chew my food. It was a city cop this time, not a sheriff's deputy. The cruis-er kept going, to the other end of the strip-mall parking lot,

180

down toward the Big Lots. It seemed to take forever. If they were looking for me, they weren't acting like it.

Or maybe that's what they want you to think. Maybe they spotted you looking at them and are trying to play it off.

Christ, Alton, get a grip. Paranoia will fucking kill you if you let it.

Which is true, of course, but I didn't think of it as paranoia. It was more like . . . hyperawareness. It was keeping my edge sharp. Staying one step ahead. I picked up my bacon double cheeseburger and took a generous bite. Ketchup oozed out around the side of my mouth, smearing itself between the bun and my cheek. I chewed slowly as I watched the cruiser roll out of the parking lot and head north, swept along by a current of heavy traffic.

They hadn't approached me, didn't even appear to be watching me at all. But that meant nothing. A cop pounding on your motel room door has a way of focusing the mind. And even though the guy poking around the Royal Rest didn't look like much of a go-getter, I knew not to underestimate him. Bored cops are sometimes the most dangerous. For example, my parents used to live in this one-stoplight town in upstate South Carolina, just a blink of a place called Foster's Creek. The police there had nothing much to do with their time, but they'd built themselves a reputation for picking up fugitives wanted in other places. Turns out, the secret to their success was that they would drive into a random parking lot and run license plate after license plate through their computer. "Hey, here's a guy wanted for armed robbery," they'd say when they got a hit, and then just wait for him to come out of the Circle K. "How'd you guys find me?" the guy would probably ask once the cuffs were on. "You musta been looking for me for months." And the cops probably just laughed.

My point is this: Boredom and a little bit of luck. That's all it would take for them to find me. I couldn't let myself forget that.

It was at that moment I remembered Clara's Matchbox car. The one I'd taken from the house a few weeks back. The same one I had just forgotten to take with me from the Royal Rest.

Shit. That was sloppy as hell.

I didn't even remember seeing it when I left. In fact, I couldn't remember the last time I had seen it. Was it even still there? Where would I have put it?

Maybe the maid took it. Maybe I accidentally swept it into the trash bag when I was bugging out. In any event, I couldn't let myself worry about it. I certainly wasn't going to go back there and look for it.

I finished my dinner, then drove out of the parking lot. I headed south, away from the cruiser, looking for a place to sleep that night.

THIRTY-FIVE

Alton

That morning I dreamed of the jungle, of the mountains I had not yet seen, in a country I had never been to but in which I would likely spend the rest of my life. I dreamed of mosquitoes and snakes and alluring, brightly colored flowers that secreted the deadliest of poisons. I dreamed of tree frogs and piranhas and quicksand. I dreamed of a house with a wraparound porch, just steps from the beach, ocean breezes flushing the heat and humidity from it during the interminable sweltering afternoons. It was mine—I knew this, the knowledge came with the dream—my new home as an expat, and Clara was there and Nicole was there and from the porch we all watched the boats meandering around the harbor. But then Nicole was someone else, someone I didn't recognize, someone who smiled at me even though I had no idea who she was, and Clara was gone but nobody else seemed to notice. Then I turned my head for just a moment and I was on a boat somehow, not one of the sleek polished sailboats but a freighter or something, crowded with men who all seemed to know each other and seemed not to be surprised to see me, a complete stranger, among them now. Toilets overflowed and showers reeked of urine. I had no idea how I had gotten there, and the freighter felt too big to be real, like a city almost, too big to float. It was my turn to steer the boat, but I couldn't find the bridge, didn't know where it was, but kept climbing anyway, trying to get to the top of the ship, because the bridge must have been there, but it never was, just deck after deck of tiny rooms—

—and then suddenly I was out, but I wasn't on the ship anymore, I was on a ribbon of highway that stretched upward, almost to the sky, steeper than a roller coaster and miles long, and instinctively I knew it was too steep, too high, and I felt like I would flip backward any second and tumble all the way down, so I leaned forward, but that didn't help, and it got steeper near the top, and then I looked again and saw more highway, a bridge that went on as far as the horizon, and I was falling backward again and—

My eyelids snapped open, and I sat bolt upright in the bed. I was already forgetting the dream—even then, just moments after waking, I could only try to grasp snippets, loose frames of film decontextualized from whatever movie they came from, the random imagery almost completely meaningless to me. I did not feel refreshed after my nap. Instead I was uneasy, and trying to hold on to those brief flashes of my dream only reinforced the feeling. It had been a bad dream; I knew that, even if I could not actually remember much of it. At that point I was only too willing to let it go.

I checked my watch: two forty-three in the afternoon. I hadn't meant to fall asleep at all, yet I'd been out for over two hours.

Idiot. What if they came home early again? What then?

It doesn't matter. They didn't. They're not here.

You should never have come back. This place has made you dull.

Another hour and a half to kill. Waiting didn't annoy me as much as it used to. I guess I had gotten accustomed to it over the last few weeks. Waiting to go outside, for my wake, for the house to be empty, for Davis to show me where he lived, for the cop to drive off, for Clara to be home so I could say good-bye. I was on other people's time, all the time.

The real problem with being dead is that you lose the power to set your own schedule.

I took a quick visual inventory of everything in the bedroom, bathroom, and kitchen to make sure every last detail was exactly how I had found it. Then I headed upstairs, to the study. Maybe I would read while I waited.

At three fifty-five I got up from the chair in my study and sat down on the floor of Clara's closet, drawing my knees up to my chest. I heard the back door pop open about fifteen minutes later, followed by the beep-beep-beep of the alarm control panel. Then a series of rapid-fire thumps, which could only be Clara clambering up the steps at top speed. Top speed's the only speed she has, I used to say to Nicole whenever we would take her to play at the park, back in the good old days. I smiled to myself just then, savoring the memory, but in the moment I felt more sadness than anything else.

And then she was in the room, just beyond the door. I listened for a moment to make sure Nicole was still downstairs before stage-whispering my daughter's name.

"It's okay," I whispered. "It's Daddy."

"Daddy!" The door flew open and there she was. My heart swelled and I smiled again, unable to stop myself even if I had wanted to. This time, the smile was a happy one.

"Shhhhhhhhh," I reminded her, holding a finger over my lips. "Remember, Mommy can't know. She's afraid of ghosts."

"No she's not, Daddy."

"Oh, she's not? How do you know?"

"Because the other day I told her you were a ghost, and she wanted to see you too, so she came up to my room to look in the closet, but you weren't here, but she said you would be."

"Wait—you told her I was a ghost? Did you tell her I came to visit?"

"I don't know," she said. I recognized her tone immediately: guarded, like she wasn't sure exactly how much she should admit to. I sighed.

"Honey, it's okay that you told, but why? You remember I asked you not to, right?"

"I remember," she said. "I don't know why I told. I just wanted to."

185

"Well, what did she say when you told her?"

"She said you weren't real," Clara said. "But that's what Miss Mari said when I saw you at school, but she was wrong because you are real." She reached out to touch my arm, reassuring herself that she was indeed speaking to a real live ghost.

"That's right, honey. I am definitely real." I took her hand and kissed it. "But if Mommy didn't think I was real, why did she come up to look for me?"

"I don't know," she said. "Mommy said you would be here, so I came up to find you, but you weren't here."

This is the problem with relying on four-year-olds for reconnaissance work. Their field reports are usually too garbled to provide any useful intelligence. I tried to filter what Clara had just told me. What did Nicole actually think was going on? Had she somehow figured out that I really was still alive, or was she just humoring her four-year-old daughter?

But it didn't matter either way, really. She could believe what she wanted. In four days I'd be on the beach in Costa Rica, where the fish were jumping and the cotton was high. Nobody could touch me then.

I took a deep breath and released it slowly.

"Honey," I said. "I have something important to tell you."

"Okay, Daddy," Clara said.

"I came to see you today because I have to tell you something. This is the last time I can visit you," I said. "I have to go back to where I live, under the water, and I can't come back for a really long time."

"Maybe not ever?" Clara asked. Her face was serious. A preschooler's face should never look like that.

"Maybe not ever, baby. I wish it wasn't like that, but it is."

"Why?"

"Because . . . because the new king of the ghosts said we have to stay under the water where we belong from now on." I know, I know. I'm not good at that kind of thing. And I could tell from her face that she wasn't buying it.

"But why?" she persisted. "I don't want you to go back under the water. I want to play with you every day."

"I know, baby," I said. I tried to stifle the tears welling up. This was already so much harder than I had expected. "But I can play with you now. Do you want to play now? We could play cars this time."

"Okay, Daddy," she said, and she got up to get some toys for us to play with. But her spark was gone. She didn't sing or bounce across the room. She just picked up a few pieces of plastic and metal, brought them back to the closet, and dumped them at my feet.

"Cars and dinosaurs," she said.

"That sounds great, honey."

"But dinosaurs can't drive the cars," she admonished. "They don't know how to drive."

"Then what can they do?"

"They can step on the cars and smoosh them," she said. "And sometimes the cars can run over the dinosaurs."

"Okay," I said. "Sounds good." And it was. We played like that for a while, quiet, in the closet doorway. She liked making the dinosaurs stomp the cars deep into the carpet and always seemed to find an excuse not to let me run over any of the dinosaurs. This one's too big. That car is too fast. Or too slow. The dinosaur moved at the last second. Always something. But I could not have cared less.

"Clara," Nicole called up from downstairs. "I made mac and cheese for you! Come eat, please!"

"I don't want to, Mommy!" Clara yelled back.

"I don't care what you don't want." Nicole's voice had an edge to it. "Get down here. Now!"

"Clara, honey, you'd better go," I said. "But give me a hug first, okay?"

"Okay," she whined. I scooped her up and held her tightly.

You know, it would be so easy to just carry her away like this.

Stop right there.

She doesn't weigh much, and she probably wouldn't even scream.

"Daddy," she said, and I relaxed my hold on her.

"Yes, honey?"

"I have made a decision," she said.

"Oh? What's that?"

"I want to go live under the water with you. Can I? Please?"

"Oh, honey," I said. "I—I don't think—"

"But I want to live with you," she whined. "I want to be a ghost and live under the water and then I can come back and visit Mommy and my friends at school and then go live at your house."

Of course I knew I should shut that down right then and there. It was absolutely a nonstarter. It would make the trip so much more complicated, to say nothing of what it would do to Nicole, who, regardless of what else she deserved, certainly didn't deserve that. No, Clara, I knew I should say. You cannot come with me to live under the water, because it's no place for a little girl. It's cold and wet and there aren't any toys or parks there. Besides, Mommy needs you, and she would miss you so much, and it just isn't a good idea. I'm sorry, baby.

But you know, I didn't say that. I should have, but I didn't. What I said instead was, "Maybe."

THIRTY-SIX
Nicole

I continued to see Davis pretty regularly, even as I started to question the entire arrangement more and more. And I don't know, maybe it was because of that questioning, but I noticed after a while that I was relying on him less and less. Instead I turned to wine for support.

The relationship wasn't really paying off for me the way it used to. I probably should have just ended it. I mean, it's not like I didn't have enough to deal with as it was. But I think maybe that was the reason I didn't end things. I didn't want to have to explain everything to someone else. The idea of bringing anyone else up to speed on what had been going on in my life for the last several months . . . well, I just didn't have the energy for that, and I couldn't think of anyone whom I'd be comfortable telling all that stuff to anyway. And Davis, he was the incumbent. He was in place. So I guess I just decided to take the path of least resistance and stick with the status quo for a while longer.

That night, I met him at the door around nine thirty, a glass of red wine in my hand.

"The rugrat sleeping?" he asked when I answered the door.

"I wouldn't have let you in if she wasn't."

He pointed at my glass of wine. "That for me?"

I lifted it to my lips and took a long sip.

"Guess not then."

"You know where the bar is," I said.

"That I do," he said, and I followed him into the living room. That was when I first noticed the plastic shopping bag in his hand.

"Whatcha got there?" I asked. I waved my glass at the bag.

189

"In a minute," he said. "Let me fix a drink first."

"Take your time," I said and dropped myself back down on the couch. I had been watching some trashy show on the Murder Channel, this ridiculous hyperventilating true-crime thing about children's beauty pageants. It was an awful show, even by the Murder Channel's standards, but I couldn't look away. That world, that glamorous exploitative broken world—it fascinates me. I have no idea why.

Davis moved behind the couch and looked on over my shoulder. I could smell his drink—Southern Comfort and lime, disgusting stuff, the only reason I even kept it in the house was as a favor to him—and I could almost hear him slowly shaking his head.

"You know," he said, "if you're worried about not sleeping at night, I don't know, maybe you might want to consider not watching shows like this one before bed. Just, y'know, putting that out there."

"Mmmm-hmmmm," I said. "Suggestion noted."

"Seriously," he said. "This is crap. I can actually feel myself getting dumber just standing here watching it."

"Well I'm afraid I forgot to DVR the Jackass marathon, so I guess we're stuck with this." I heard the sharp clink of glass on glass as he put his drink down on the library table behind the couch, and then he sort of positioned himself between me and the television. I made him stand there for twenty seconds or so before I dragged my gaze up from the screen and looked at him.

"What is your problem tonight?" he said.

"I'm sorry," I said, even though I wasn't. "I'm a little drunk." That part was true.

"You wanna see what I brought you?" he asked.

"Yay, presents," I said, clasping my hands together. "What's in the bag, baby?"

"Now, that's more like it." He emptied the bag onto the coffee table. Eight or nine small boxes, each one maybe three inches square, clattered onto the glass tabletop. I sat up and leaned forward.

"Nanny cams," he said. "Each one with built-in recording capabilities. Got four sets."

"Uh," I said, "okay."

"We talked about this. You need these."

"But I already changed the locks," I told him. I honestly had no idea why I was resisting him. I knew he was right. I think it's just because I'm a stubborn drunk. "Alarm codes too."

"Yeah, well, just in case, I guess," he said. "I wanted you to get these things before. Like, weeks ago. We talked about it. And yeah, you got the locks changed, but what if whoever it is finds another way in? Now we can catch the fucker on video."

"Fine, okay, sure," I said. "But could you do it? I'm no good at that kinda thing, and I think I mighta mentioned this, but I'm a . . . just a little drunk tonight."

He sighed. "Yeah, you know what, I'll just do it. You just go ahead and keep doing what you're doing. Sounds like a plan to me."

"Thanks, babe," I said, and then I sort of looked past him to the screen again. He shook his head and picked up two boxes from the table.

Yes, I was a little drunk, but beyond that, I was in no mood to think about home security right then. I had finally just started to feel comfortable in the house again. I wasn't jumping at every random sound or every stray flicker of the lightbulbs anymore. Personally, I considered this to be a significant accomplishment, and the way I had accomplished it was by not thinking about any of it.

I know what you're going to say about that. You're going to say the same thing you always say, and I'll just acknowledge that I know you're right and that I'm working on it. Like I'm working on a lot of things. Okay?

So Davis stalked around the living room, hunting for places to mount his great fun new spy toys. He set one of them up on the plant shelf, opposite the French doors. It looked like a pretty obvious hiding place to me. I could see it peeking between the leaves of a couple of wandering Jews, but maybe that was just because I watched him put it there. He set another on top of Alton's record cabinet and pointed it toward the front door. Then he carried a couple more boxes into the kitchen, for the back door.

A couple minutes later I heard the third stair creak and groan—Davis heading upstairs to rig up a camera, I guessed. I wasn't comfortable with him just wandering around up there with Clara sleeping, but having a camera up there was probably a good idea. Besides, I had by then realized that I'd had more wine than I'd originally thought, and I was in no condition to stop him even if I wanted to.

The next thing I knew, Davis was on the couch with me. I must have dozed off. I looked around for my wineglass, hoping I hadn't knocked it over. There was a basketball game on TV now.

"You fell asleep, so I changed the channel," Davis said.

"That's fine," I said.

"You've got two cameras in here, one pointed at each door," he said. "I put one in the kitchen, under that thing you hang the bananas on. Whatever you call that. The banana hanger? I don't know. And then there's one in Clara's closet. That was the only workable place upstairs I could find."

"In her closet? You didn't wake her up, did you?"

"That kid sleeps hard. She didn't hear me. And she won't see the camera either. I pushed it way in the back to make sure. The only thing is that she should keep the closet door open from now on."

"Shouldn't be a problem," I said. "You might not have noticed this, but she isn't exactly a neat freak or anything."

"You don't say," he deadpanned. I leaned over and kissed him.

"Thank you," I said. "For taking care of that. Of us. Of me."

"It's cool," he said. "Want me to show you how they work?"

"Can we do that tomorrow? I'm way too tired to concentrate right now." Which was true, if "tired" means "drunk."

"Sure," he said. "No problem. I'm gonna get going then. You okay to lock up and get to bed on your own?"

"I got it." I said. "But thanks."

He really could be sweet sometimes. I don't think I ever really gave him enough credit for that. It's probably what I miss the most about him.

THIRTY-SEVEN
Alton

As cliché as it sounds to say this aloud, it really did come to me in a dream.

I woke up around two thirty in the morning in the reclined front seat of my car. My lower back ached; moving just made it feel worse. I had parked on the top floor of the garage attached to the university library and fallen asleep there a few hours earlier. And while I slept, my subconscious mind sorted a few things out for me.

Specifically, that Clara would be joining me for my trip to Costa Rica after all.

It made sense. A girl needs her father. She'd never be more than an irritant to a guy like Davis Spaulding, assuming that whole thing between him and Nicole even lasted long enough for any kind of family relationship dynamics to develop in the first place. I mean, that much was obvious. Anyone could see it. As for Nicole, while she was a decent enough person—we had some good years, I can't deny that—could I really trust her with my daughter when it took her literally weeks to get around to calling a locksmith? Weeks! And she knew someone was getting into the house. She had to know. And even if she didn't, it just made sense to change the locks when a house key goes missing. Even if you think it's under fifty feet of water or whatever it was, you still change the locks. Because you don't actually know, do you?

That sort of negligence . . . well, I found it troubling. It was a legitimate concern. My daughter deserved a real chance, the love of a real family, and she certainly wasn't going to get it in an unstable home environment like that one.

I'd never noticed Nicole's questionable judgment before I disappeared, before I'd had the chance to observe her—

indirectly, at least—when she had no idea she was being observed. There was, for example, the matter of all the empty wine bottles. They'd been accumulating so quickly lately that the recycle bins had no room for anything else. Had she drank that much before? I couldn't remember. I didn't think so, but then again, maybe she'd been sneaking it the whole time. Isn't that what hard-core alcoholics do?

And speaking of poor judgment. Two words: Davis Spaulding. I knew what he was all about the first second I saw him. Bros before hoes? Isn't that what guys like him said? It was like their mantra. At any rate, certainly not the caliber of person I wanted having any influence whatsoever over my daughter.

So pick her up tonight.

I could, couldn't I? I could just go get her that night. We'd be almost the whole way to Pensacola before anyone even noticed she was gone.

It was so simple. And it would solve everything.

The decision made, I slept, and this time I slept well. I didn't wake up until an hour after sunrise.

When I did wake up, I thought about going back to the house to grab a shower but decided against it. I just paid the day rate at the university gym and used theirs. That would fit my schedule better than driving home before setting out on my errands for the day. Had a lot to do before fleeing the country.

I stopped for breakfast at Dave's Classic Diner. Cheeseburger omelet, two sides of bacon, wheat toast, and four cups of coffee. Definitely more than I usually eat. But I didn't know if I'd have time for lunch, and I wanted to make sure I kept my blood sugar up throughout the day. The day you're preparing to make a run for the border with almost three million dollars in stolen cash stashed in the trunk of your car is not the day you want to have to push through a hypoglycemic crash. Maybe I should have skipped the bread,

I thought when my plate arrived, and then I scarfed it down anyway. I felt like I hadn't eaten in days. After, when I was in the car driving away, I could still smell the place on my clothes.

That time of the morning, I figured it would probably take me about half an hour or so to drive the six or seven miles up to Highpoint. I wondered for a moment what the traffic in Puerto Limón was like before I remembered that I didn't have to care—I would never be a commuter again. Old habits die hard, I guess. I smiled at the thought, sitting a dozen cars or so behind the red light, waiting.

I had already been going back and forth about reclaiming the cash in the safe deposit boxes for a few days by then. But now I figured there was no real reason to leave it anymore. If I left it behind for Nicole, it would almost certainly find its way into the pockets of that odious little car salesman, and I'd be damned if I was going to let that happen. I'd worked hard for that money. It was mine. Besides, he was probably going to enjoy some of the runoff from that sweet insurance payout that Nicole was almost certain to collect any day now.

That wasn't it, though. Or rather, that wasn't all of it.

Part of me—not the rational part, obviously, or the part with all the brains—still hoped that Nicole would make the trip down and stay with us in a couple years. It was possible. It could happen. Maybe. And if it did, I certainly wouldn't want to put her in a position where she would have to smuggle something like two or three million dollars in cash over the Mexican border. Twice, even, and then through Nicaragua. At least, I think that's how the geography goes. I can never keep those countries straight down there. At any rate, Nicole just wasn't equipped for that sort of thing. So I thought it would be better if I took on that risk myself.

I spent my morning driving all over suburbia, visiting Bank of America branches and emptying out safe deposit boxes. All but one.

I had decided to leave one safe deposit box untouched. There was over $650,000 in it. It wasn't three million, that was true. But it was certainly enough to notice.

I tried to grab a car nap that evening. Just a couple of hours' worth would have been more than enough. But even that was too much to hope for. The folded T-shirt draped across my eyes did a passable job of keeping the ambient light out. But I couldn't get control of my breathing, couldn't get it to slow down, couldn't get to the deep breathing patterns that always relaxed me. A couple of times I caught my right foot tapping out a beat against the side of the foot well. My mind raced and sprinted and jumped from track to track to track.

But that was okay. Something like 80 percent of sleep is just basic rest anyway. Energy conservation was what was important. So it didn't really matter if I slept or not. Just lie still. I'd be fine.

I had planned to wait until after one to prowl out to the house and liberate Clara, but that was when I'd expected to spend a few of the hours in between asleep. Lying there awake, turning what I was about to do over in my mind—it was wearing on me, and by eleven forty-five I just couldn't stand it. I popped the seat back up, swung the car out of the space, and rolled down the tight spiral of the exit ramp.

Ten minutes later I was parked in the darkness on Reedmere, less than a block from the house, hidden from the streetlights beneath the sweeping canopy of a classic Florida live oak. I needed to gather my thoughts, stitch them together into some kind of coherent plan. I was halfway home when I realized that for all the thinking I'd done earlier in the day, I still didn't know exactly what I was going to do once I got inside. It had never occurred to me to take a minute and plan this out. But then again, it was my daughter and my house and who needs a plan to just pick up your daughter and take her to live with you?

Think, man. I could see the house from where I sat. The stoop light was on, washing the entire front yard in an antiseptic fluorescent white light. There was no cover there, no shadows to lurk in, nowhere to hide the fact that you've got a four-year-old girl draped over your shoulder and you're trying to carry her out of her house like a bag of laundry in the middle of the night without being seen.

I started the car again and drove into the alley on the north side of Reedmere, headlights off, creeping up on my back gate. It was probably late enough that Todd Edgecomb wouldn't be in his kids' tree house, pretending to clean it while trying to catch a glimpse of Nicole through an untended window. I saw no signs of wakefulness in any of the houses that backed up onto the alley. Everything was quiet, as quiet as a calm summer sea. I cut the engine and got out.

The gate is easy to open up when it's locked, if you know the trick. What you have to do is lift the handle and pull the gate toward yourself, and then push your thumb on the latch and shove the gate forward again. But you have to do it all in one single motion or it won't work. I'd done it so many times over the years that it was just muscle memory, and the gate swung open without resistance or sound. I scurried toward the back of the house, an empty black backpack slung over one shoulder.

I got to the French doors and stopped, credit card in my right hand, left hand on the doorknob. If I opened the doors, the alarm would start beeping and wouldn't stop until I punched in the code. It would take me at least four steps to get to the panel, which almost certainly wasn't fast enough to deactivate the alarm before it woke Nicole up. But I couldn't see any other way. If it came down to it, I mean if I really had to, well, maybe I could overpower her and tie her up or something. Could I get us to the Mexican border by the time she freed herself? Would they even know to look there?

Fuck it, I remember thinking. I'll burn that bridge when I come to it. And I slid the credit card into the gap between the doors until I felt the bolt give way with a satisfying chuk sound.

Moment of truth now. I took a deep breath, turned the handle and pushed.

Beeeeeeeeeeeeeeeep, went the alarm panel. Beep beep beeeeeep. Beep beep beeeeeep.

It only took me three steps to get to that panel, and once I was there, I shut it down quick. My finger was trembling. Probably the adrenaline. I froze, listening for Nicole, for Spaulding, for Clara, for anything. There was a noise, a high-pitched whirring, coming from the bedroom. It took me a second longer than it should have to recognize it as Nicole's hair dryer, and I realized I'd been holding my breath since before I even opened the French doors. I let the air escape from my lungs, slowly, quietly. You got this. Don't fuck it up now.

I eased open the door to the guest bathroom and, without turning my flashlight on, removed a safe deposit box key from my pocket and placed it on top of the cabinet directly above the toilet. I slid the key as far back toward the wall as I could reach, and then I slipped back out of the room and closed the door.

Up the stairs now, two at a time, careful not to catch a toe on a step and end up clattering back down the staircase. I ducked into the study and left the door open just a crack. I could see the light from the bedroom seeping into the foyer at the base of the stairs, softly illuminating the white tile—yes, it was white, even though Nicole always insisted on calling it ivory; I never could tell the difference. A few minutes later the foyer went dark. Even though Nicole always fell asleep quickly—I'd always envied her for that—I still decided to wait where I was for another half hour or so. That should be plenty of time.

The minutes ticked by at an agonizing pace. Eventually I stepped out into the pitch-dark hallway and considered, just for a moment, what I was about to do. I was about to depart from my prepared remarks and improvise a whole new plan, and in a way that couldn't help but have repercussions on everything that happened from that point forward. Being an expat fugitive was one thing. Being an expat fugitive with a four-year-old girl in tow was quite another.

But that four-year-old was my daughter. How could I abandon her, knowing the fate I would be dooming her to?

Fuck it, I thought. Just do it and be done. And I turned, pushed open Clara's door and crept into her room, flashlight in one hand, backpack in the other.

THIRTY-EIGHT

Nicole

The days that change your life start out just like all the rest of them.

I remember floating through my usual routine that morning. Spooning three small piles of ground coffee into a plain brown filter, slapping the filter drawer shut, pressing the "Brew" button. I remember how the machine churned and rumbled and the sound a few seconds later when a steady stream of hot liquid hissed downward into the waiting pot. I closed my eyes, inhaled deeply. I'd slept terribly the night before, and I was already planning to make a second pot just to get through the morning.

I could tell that day was going to be a scorcher. Some days, you just know. You can just look out the window and actually see the heat about to burst out of the bright sunshine. It was barely seven in the morning, and it was already blazing out there. Summer just keeps getting earlier, I remember thinking. I was a little preoccupied that morning; I had to come up with a plan for Clara during the two months when Pineview's preschool closed down in the summer. I had, or thought I had, this vague memory of someone—possibly Lindsay, I don't know—mentioning something about an arts day camp not too far away. But I couldn't quite pull it together in my head, not before that first cup of coffee, and it might not have been Lindsay, maybe Lauren, but no, why would she know anything about a day camp, she doesn't have kids—

Speaking of which, where was my kid? It was already five after seven. Clara usually beat me to the kitchen in the morning. She better not be sick. And as soon as the thought crossed my mind, I knew that was it, that had to be it, because that was the only thing that ever kept Clara in bed after

201

sunup. Great. Just fucking great. I had no personal days left to spare, and the last thing I needed right now was to get docked a day's pay. I poured myself a cup of coffee and felt the haze start to burn off. Finally.

"Clara," I called up the stairs. "Time to get up, kiddo." I waited for one of Clara's standard responses whenever she was taking too long upstairs, something like Okay, Mommy or I'm coming, Mommy or I can't find my shoe, Mommy. "Come on, bug. I have to take you to school and we cannot be late today, okay?"

Definitely sick. Bad luck for me. I wondered for a moment if there was maybe anything I could work on at home, but no, that wouldn't fly, because I'd have to go back to the office anyway, for the notes and files I would need, which meant either leaving Clara by herself or lugging a sick four-year-old across town in the car. Neither sounded all that appealing.

Either way, I had a schedule, and it was time to get things moving. "Clara," I yelled, climbing the stairs. I do not have time for this shit, oh no I don't. "Let's go! Are you sick or just a little lazy head today?"

Still nothing. Hmm.

When I got to the top of the stairs, Clara's door was halfway closed, the way she liked it at night. I had no reason to think I hadn't left it exactly like that when I put her to bed. But something just felt off about it. Nothing I could quite articulate, exactly. Just . . . I don't know, off.

I pushed the door open. Clara was not in her bed.

"Clara?" It's funny how, with all the uncountable thoughts that were rushing through my head at once at that exact moment, I can so clearly remember noticing the sound of my own voice just then, how it caught, then squeaked on the second syllable. The human brain is so stupid.

I lurched over to the open closet and looked inside. No Clara.

Maybe the bathroom, I thought, and I flung myself out of the room and down the hallway, the hallway that suddenly felt as long as a jet runway, the hallway with the closed bathroom door at the end of it—

I knocked on the door but didn't wait for an answer.

"Clara? Clara, honey, are you in there?"

I pushed the door open. Clara was not inside.

Okay.

Breathe.

Don't panic, I warned myself just as I felt the panic start to build. She's around here somewhere. She has to be.

"CLARA!" I shouted as loud as I could. My voice trembled with fear of—well, of the unthinkable, I guess. "CLARA, WHERE ARE YOU, HONEY?" I was whirling, spinning from room to room, down the stairs, scouring every one of her known hiding places, checking every crevice big enough to fit a small child. The house bobbed around me.

Outside. Of course. She went outside.

Yes, of course that's what she did. She went out to play in the yard while I was making coffee. Of course.

I sprinted toward the French doors, clinging to this obviously ridiculous shred of hope even while my own mind was already trying to undermine it. But the alarm—you'd have heard it if she opened the door. I glanced over at the alarm panel and stopped.

The alarm was off.

How was that possible? I specifically remembered setting it before taking my shower the night before. I did that every night. It was part of the new routine I had built for myself. You know, like we've talked about. I knew I'd set that alarm.

Okay. But then who turned it off? Clara was too short to reach it, and besides, how would she even know how to work it?

I threw open the French doors and sort of half walked, half wobbled in a tight circle on the patio. "Clara," I called out. "Clara! Time for breakfast! Come on in, honey!"

No answer.

My knees buckled and my stomach boiled over as the cold realization hit me. Clara was gone. Somebody took her. Somebody took my daughter and oh fuck oh fuck oh FUCK. The next thing I knew, I was on the phone. I wasn't even sure who I had called until I heard Davis's voice, all groggy and caked over with sleep.

"Uhnnngh," he said.

"Clara is gone," I blurted. "She's gone. That fucking lunatic took her and I don't know where she is and I don't know what to do. She's gone. Gone."

"Wait, what?" He was awake now. "Gone? You checked everywhere? Even outside?"

"Of course I did," I snapped. "Jesus. What do you think?"

"Fine, okay. So you've called the cops?"

"No. I called you first. I didn't know what to do."

"Um, well, the thing to do in this situation would be to call the cops."

"Okay," I said.

"So did you recognize him?" he asked, and for a second I thought I must have misheard him.

"Who? Recognize who?"

"The guy. You said that fucking lunatic took her. Did you recognize him, or—"

"Jesus, you think if I saw him kidnapping my own daughter in the middle of the night, I'd wait until now to do something?"

"What?" Davis said. "No, I—wait, you did watch the nanny cam video, right?"

"Oh shit, you know, I forgot those were even here."

"What the hell, Nicole. That's the whole reason I—"

I hung up on him and scanned the room. Where the hell had he put those damn things? I spotted one of them way up on Alton's record cabinet. There was the other one, on the planter. I grabbed them both and dumped them onto the coffee table. Weren't there more? I was almost certain there were, but I couldn't remember exactly where Davis had put them. It didn't matter—I could find them later. This first.

But I couldn't remember how to work these things. I couldn't even find the little slot for the memory card. I kept turning it over and over, but the plastic casing was completely smooth. My hands started to shake. They are getting away, I remember thinking. While you try to figure this thing out like a moron, they are getting farther and farther away and soon it'll be—

And just then my fingernail caught in a tiny crack in the plastic, and out popped the memory card. A few seconds later, I was watching grainy, stop-motion footage of myself from the previous afternoon on my laptop screen. It looked like Davis had set these things up so they would only record when there was something moving in the room. More efficient that way, I guess. He was always impressed by efficiency.

The video I was watching had come from the cam on the plant shelf, the one with the best view of the French doors. There I was, moving through the room. There was Clara, playing, running, carrying her books downstairs so she could read on the floor while Mommy watched TV. Then the light through the French doors darkened suddenly, which I figured must mean the camera had switched itself off for a while.

I was losing patience with this shit. My daughter was out there somewhere and I didn't know where. I clicked forward until I saw myself setting the alarm—See? I fucking knew I did that—and then let it play from there. My pulse quickened. What was I about to see? And suddenly I didn't want to see, didn't even want to imagine the possibilities. But I had to. So I flushed everything out of my mind and watched, noticing but not caring that my hands were clenched into hardened little mallets, ready for battle.

There—a shadow moved outside the French doors.

I stared at the screen, my mouth hanging open like a fool, unable to believe what I was watching as my deepest fears came true in front of my eyes. Then the French doors opened, and the man—definitely a man—went straight to the alarm panel and punched the keys. I suddenly realized that the light from my bedroom was still on in this video, which meant that I was awake when this had happened. Why hadn't I heard anything? Was the alarm broken? And how the hell did this person know my alarm code?

The light from the bedroom came from the wrong angle. It draped the intruder's face in shadows. I couldn't make out his features. But there was something familiar about him. I knew that, knew it for sure. I knew my stalker, my daughter's kidnapper, the evil person who had been terrorizing me for weeks.

Who the fuck was he?

Then he disappeared, stepping out of frame for a moment, and suddenly he was back again. The bedroom light was off now, so I could only make out silhouettes by the moonlight reflected through the French doors. One was the kidnapper, carrying what looked like a backpack, as well as something I couldn't identify. The other, slung over his shoulder, was almost certainly a sleeping Clara.

Or at least you hope she's sleeping, I thought.

Of course she's sleeping. Why would he bother carrying her out if she was—

I cut myself off right there and fumbled for the memory card from the other cam.

This camera—the one from on top of the record cabinet—gave a different view of the room. The picture was noticeably brighter, though maybe not what I would actually call bright. Still, I could see a lot more, mostly from the light outside. But I still couldn't see the guy's face as he punched in the alarm code before disappearing around the corner and heading upstairs.

Then he was back, carrying Clara over his shoulder, and I could see his face in the blue reflected moonlight, and it was simply not possible, not possible at all what I was seeing, that face, that face of all faces, it could not be the face I was seeing. It was Alton. It was Alton's dead face come back to life.

My hand shook as I picked up the phone and called Davis back.

THIRTY-NINE

Alton

I watched the sunrise in the rearview mirror that morning, the breaking daylight gauzy and blue tinted. We cruised west on I-10; the highway signs told me we were near someplace with the unlikely name of DeFuniak Springs. I had never heard of it, but a cluster of sun-bleached billboards alerted me to the proximity of food, available from at least six different drive-through windows within spitting distance of the exit ramp. And I had to admit, I was famished.

Clara slept in her car seat. She'd been motionless for hours, both arms wrapped tight around Brownie, like she was worried that he'd escape and run back to Mommy. Mommy probably has no idea you're even gone yet, I remember thinking. We had a six-hour head start so far, with probably another hour yet before Nicole woke up and discovered that she had the house all to herself now. Well, her and Davis, anyway. Even so, it still didn't feel like enough time. I doubted it ever would, not until I got to Costa Rica. Which was probably why I was still reluctant to pull off the highway even for the six minutes or so it would take to grab a paper bag full of grease and starch and artificial flavors and preservatives, but since I was right there, I figured I might as well eat something.

The landscape around the exit had clearly evolved over the years to service travelers whose only business with DeFuniak Springs was to pass through it en route to somewhere else. Somewhere better, no doubt. A couple gas stations; some fast-food restaurants; a solitary hotel, its beige paint faded and peeling; weeds sprouting from the asphalt of every parking lot in sight. A few trailers scattered nearby. A little farther up the road was an equipment rental depot, where you could apparently get a good deal on renting a Ditch Witch, whatever that is.

Three of the six fast-food joints didn't look open yet, and I refused to go to McDonald's on general principle, because I hate the way they market so aggressively to kids. I'd always resented the hell out of it when they told Clara to nag me for a goddamn Happy Meal, complete with yet another plastic piece of crap that she didn't need and most likely wouldn't ever play with after she lost interest in it that same afternoon, like she always did. It's unethical. Immoral. So I picked the nearest of the other two places and drove through, ordering a chicken biscuit, hash browns, and coffee for me and a box of chicken nuggets for Clara. She could eat them when she woke up. My teeth sank into the soft biscuit as we climbed the highway ramp. The salt and juices from the chicken spilled across my taste buds. Mmmmm. Damn. I was hungry. I devoured the whole sandwich in four bites. I remember thinking that if Clara didn't wake up soon, I'd eat those nuggets I'd bought for her too. You might think that makes me an awful parent. What kind of a man eats his daughter's breakfast? She'd be fine. There was plenty of fruit and cheese and even a few packages of cookies in the Styrofoam cooler on the passenger's seat.

I was so tired that parts of me were going numb. My limbs felt heavy and leaden, and I knew that the cup of black coffee I'd just bought was only going to make things worse for me later on. I figured by the time we made Pensacola, the caffeine bounce would be gone and I'd be in full crash mode. I'd never get us even as far as New Orleans without a nap, there was just no way. I took a greedy sip of the coffee and savored the warmth of it sliding down my gullet.

I was only a couple of days from making it to Costa Rica and beginning a new life of leisure with my beloved daughter. So much to look forward to, and it was finally within my reach. But I couldn't focus on anything but last night. It all ran through my head in a loop: Me rifling through Clara's dresser and shoving clothes into the backpack. Cramming as many books as I could get inside of it. Holding my breath the whole time, irrationally certain that even a loud sigh would wake Nicole all the way downstairs and give the game away. Bending over Clara, touching her shoulder and saying, "Daddy's here, honey, it's time to go," and Clara not really coming out of her sleep, not all the way anyway, but just enough to remind me, "Don't forget Brownie."

Okay. That seemed reasonable. I could do that. So where the hell was he? He wasn't in the bed with her, not under the covers, not wedged between her pillows. I swept the flashlight over the floor, the beam illuminating for a brief fraction of a second every other toy she owned—that was the exact moment I decided not to bring any of her other toys; if she didn't care enough about it to put it away properly, it wasn't worth bringing—but not settling on Brownie until I shined it into the closet. There he was, resting like a king on top of a pile of what might have been clothes. Or possibly towels. I bent down and grabbed the walrus by a tusk. But then as I stood back up, the flashlight passed its beam across something sleek, black, and plastic, something I hadn't seen in Clara's closet before. But I recognized it the instant I saw it.

I reached up for the nanny cam and yanked it off the shelf. My heart thudded away in my throat. Shit. For the first time I wondered if maybe I might have underestimated Nicole, might have pushed my luck too far, might have ruined everything. All because I couldn't stick to the goddamn plan.

Panic later, I remember thinking. First things first. What am I looking at here?

I held my flashlight between my teeth and examined the cam. I could tell right away it wasn't one of the wireless streaming models. I found the memory card slot, ejected the card and dropped it into my shirt pocket. Then I set the camera in a clearing on the floor and ground it to dust it beneath my shoe.

There had to be more. How many more? But it didn't matter. I knew I'd never find them all in the darkness, and looking for them would be a waste of time. My face was almost certainly on at least one of them, and there wasn't a damn thing I could do about it at that point. So I swept Clara up out of her bed, draped her over my shoulder, and padded down the stairs and out the French doors.

I kept asking myself how Nicole would react as I drove farther west. It was pointless, I knew that, but I kept going back to it anyway. I couldn't control anything that happened in Florida now. All I could do was game out the possibilities in my mind and hope for the best. I opened the box of chicken nuggets and popped one into my mouth. It was a hot cascade of spices and salt and fatty juices, everything I had hoped it would be.

An hour or so after I finished eating her breakfast, Clara woke up and announced her need for the bathroom. She didn't seem at all surprised to find herself waking in her car seat, or by Mommy's absence. I remembered seeing a sign for a rest area coming up—the last one for thirty-odd miles, I think it said—so I pulled off the highway about a mile farther up.

"Daddy, I'm hungry for breakfast," she said after she was done, as we walked out of the facilities and back toward the parking lot.

"Okay, honey," I said. "I have an idea. Let's eat at the picnic table over there." The entire rest area had been carved out of thick pine forest and was set back about a quarter mile from the interstate itself. A dense thicket of tall trees separated us from the highway. I wouldn't have known the highway was even out there if I hadn't just come straight from it. The place was perfect, secluded and quiet. A natural choice for our fugitives' picnic.

"A picnic? For breakfast?" She scrunched up her face.

"Oh come on," I said. "It'll be fun."

"Can I have juice?"

"Sure you can," I said. "Why wouldn't you?"

"Okay," she chirped before asking the question I had spent the last eight hours dreading: "Is Mommy coming too?"

I could feel my ears redden as I answered. "Later, honey. She's coming later." In that moment, I hated myself.

"To live under the water with us?" Her squeaky little voice seemed to keep rising even after she'd finished the question. She skipped ahead of me, toward the picnic tables.

I sighed. "Yeah, but remember, she's afraid of ghosts, so it's gonna be a little while," I said without energy. "Maybe a lot of a little while, actually." I kept one eye on Clara while I opened the passenger-side door and grabbed the Styrofoam cooler. It felt heavier than I remembered. I heaved it out of the seat and shuffled after her.

A few minutes later, Clara sipped from a box of apple juice and picked at a small bag of grapes. A wrapped cylinder of string cheese lay there on the table in front of her. I closed my eyes and felt the fatigue wash over me, battering me, like the waves did to my kayak that night all those weeks ago. Weeks. That seemed like something that happened in some other year, another lifetime. My eyes were cracked. The front lobe of my brain—I could never remember which one that was—felt fuzzy and useless. I couldn't think. I was irritated with nothing in particular and frustrated with everything in the world. How was I going to get us to where we were going in this condition? Could I?

People walked past us, shuttling from car to restrooms and back again. Most smiled at the wholesome family scene of an impromptu father-daughter picnic. But that changed once the smilers got a good look at my face. I must have looked a sight, judging from the way those smiles would either freeze into a conscious imitation of an expression of actual pleasant emotion, or just disappear altogether. It was as if they discovered they'd been tricked into grinning at an abductor, a negligent father, a child-eating troll. If I looked anything like I felt that morning, I can't really blame them.

"Okay, bug," I said. "It's time to hit the road. You ready?"

"Daddy, I'm not done with my cheese yet," she scolded.

"You can eat that in the car, sweetheart. Come on."

"I don't want to," she whined. "I want to stay here at the park."

"It isn't a park, honey," I said. "It's a place where people stop to go to the bathroom. That's it." I stood up. "Come on, let's pack up and go. Don't forget your trash, okay?"

"Just a minute," she sang, and she nibbled the end of her string cheese.

"Clara," I growled. "Damn it, I'm not kidding. It's time to go."

Her face wrinkled and folded on itself. Just what I need, I thought as the tears started rolling.

"But. I. Don't. Want. To," she hiccupped out between sobs. What would a good father do? Calm things down? Convince her that we wouldn't be in the car long before we could stop again? Compliment her on her maturity for doing something she didn't want to do but still had to do? Make a deal with her?

I didn't have the time or the inclination for any of that crap. "I don't give a shit," I exhaled through clenched teeth. "We're going. Now."

It didn't take long for things to settle down once we were back on the road. She seemed to have forgotten all about the picnic's abrupt ending. There were things to look at and point at just beyond her window, like big trucks, and billboards with giant cartoon beavers, and cows. She was especially excited to see them.

"Look, Daddy," she would say every time she spotted them. "Cows!"

"Yes, dear," I would say, completely absent from the conversation. "Cows."

"But you're not looking," she would say.

"Sure I looked. They looked delicious."

"Daddy, I want Kidz Bop."

My ears couldn't parse whatever it was she'd said after I want. "What do you want, honey?"

"Kidz Bop." She dragged out the O and overenunciated the rest, as if she were speaking to a much smaller child. Or an idiot.

"Baby, I don't know what that is," I said.

"On the radio," she said, her voice full of exasperation. I watched her in the rearview mirror, and I swear I saw her roll her eyes as she said it.

"Honey, I don't have your music in my car. I'm sorry."

"This isn't your car," she said. "I don't know whose car this is."

"This is my new car. The other one broke."

"I don't like this car," she whined. Four years old and already too good for a Toyota. That's my girl.

About forty-five minutes later, a little while after we crossed into Alabama, Clara had to go to the bathroom again. I got off the highway and stopped at a McDonald's, mostly because there was no other option nearby and we weren't buying food. Clara immediately spotted the playground in the front of the restaurant, with its slides and ladders, all bedecked in bright primary colors.

"Look, Daddy." She pointed. "They have a playground!"

She wanted to play, to climb and fall down and laugh, to be a kid, like she was the day I watched her at recess. And I was too tired to argue about it, too brain-scattered to do anything but go with it. No, that wasn't it, really. It was that I wanted to watch her play. I wanted to watch her enjoy being a four-year-old child. I shambled over to the counter and leaned on it, waiting for the cashier to notice me.

"Coffee please," I said, not looking at her. She brought it quickly and I breathed in the acrid aroma, which was enough to perk me right up in a pure Pavlovian reaction. Again, I knew the boost wouldn't last. But drinking it felt like the only choice I had. So I gulped it down.

Clara was the only kid in the PlayPlace, but if she noticed it, she didn't care. She climbed the ladders and slid down the twisted tubes of molded plastic. She crawled into a red bulb sprouting from the side and pressed her face against the Plexiglas, looking like an astronaut in an escape pod from some low-budget 1970s sci-fi flick. She laughed. I smiled at her. She waved to me. This, I thought. This is all right. I stretched out my left leg, slid down a bit in the booth and made myself comfortable. I watched her play at that McDonald's on the outskirts of Mobile until the lunch crowd stampeded through.

Clara wanted to stop again almost as soon as we were back on the road. She refused to explain why. She also discovered that she could reach the Styrofoam cooler I had foolishly set in the backseat. I'd filled it with ice before we got on the highway, but it had mostly melted by then, and so of course she spilled the meltwater all over the floor when she tipped over the cooler, trying to get a package of Oreos that I specifically told her she couldn't have. Sometime after we passed Biloxi, she took off one of her shoes and threw it at me, then wailed for ten solid minutes—and yes, I did actually time it, in case you're wondering—when I yelled at her for it. And more demands for Kidz Bop, whatever the hell that is.

Originally, the plan was to stop in New Orleans for the night, but sometime during the day's driving I changed my mind. Showing up now in the same city where I went to law school would probably not be an advisable course of action. Especially since I was still supposed to be, you know, dead. No, we would press on and stop in Baton Rouge instead. I didn't know the city, didn't know anything about it, was pretty sure I'd never even passed through it. Which would make it an ideal place to stop for the night, even though we still had a couple hours' worth of daylight left. But by that point I just didn't care. I was done.

I figured I would just drive around and find a cheap motel for the two of us, the kind of place that's not too picky about credit cards or IDs. Almost as soon as I got off the interstate, I found myself driving through a sprawling greenscape of parkland.

"Daddy," Clara said, "can we play in the park?"

I sighed. Yes, yes we would play in the park. Of course we would. "Sure, baby," I said. "Let me just find a place to park the car."

"I wish Mommy could play in the park with us," she said. "Maybe we could call her and tell her to come."

I started to tell her no, Mommy's phone was broken, but I stopped. What could Clara tell her that she didn't already know? She had no idea where we were. She couldn't give anything away except that we'd stopped at McDonald's and seen some cows.

"Sure," I said. "Of course we can call her. Just as soon as we're out of the car."

FORTY
Nicole

"It was him," I hissed into the phone. I was breathless. My heart was racing. I couldn't string two coherent thoughts together.

"I'll be right over," Davis said. "Don't call anyone else until I get there." Then he hung up.

I dropped the phone on the couch cushion and stood up. And then I pinched my thumbnail—recently manicured too—between my front teeth before I even realized I was doing it. I hadn't bitten my nails since I was twelve years old—*Such a disgusting habit for a young lady,* my mother always said, usually just after she slapped the finger right out of my mouth, never caring whether she made contact with my hand or my cheek. I broke the habit through sheer force of will a week before my thirteenth birthday. It was the first thing I felt like I ever accomplished, the first really hard thing I ever succeeded at doing. In all that time I'd never once been tempted to relapse until that moment.

I pulled my hand away from my mouth and circled the couch once, then a second time. *What do I do?* I kept thinking. *What do I do?* over and over. *How do I get my daughter back? Where the hell is he taking her? What do I DO?*

Okay, the cops. Call them? Don't call them? What should I do? I should call them. But Davis specifically said not to call anyone. I assumed that included the police. Maybe he was right. Because what would I tell them? Here's a video of my supposedly dead husband sneaking into my home and carrying our daughter off in the middle of the night. Clearly he was not dead. He fell off his boat somehow and then made it all the way back to shore. Somehow. Right. And then he didn't tell anyone. So. Why hadn't he come home?

217

Because he wanted everyone to think he was dead. Because he wanted to beat that investigation. Because . . . because he had some money? Yes. He must. He wouldn't have done this without money. He'd never last, trying to live off the land or on whatever he could scrounge together. He was too soft for that.

So. Okay. He had some money squirreled away, most likely from those clients he defrauded, from those accounts he embezzled from, and the feds must have had him cold, or he must have at least thought they did, which meant he was guilty as hell. I wondered how much it was. More than the insurance payout? That was a three-million-dollar policy, or it would have been if I had been allowed to collect it, and wasn't I glad now that all that had gone the way that it did.

But Piedmont Insurance didn't know what I knew. And they probably wouldn't care, either. They'd probably say I attempted to commit insurance fraud by filing that claim, just like those stupid detectives said. Surely the police would have to look into it, at least. Maybe they'd believe me. But maybe they wouldn't. So . . . maybe don't involve them.

Okay, fine. No cops. Then how would I get Clara back? A private investigator? A bounty hunter? Is that even a real job? How would I pay for that? Without that insurance money, I . . . well, let's just say things were already pretty tight. Would Alton call me? Did he want something from me? I had no idea. I was just beginning to realize how much I didn't actually know him. I had no idea what he'd told Clara about why she was with him now—Maybe he told her Mommy died, or Mommy didn't want her anymore. I had no clue where they were going.

Then I guess I picked up the phone and made a call. I don't quite remember doing it, and I think I was actually surprised when I heard the voice on the other end say, "Pineview School."

"Yes, hi, this is Nicole Carver, and I just wanted to let you know that Clara isn't feeling well today so I'm keeping her home." I said that whole thing in a single breath.

"Oh, I'm sorry to hear that," the woman on the other end of the line said. "Hopefully nothing serious."

"Um, no, nothing serious," I said. "But she might be out a few days."

"Oh. Out a few days for nothing serious?"

"Yes. Um, no, um, we've got family stuff, obligations and—"

"Mrs. Carver, are you okay?" I thought she really did sound concerned. A lot of people just fake like they care about whoever they're talking to. It was kind of touching, in a way. "Is everything all right?"

"Oh sure, of course. It's just the wrong day for her to get sick, you know? I was supposed to be at the office half an hour ago and here I am, still trying to figure out how today is going to work." I wondered if I sounded as convincing as she did.

"Well, the most important thing to keep in mind is that it's times like these that a girl needs her mother the most," she said. "But I'm sure I don't have to tell you that. Take care, and good luck."

Yes. A girl needs her mother. Her mother.

And that was all it took. Right then, in that precise moment, I completely changed my mind, a hundred and eighty degrees in reverse. I was going to call the cops. Screw their suspicions. I didn't care. I had nothing to hide and way too much to lose.

I was just about to call them—in fact, my index finger was literally hovering over the "Call" button—when Davis arrived.

"I'm calling the police," I said. "I shouldn't have even waited this long."

"No no no no," Davis said. "Don't do that. Hang on. Let's think this through."

"I have thought it through. I've been doing nothing but thinking it through. Jesus, what is wrong with you?"

"No you haven't. Not all the way." He folded his hands over mine, over the phone. He'd never done that before. It felt put on, like a tactic, like something he might do at work to close a sale. "I think you're missing a very, um, lucrative option here."

"Am I."

"How much money do you think he stole?"

"No idea," I said. "A lot, though."

"Think he has it with him?"

"I don't know. Maybe. Or he has it stashed somewhere. He probably wouldn't just carry it around with him, right? I mean, it would have to be a lot of money. Alton's not really a risk taker."

Davis nodded, his eyes far away. I could tell he wasn't listening.

"So why, I mean, okay, hear me out here, but why don't we just get it off him?"

"Oh Jesus." I knew it.

"We could set ourselves up for a long time. Maybe even the rest of our lives."

"Get it off him? You mean, like, rob him?"

"I mean take it. It's only robbing if you don't have a claim on it. And you definitely have a claim on it. You have earned that money if anyone has."

I shook my hands free from his. "No," I said. I had my arms folded across my chest. "It's a terrible idea. What, am I supposed to point a gun at my husband?"

"Tell me you wouldn't love that," he said.

"Don't act like you know me," I said, but I knew, at least in that specific moment, that he was right. About all of it.

"Uh-huh." He was smiling now.

"Fine, okay, a lot's happened over the past couple of months that might make me want to do that, but he's still the father of my daughter. She cannot see that. I think she's been through enough, wouldn't you say?"

"Well, I kind of only thought of this while you were talking just now, so forgive me if I don't quite have all the details fleshed out yet," he said. "Okay?"

But no, it wasn't okay, and I told him that, because nothing was okay and then everything just hit me all at once and I couldn't hold it back anymore and there I was, crying in front of him, and his arms were around me and I pushed at his chest, trying to get some separation from him—

—and then we were in the bed somehow. I shouldn't be doing this right now, I remember thinking, my daughter, but then again, I knew Clara was safe, she wasn't with some pervert or serial killer or white slaver, she was just with her father on some road trip somewhere, and yes he was a son of a bitch, but he'd never hurt her, not his own daughter, and then Davis was on top of me and inside me and I let him, just let him do what he wanted, just let myself relax, enjoy it, pleasure and guilt swirling together the entire time.

When we were done, neither of us said anything for a few minutes. I watched the fan spinning above us, watched the shadows on the ceiling race against the blades that created them. Davis cleared his throat.

"Look, if you don't want to . . . well, if you don't like my idea, that's cool. We don't have to do it. But just do me a favor and, like, think about it for a little while. You know? I mean, if you really give it some thought and you still don't want to do it, I'll shut up about it and never mention it again. Like it was never even a thing."

I rested my hand on his forearm. "Okay," I said. "I'll think about it."

But that was a lie. I was already thinking about it. Already had thought about it. Why shouldn't I take that money? Davis was right. Wasn't he? After everything Alton had put me through, I deserved it. He may have stolen it, but I'm the one who actually earned it. The idea had frightened me so much that I'd just buried it the very instant it poked its snout out of its hole, weeks ago. But then Davis went and spoke it aloud, giving it a life of its own, and there was nothing I could do to push it back down this time.

My phone rang at a little after seven. Davis and I were in the backyard, splitting another bottle of wine. We spent most of the day not talking, just lying in bed, wide awake, or out there, drinking in the accelerating dusk. I had expected him to try to sell me on his idea, this still-unfocused little plan of his. Not that he needed to at that point. But he didn't. I was surprised he was able to stay quiet about it; I would never have told him this, but I always thought he was a little in love with the sound of his own voice. Which feels horrible to say out loud now. I mean, after how things turned out.

The phone. Ringing. I blinked through a Pinot-induced haze and looked at the number. I didn't recognize it. But I knew who it was. "Alton?" I nearly barked into the phone. "Alton? Who is this?"

"Hi, Mommy!" Clara sang, her voice as light as spun sugar. "I miss you. When can you come?"

"Hi, Clara." I gripped the edge of my seat. Oh god. My little girl. "Hi, baby. How are you? Are you okay?"

"Me and Daddy are at the park. It's really big. I saw dogs and a man on roller skates and I want to play on the monkey bars but Daddy said no. They're all rusty."

"Well, you should listen to Daddy."

"We're going to live under the water, Mommy. And guess what—you can come too!"

"I can? Oh, that's terrific, honey. I'm so glad." I remember wiping tears from my eyes. "Sweetie, do you know where you are right now? I mean—"

"I just told you," she said. "We're at the park," and then I heard a deeper voice in the background, Alton's voice, but

222

I couldn't make out what he was saying. And then there he was, right in my ear, alive after all these numbing and wrenching weeks.

"She can't read maps yet," he said. "Though for what Pineview charges, she probably should be able to by now."

"Alton, what the fuck? Seriously, what the fuck?"

"Okay—"

"No, goddamn it. Not okay. You do not get to 'okay' me!" I was boiling. I shot up and sent the chair skittering three or four feet behind me, almost all the way to the grass. I thought I had prepared myself for that moment. I'd spent the whole day thinking about the conversation that Davis had explained would inevitably happen, had to happen, before Alton could just go ahead and slip off to wherever it was he thought he was going. But it was too much. I couldn't wrap my mind around it. Not even close. "What gives you—I mean—to fuck with my life like this—I—we had a wake for you, everyone thought you were dead—the police—and then now, my daughter, no, don't you dare use that word to me, that is not okay at all!"

"I know this has all been tough on you," he said, "and I'm sorry about that. But I'm sure your friend the car salesman was a great comfort through it all." His voice had that tone, that smug monotone he always used whenever he thought he had the moral high ground. I hated it so much.

"Ah, aha, no no no no no," I said. I think I was even wagging my finger, like he was right there in front of me. "You do not get to do that, you son of a bitch. You do not get to throw anything in my face. You, you you you ran away, abandoned your family—"

"I came back for my family." He was trying to talk over me now. "My family is all right here in this park with me."

"—because, what, because of an investigation? Into what you were doing? I mean, whatever the fuck that was, because I have had no idea what has gone on in your life for the past two years now—"

"My reasons don't matter," he interrupted. "Whatever they were, it's pretty clear to me now that I made the right choice."

"How much did you steal, Alton? How much was enough to make it worth it, to make it worth giving up your family, to ruin your own wife's life? Your daughter's life?"

Suddenly I forgot all about Davis's big idea. In that moment, all I wanted was to see Alton wearing orange, rotting away in a dank prison cell and forgotten by everyone but his jailer.

"You know what, it doesn't matter," I said. "I don't care how much, but I'm sure the police will care. Yeah. The FBI? They'll probably care plenty, they'd probably be very interested to know that you're still alive and on the run with a child. Across state lines. I think that's something they take seriously."

"So you haven't called them," he said. "Huh. That's . . . interesting. Why wouldn't you have called them right away, I wonder?" Which was, I had to admit, a pretty good fucking question.

"I'm hanging up now, Alton. And then I'm going to call the nice detective who stopped in to see me the other night to ask about you."

"There is something you should know," he said. He sounded like he was rushing to get the words out. I waited. "Before you make that call. I . . . well, I left something behind, just in case it came to this. Some of the money I stole. Well, not the money exactly. But a key to where the money is. It's hidden somewhere in the house. I put it there on one of my visits."

"Bullshit," I said. But it was weak.

"Anyone stops me, I tell them you were in on it with me. Simple as that. I get to where I'm going, I tell you where that

224

key is and what it opens. Then the money's yours. To keep. I won't say how much it is, but it's enough to keep you comfortable for a while."

"I don't want money," I said. "I want Clara."

"She asked to come with me. I didn't take her anywhere she didn't want to go."

"Give me back my daughter," I whispered. I could barely even see through how much I hated him right then. "Goddamn you."

"You know what," Alton said. "I'll think about it." And he hung up.

Fuck, I thought. That could not have gone worse.

"We couldn't have done that inside?" Davis demanded. "You do still have neighbors, you know. And the cops? Seriously? Like, what the hell? We talked about that. We—"

"Shut up," I said. My voice was distant and my head was pounding, floating in a cocktail of red wine and adrenaline. "Just . . . shut up for a while. Okay?" Sometimes I just liked him better when he wasn't talking.

FORTY-ONE

Alton

I didn't intend to sleep in the next morning. I woke up only when the daylight from the hotel room's sole window had soaked into every corner of the place, pounding at my eyelids, demanding immediate compliance. My hand flopped around like a gasping fish on the particleboard nightstand until I felt the smooth glass plane of my phone. It was eight thirty-four. My alarm was more than two hours late.

I sat up and rubbed my face. All I wanted to do was lie back down, pull the covers over my head, and sleep for another couple of hours. Yesterday had been draining. Clara and I both must have fallen asleep quickly that night. In the bed next to mine, she was still curled in the exact position she'd been in when I set her down eleven hours earlier.

"Come on, bug." I reached down to her shoulder and gave a gentle nudge. "Time to wake up."

"Hmmmmmmmmmmph," she whined at me, and rolled over to bury her face in the pillow.

"No no," I said. "No going back to sleep. Can't do that today, honey. We gotta go."

"I'm hungry," she grunted through the pillow. "For breakfast."

"We can get some breakfast on the road."

"I want cereal," she mewled. "In my Dora bowl."

My shoulders sagged. This was new, Clara being difficult to get going in the morning. Hell, most mornings she was the one dragging us out of bed. "But going through the drive-through is so much fun." I wondered who exactly I was trying to convince, her or me. "And you get to eat in your car seat there, and drink your milk out of that little box, carton, whatever, and—"

226

"I don't want to eat in the car!" she said. "I want my cereal in my Dora bowl!" And she grabbed one of the other pillows and clamped it over her head.

Goddamn it. We do not have time for this.

"Okay, listen to me," I said. Every muscle in my jaw tensed. "I don't have your bowl. I don't have any cereal. I don't have any milk. I don't have a spoon for you to use to scoop the cereal and milk into your mouth. What I do have is a set of car keys, some money, and a schedule to keep. And that spells breakfast in the car. Understand?"

Instead of answering me, she burrowed further into the covers, where she wouldn't be expected to put up with this sort of indignity. I breathed in, held it, and counted to three. Then I yanked the covers off the bed and flung them onto the floor. Clara didn't move for a few seconds, then her head shot up from the pillows to see what had just happened.

"Noooooo!" she wailed. "Daaaaaaaa-deeeeeeeeeeeee!"

"I told you. We're on a schedule, and we're already late. Get out of that bed, get dressed, and let's go get some breakfast."

Clara sprung out of the bed and bolted for the bathroom door. Just before she slammed it, she threw me the sourest look I'd ever seen her put on.

We crossed the Mississippi River about half an hour later. "Clara, look," I said, pointing out the window at the wide, languid stripe of brown water wending its way from under the bridge all the way to the horizon. "That's the Mississippi River. It's the biggest river in America. It comes all the way from Minnesota, which is . . . well, I don't know how far exactly, but it would take a couple days to drive there. More than a thousand miles, I can tell you that much for sure. A thousand miles. Pretty neat, huh?"

She sat in her car seat, arms folded, saying nothing, just glaring at the back of my head. I caught her gaze in the rearview mirror. She didn't flinch.

"Yeah, you're right," I muttered. "Who gives a shit about Minnesota."

We settled into a tense but somehow comfortable silence after that. Once we were a few miles out of town, I bought us breakfast from a drive-through window, just like I promised. Then we were back on the highway, and soon the sky darkened, splattering the windshield with drops of rain the size of killer bees, drops so big their shape could barely contain them. But the shower itself was short and half-assed, and we were through it quickly. The sky lightened a bit but did not clear, the gray of it adding a pall of bleakness to a landscape that was bleak enough already without it.

I felt a sudden jolt in my left kidney. Not sharp; more like a dull thudding. Then I felt it again, but in the right kidney this time. Then back to the left. Then right. Thunk. Thunk. Thunk.

"Stop kicking the seat, Clara," I said.

Thunk.

"I'm warning you."

"Your seat is stupid," she informed me. "Your car is stupid. You're stupid too." Thunkthunkthunkthunkthunkthunk.

"I've told you before about that rude mouth of yours, young lady." Had I? I couldn't remember. Probably, though. "Do you want a spanking? Do you want me to put you out by the side of the road? I don't allow rude little girls in my car, you know."

"I want to go home," she said, and the words kicked me in the solar plexus and squeezed the air out of my lungs.

"That's exactly where I'm taking you," I said. "To your new home. Under the water. With me."

"Nooooo," she moaned. "I want to go to my real home. With Mommy."

I watched my own eyes narrow, my jaw set as I looked at her in the rearview mirror. "Well I'm sorry you feel that way.

228

But the only home you have now is with me. I went to a lot of trouble to come back from under the water to get you, you know."

"I have to go to the bathroom," she announced. It was already her fourth time since we left Baton Rouge, and it wasn't even lunchtime yet.

"Fine. The next chance we get."

Go home? Back to that, that, that pit of neglect? Not on your life. What kind of father would I be? Then the next exit came up, and wouldn't you know it, there was a McDonald's where she could relieve herself. Which is about all they're good for, if you ask me.

"I can go by myself," Clara hissed at me once we were inside, and she yanked her hand from mine and ran into the women's restroom. I just shrugged. If she wasn't out in five minutes, I'd go in after her. I took a seat in a booth in the back of the restaurant, right next to the lavatories.

The place had already started to fill up with the pre-lunch-time rush. I looked at my watch. I'd forgotten to change it to Central time yesterday. I looked up to notice a red-faced cop with no neck sitting at a table on the other side of the aisle. He chewed his two all-beef patties and whatever else went with them slowly, deliberately. His eyes sat squarely on me the whole time.

There must be an APB on me by now, I thought. I wondered if they'd know to look in that part of the country, if they could have guessed so easily where I'd be headed.

Of course they'd guess it, you idiot. It's an interstate highway. It's the fastest land route out of the country. If they didn't think to look for you here, then they don't deserve to catch you.

I half-waved to the cop. "My daughter," I said, hooking a thumb toward the bathrooms. "Insisted on going by herself."

The cop nodded but did not smile. "Grow up fast, uh-huh," he said, or at least that's what I thought he said. It had been years since I'd been to Louisiana—with good reason, I think—and in that time I guess I'd lost my ability to parse the peculiar, mush-mouthed dialect of the swamplands.

"Yeah, sure do." I partially swallowed the words in case the cop had actually said something else entirely. He continued to stare me down for what seemed like an hour before Clara finally emerged from the ladies' room.

"I went by myself, Daddy!" she squealed, all the animosity forgotten, nothing but vapor in the glow of this momentous achievement.

"That's great, honey," I said. The cop was still watching. "Did you wash your hands?"

Her face faltered. "Ummmm, yes." She stretched that second word almost until it snapped back on her. She was lying, and ordinarily I would have made her go back and do it again. But not today.

"Okay then, let's go," I said, grabbing her by her unwashed hand.

"Daddy, can we get some chicken nuggets?" she asked.

"No, not this time." I looked over my shoulder for just a second and saw the cop get up from his seat, ball up his trash, and walk after us, to the door. "We had a late breakfast. But maybe later if you're good, okay?"

"But I want some now," she whined. I wasn't listening. I bundled her into her car seat and strapped her in, all the while trying to keep one eye on that trooper. And then I couldn't see him. Goddamn it. Where the hell did he go?

I caught sight of him again just as I was about to merge back onto the interstate from the on-ramp. A white Chevy Tahoe lumbered up the ramp behind me; I saw the flashers on the roof, and I just knew it was the same cop. My breath hitched and everything went cold. So this is it, I remember thinking. I'm not even going to make it out of Louisiana. I thought—for one crazy moment—about punching it, gunning the engine, and trying to outrun him, but then I remembered I was in a 1997 Toyota Camry, and the cop was driving a late-model police-modified Chevy freaking Tahoe, for Chrissakes. I sighed and eased off the gas pedal, wondering how I was going to explain all this to Clara.

Then the Tahoe sped up and passed me. Like I was standing still. Like I wasn't even there.

It . . . wasn't for me. He didn't. He . . . wasn't. Holy shit. And suddenly I was shaking, shaking with tension and relief at the same time. My breath was ragged and loud.

Jesus, that was close. But it really hadn't been close at all. The cop didn't know who I was, couldn't have cared less about me and my little girl. I had never been in any real danger.

But I'd had no way to know that as it was happening. Staying in a constant state of heightened awareness was grinding me down. No matter how many hours of sleep I got—and it was never that many, really—I never felt rested. My shoulders ached from the constant tension I carried there, but I had been doing it for so long now that I barely even noticed it.

And suddenly we were in Texas, at least according to the no-frills green sign just off the highway shoulder. "Texas State Line," it read, and that was it. No state insignia. No state motto. No greeting from the governor. And certainly no need to impress anyone coming from Louisiana, that was for sure.

"Hey Clara, guess what?" I called back to her. "We're in Texas now, honey. You've never been here before."

She said nothing, just stared at her shoes.

"Come to think of it," I went on, "I've never been here before either. It'll be a new adventure for both of us. Sounds fun, huh?"

"I want to go home," she said. "I miss Mommy." It was the last thing I wanted to hear from her, and suddenly I could feel the anger and resentment and bitterness beginning to bubble up from my core, threatening to spill out of my mouth and onto my daughter's shoes and pants and soul. But just as it was about to cascade all over the car's faded and stained interior, I stopped.

She does have a point, you know.

Of course I knew. How could I not know? How could I not know that a girl needs a mother, someone to take care of her and show her how to grow up and become a woman someday? I couldn't do that. How could I not know that by taking her to Costa Rica like this, I would be cutting off worlds, universes even, of possibilities for her future before she could even begin to understand what that meant? There was nothing for Clara in Costa Rica. This thing I was doing, it wasn't for her. It wasn't for her salvation, for her future, for any of it. No, it was all for me and me alone. I knew that. At some level, I always had. I just hadn't been able to admit it.

Still, though.

What kind of a man abandons his daughter? No kind of man, that's what kind. That's what cowards do. And if I was being honest, I didn't really know for sure what Costa Rica had to offer Clara. Everything I knew about the place, I'd picked up through my own research, and while I was confident I had done a thorough job, it was all still second-hand. I couldn't vouch for any of it.

Then another random thought: A man traveling alone draws less attention than one traveling with a small child and no wife.

I rolled that notion around in my head for a few minutes. It made some sense. Yes it did. Countless men cross that border every day. No reason to give any of them a second glance if you're a tired, underpaid border-crossing checker. But a kid? Someone might notice a cute kid. That same cute kid might say something at exactly the wrong moment. This particular kid in question had no fake papers, because I hadn't been planning to do this when I'd had my own set made, and Jesus Christ how could I have—

Wait—do kids that young even need passports? Fuck, I didn't even know! I pounded the steering wheel. How could I not know that?

My heart thudded against my sternum, hard, like it was trying to burst free. What if I hadn't thought of this before I tried to cross? What then? I was starting to panic, this time for no good reason. I gripped the steering wheel hard enough to whiten my knuckles, the cracked vinyl suddenly slick with my own palm sweat. I was certain, with all the nervous energy collecting in my arms just then, that I could have twisted the whole steering assembly right off its column, with no more trouble than I'd have had with the cap on a bottle of ginger ale.

So this is what defeat tastes like.

"Daddy, look at all the skyscrapers!" Clara shouted when we got close to downtown Houston. I had actually planned to point them out to her, to try to bring her out of her funk. She'd always been fascinated by tall buildings, the way the sheer walls of glass reflect the world back onto itself, only brighter. Now she didn't need me to help with her mood, and I wondered if she knew what I'd been thinking.

"Wow, honey," I said. "Pretty cool, huh?"

"Yeah!" she yelped. "I want to live in one!"

"I thought you wanted to live with Mommy," I said. "You know, in your real home."

"I mean after that."

We drove west, through Houston, passing above the endless sprawlscape of parking lots and chain restaurants and apartment complexes and cell phone stores and car dealerships out beyond downtown. I tried to sort out in my mind what to do next. I'd originally planned to drive to San Antonio and then head south on I-35 until I hit Mexico. But now I wanted to put off that moment as long as possible. So instead I branched off the interstate about an hour before I would have gotten to San Antonio and headed northwest, toward Austin. I'd always heard good things about Austin. This might be my last chance to see the place.

I stopped for gas a few miles past a sneeze of a town called La Grange. My gaze wandered past the pumps, past the dumpster at the end of the parking lot, and into the empty landscape beyond. It looked exactly like what I had expected Texas to look like. Flat, mostly. Just a handful of spindly trees. Endless grass, dried out and yellowing.

There was no reason to put this off any longer.

I stepped away from the pumps and punched a string of ten familiar digits into my phone. A thousand miles away, I could hear ringing on the other end of the line. I closed my eyes and focused on the sound of the purring phone, to the exclusion of everything else, and for a moment I began to relax, to let go of the tension and nerves I held in my—

"Where are you?" And there was Nicole's voice, and it was over. "Is everything okay? Is Clara okay?" I took a deep breath and let it out slowly.

"I'm in Texas," I said. "You should probably come and pick up our daughter." And I tried to convince myself that I hadn't almost said your daughter.

FORTY-TWO

Nicole

So that was it. All that was left for me to do was fly to Texas and get Clara. Then I could start forgetting that Alton ever existed. He could run away to South America or Bora Bora or Mount Everest for all I cared. After a while he would be nothing more than a bad dream, or a character half-remembered from a movie I watched when I was sick one afternoon years ago.

Before I go any further with this, I want to make sure you understand that I am not blaming Davis here. Because we've talked about my issues with taking responsibility for my own choices, and I've been working on that, I really have. But this part of the story, it might sound like I'm trying to blame him for everything. I'm not.

Not only was Davis right about how I deserved that money, but I couldn't overlook the fact that he had also been right, exactly right, about how everything had unfolded so far, from the fact that Alton would call to the fact that he wouldn't make it past the border with Clara, if that's where he was going, mostly because she doesn't have a passport.

It would have been foolish of me not to trust his instincts here. Negligent, even. I'd have been doing Clara a huge disservice if I let this opportunity slip past.

And once I convinced myself of that, the rest was a fait accompli.

As soon as Alton and I were off the phone, I got online and bought two plane tickets to Austin for the next morning.

"Pack a bag," I called out to Davis. "For a couple of days or so. And you should probably call in sick or something."

"What's that?" he called back from the bedroom.

"Or just quit. Or you know, don't even bother with that. By next week, you won't need that job. We'll be coming into some money soon enough."

I looked up and he was standing in the bedroom doorway, fresh out of the shower, a navy blue towel wrapped around his waist. "What's happening?"

"We're going to Texas," I said. "To get my daughter. And maybe a couple million dollars."

His face lit up.

"You work out the plan," I told him. "That's your department. But yeah, we're doing this. We're taking what's ours." I didn't even hear what he said next. I was thinking about how much smaller three million dollars looked when you split it in half. I was wondering about how he'd react later, when he finally figured out he'd been used.

FORTY-THREE

Alton

Compared to Houston's, the Austin skyline wasn't all that impressive. Clara pointed this out to me from her car seat as we drew closer to downtown. I used the skyscrapers as a beacon, holding a steady bearing on them even as the surface streets worked in tandem to shunt me off to one side of town or the other. I had no intention of spending my last night with my daughter in some dingy roadside motel on the outskirts of town, some forgotten hole that reeked of mold and failure. The Lone Star version of the Royal Rest. Absolutely not. Tonight we'd sleep high above the city, in a sparkling silver tower, with soft, freshly laundered sheets and air-conditioning you couldn't smell, not even a little.

"How would you like to sleep in one of those skyscrapers tonight?" I asked.

"I would love to!" she nearly shrieked. "Can Mommy come too?"

"Not tonight," I said. I watched her face change in the rearview mirror. "But she'll be here tomorrow sometime, I think." That was the arrangement we'd made, less than an hour earlier, when I called her from that middle-of-nowhere gas station.

"Are you serious?" Nicole asked me. "Because if you aren't, if you are screwing with me, I don't know if I could take that. So just . . . don't fuck with me here, okay? Please."

"It won't work," I told her. "This thing I'm doing. I'm not . . . I'm not up to this." And admitting to another person—even my own wife, especially my own wife—that I knew I was incapable of raising my daughter on my own, that was a lot harder than I had expected. "Besides, she misses you. She needs you. She needs her mother more than she needs her

237

father, I think." A speck of dust blew into my eye, deposited there by the desert winds. I allowed myself a couple of tears to flush it out. "Plus—" And then I stopped. I almost told her about the passport problem but stopped. That wasn't her concern. And who knows who else might have been listening.

Nicole just let that last word hang there for half a minute or so before speaking.

"Well, I'm not trying to talk you out of anything here, but she's four. She misses whoever isn't with her at that exact moment. You should have heard how much she talked about you when you were . . . well, wherever you were."

I shook my head. "I'll get to say a proper good-bye this time. I got to spend a little more time with her than I would have otherwise. That's enough. I guess I can't realistically expect to have everything I want."

"Thank you," she said, her voice cracking a little. Or maybe I imagined that. "Just, please don't change your mind after we hang up."

Then I heard the clacking of a computer keyboard, and Nicole said the next available flight didn't leave until 10:09 the next morning. She'd be in Austin by early afternoon. She would call me when she landed.

That would be in about eighteen hours. That's how much longer I had with my little girl, who was beyond pleased to hear that Mommy would soon be joining us.

After circling through the maze of construction, one-way streets, and sudden blasts of oncoming traffic that seemed to materialize at random intervals—Austin traffic was ridiculous, more like what I would expect in a much bigger city—I eventually settled on a Hampton Inn, mainly because I'd heard of it and because it happened to be on the right side of the street for me to just slide the car into the half-circle driveway out front.

"How's this, Clara?" I called to the backseat. "Is it tall enough for you?"

She leaned over and pressed her face against the window, looking up at the building's façade as we pulled up. Twelve stories, tops, but a four-year-old looking straight up at it might be fooled.

"I can't see the top of it!" she said. "It's a million feet tall!" Her grin stretched nearly the entire width of her tiny face.

I checked in using a credit card I'd opened a couple months back in the name of my least-favorite client, back when I first started planning this thing. Our room was on the eleventh floor. The minute I had the door open, Clara bolted for the window, scrambling on top of the air conditioner so she could get the highest possible vantage point to see the street directly below.

"Daddy, we're up so high!" And I smiled at that, happy to be able to give her this new experience. Probably the last time I would get to do that for her.

"Yes we are, honey. Are you scared?"

"No," she said, still looking down. "It's not scary. I can't fall out. There's a window."

"Okay. Are you hungry for dinner yet?" And suddenly I was exhausted. The reserve of energy I'd thought I had left was a mirage after all. It had been a long day.

But she said, "Pizza," so I bundled her down the elevator and out into downtown Austin; I figured there must be a decent pizza place somewhere nearby. We walked around awhile, taking a couple of lefts and ending up on Sixth Street, smack in the middle of the noise of the bars and clubs, where there was already live music—loud live music—and the sun wasn't even down yet. Hell, it wasn't even seven o'clock yet. And then there were bums, street people so much bolder and more aggressive and covered in filth than the ones who kept getting into Edgecomb's backyard, so many of them that I scooped Clara up and turned around, heading back the way we had just come, shielding her with my arms from whatever these people might have in mind for

239

a tiny child like her. And then, a couple of blocks in the other direction, success. A pizzeria, someplace claiming to have been voted best in Texas by some website I had never heard of. Fine. Perfect.

"You know, Clara," I said through a mouthful of sausage and mushroom, "some people say this is the best pizza in Texas."

"Uh-huh," she said. Her own mouth was full of cheese and tomato sauce. She likes the basics.

"So what do you think?"

"It's pretty good," she agreed, and bit off another chunk. The next morning we had breakfast tacos—apparently a local delicacy—in a hole-in-the-wall just steps around the corner from the hotel. The day's agenda was Clara's to set, at least until Nicole landed. So once we were almost finished eating, I asked her what she wanted to do next.

"I want to go to the library," she said. I asked the man at the counter where the library was and how long it would take to walk there. I looked at my watch and figured we'd get there just as it opened. Perfect. Shaping up to be a perfect day already. Just perfect.

The morning air was thick and hazy. I guess that's pretty typical for Austin, but I didn't know that at the time, and I also hadn't counted on the library's being uphill. We don't have hills in Florida. It also turned out that we had to cross Sixth Street, rushing past the army of homeless hustlers and bouncing between people waiting for a bus to passersby who looked successful enough to possibly be hiding a spare five-dollar bill in their pockets somewhere. Soon our storybook father-daughter stroll was beset by a sheen of grimness, as the weather, terrain, and local wildlife all conspired against us at once.

"I'm sweaty, Daddy," Clara said. "It's hot."

"I know it, baby. I'm sweaty too."

"Are we almost there?" she whined. In fact, we were there, turning the last corner just as the words left her lips.

"This isn't the library," she said as the automatic doors opened. The lobby blasted us with deep-chilled air, and my skin was instantly dry. I shivered.

"Sure it is," I said. "It's just a different library. They have books here too. You'll like it, you'll see."

"No I won't," she said before she sprinted off toward the children's section. I picked up a newspaper and sat in a nearby chair, next to the imposing, south-facing windows, and pretended to flip through it while I watched my daughter dig through someone else's books for a change.

She spent two full hours immersed in bright, wide books she had never seen before—the Austin library is orders of magnitude bigger than the one back home. "Daddy, can we go to the park now?" she asked when she was done.

"Are you all done reading books?" I asked.

"Uh-huh."

"Well then I don't see why not," I said. When I asked a librarian for directions to the nearest park, she gave me a look, all squinty and with pursed lips, as if the very idea were ridiculous beyond comprehension.

"Well, there's one just across the street there, but I don't know if I'd call it a park exactly," she said. "There's some grass there and it's open to the public, but if you're looking for something a little girl might enjoy . . ." Her voice trailed off, and she shrugged.

"There's got to be something nearby," I said. "A city this size?"

"You know, you might just want to head on up to the state capitol," she said. "Just a couple blocks from here? Plenty of grass, plenty of people, there's a big cannon for her to play on." She shrugged again. "Best I can do, I'm afraid."

"This isn't the park," Clara said when we got there. "There's no swing. Or monkey bars."

"No, but there's a cannon." I pointed it out to her. "See? Think you can climb all the way up it?" She didn't answer, just ran off toward the cannon.

My phone rang before she made it all the way across the green. I checked the number. It was Nicole—of course, who else could it be, really—so I answered it.

"You're earlier than I expected. I thought you weren't leaving until ten."

"You're an hour behind us," she said.

"Oh yeah. I always forget about time zones."

"So where is she? Can I talk to her? When can I get her?"

"She's here, but she's busy playing right now."

"You can't get her?" she snapped. It occurred to me that Nicole generally had a pretty short fuse. Funny that I'd never noticed it before.

"I can, I guess, but I'm not going to," I said. "This is my last day with her and I'm going to enjoy it. When it's done I will bring her to you."

"Alton—"

"Seriously, no tricks. I just want to have one last day with her. Then this will all be over, for all of us. I don't think that's too much to ask."

She was silent for ten, maybe twenty seconds. "Fine," she said. "All right. Fine. I guess I don't have much of a choice."

"Okay then. Where are you staying tonight?" I asked. She named a hotel, nothing I recognized, said it was out near the airport. "Okay. Go check in and wait for me. I will call you when I'm ready to bring her over."

I watched Clara run around on the lush green expanse for almost another hour. There were no other kids playing with her, though there were plenty of children her age nearby, clustered together in awkward little groups with their families, posing for the same uninspired vacation pictures as everyone else, in front of the grand domed edifice of the capitol building. But she didn't need any of them. She was outside, she was running and jumping and falling down and chasing any birds that were heedless enough to get too close to her. Most days, that's all she needed.

"Daddy, can we go to McDonald's?" she asked, sweaty from playing. There were grass clippings in her hair from rolling on the freshly mown lawn.

"You know, honey, I don't know if they have those here," I said, and I realized that I actually hadn't seen a McDonald's since we got to Austin. "And if they do, I don't know where they are."

"Pleeeeeaaaaaaaase?" she begged.

"And our car is all the way back at the hotel."

"I want chicken nuggets," she said, pouting. A familiar irritation began to push its way into my consciousness.

"Okay, here's what we'll do," I said. "We'll take a bus ride and see if maybe it goes by a McDonald's. How's that?"

I had no idea how the buses worked there, or where any of them went. But Clara was up for an adventure, so I was too. We got on the first one to pass in front of the capitol. We didn't find a McDonald's, so we ended up having a late lunch at this tiny hamburger joint somewhere on the other side of downtown. Clara resisted the whole thing until the waitresses all started making a fuss over her, which made her forget she wasn't supposed to like the place. I bought her chicken strips and French fries and milk, and she scarfed it down like she'd never even heard of McDonald's. My own burger was the size of a small dog. I ate the whole thing—I was finally starting to find my appetite again—but I don't think I actually tasted any of it. I just chewed and swallowed, chewed and swallowed, and thought.

FORTY-FOUR

Alton

According to the map, the Austin Zoo was somewhere south of the city, but just as I got Clara all strapped into the car, the skies darkened quickly and then split open, dumping enough rain on the city to slow traffic to a crawl within minutes. I stared at the taillights stretched out in front of me and wondered for a moment if it was the same weather system we'd passed through the day before in Louisiana. Probably not, though. I think weather travels faster than that.

"I don't think the zoo is gonna work out today, bug," I said over my shoulder. "I guess we should've gone there this morning when the weather was still good. Got any other bright ideas?"

"But I wanted the zoo," she said. I could tell from her voice that she was tired.

So your answer is no, then. I might have said that aloud to myself, but maybe I just thought it instead. "I know, but it's too rainy. Tell you what, I have an idea. You just sit tight." But I didn't have an idea. That was just one of those things parents say. I was in a strange city in bad weather that was making already terrible traffic even worse, I had to come up with a way to occupy a cranky four-year-old for a couple hours, and I had to do it fast. I drove south on Lamar, mostly at random, but also because I knew I'd have to head south to Nicole's hotel soon enough anyway. Might as well save myself some of the aggravation of crosstown traffic later on. My head swiveled back and forth to scope out both sides of the street as I passed by, looking for anything that might distract Clara for even a little while. A Chuck E. Cheese's, for example. A McDonald's with one of those damn play areas. At that point, I would have even taken that.

Maybe you should just take her back to her mother now. Sure. That could work. Nicole would be thrilled to have this over with. I could call her up, swing over to the Del Rio Inn, and drop her at the door, and then I could just go, get on I-35 and head south and keep going until I hit Mexico and then finally get to where I was supposed to have been two months ago already. Then everyone could just get on with it.

Fucking passports for kids. See, those are the details that get people caught. I'd been an attorney long enough to know that attention to detail was often the difference between a well-executed plan and a merely well-conceived one. If I had tried to get her across the border without papers—

You don't need a passport to go to Montana, you know. Now there's a moment of clarity.

If the passport was the only thing between me and a life with my own daughter, then fuck the passport, fuck Central America, because we could get almost just as lost right here in the continental forty-eight, or maybe even more lost. Everyone would assume I got her across the border somehow. Nicole absolutely thought that was where I was headed—I mean, why else would I even be in Texas—and she would tell the feds everything she knew the first chance she got. Nobody'd even think to look in Montana, unless we gave them reason to. And the money I had could last a good long while there, especially if we lived in a log cabin far off the beaten path—

But almost as soon as I thought it, I knew it would never work. Clara deserved more than that, growing up in some kind of Unabomber shack. Besides, I didn't know how long I'd last on another cross-country car trip with her. This one had pushed me to my limits after only two days. Montana wasn't going to happen. My destiny was in the other direction, on the beaches of Costa Rica; Clara's was, well, wherever Nicole said it was, I guess.

Our time together was up. I knew that then. It's been a good day, I remember thinking. Don't ask too much from it.

"How about," I said to Clara, "we go see Mommy now?"

FORTY-FIVE

Nicole

The Del Rio Inn was about two miles from the airport. Everything closer looked either too down-market or too expense-account oriented, so I made Davis drive us around in the rental car until I spotted something that looked livable for at least one night. The room's air conditioner wheezed and strained to fight off the oncoming heat of the afternoon. As soon as we were inside, I called Alton to let him know I was there. Davis sat in the chair across from the bed, watching me.

"So what's the plan?" he asked when I was done.

"He's going to spend the day with Clara, then bring her here. So I guess we wait until that happens."

"I meant the other plan." I wasn't surprised to hear that he hadn't figured it out yet. But that's how Davis was. I called him an idea hamster once, because it seemed like he was always coming up with ideas and then never taking them anywhere, just consuming the energy of the idea and spinning his giant hamster wheel until the next one came along. Honestly, some of his ideas were pretty good, I have to admit. But he never did anything with them. I always found that so frustrating.

I shrugged. "I told you, that's your end," I said. "I thought you would have had all that figured out by now."

"I have some ideas. If he's coming here, that kinda narrows it down a bit. Think he'd come inside?"

"He might. But he'd have Clara with him if he did."

"Right," he said, not understanding.

"So you can't hit him or anything in front of her."

"Oh. Right. I get it."

I sighed. I was going to have to do all the work after all.

"But he might not. He might just drop her off outside instead. So in either case, the best place for you to be when he

246

gets here is outside somewhere. If he brings her inside, just steal his car. If he drops her off, figure out a way to get into his car and . . . well, get the money from him, I guess."

Like I said before, sometimes you have to show him the stick before you throw it.

"Okay, cool," he said. His face darkened. "Think he'll have a gun?"

"I don't know. He's never been a gun person. But if I were driving around with a couple million dollars in my trunk, I might get one, sure. Do you have one?"

"How would I have a gun? We just got here."

"Well, figure it out, I guess," I said. "You're a smart guy."

But I don't think he even heard me. He started talking aloud—possibly to me, but I got the feeling it was more for his own benefit than anything else—about where that money was most likely to be, whether Alton would have it on him when he showed up or whether he'd sense a trap and leave it somewhere else, and if it was the latter then we might just be shit out of luck. Or we could try to beat it out of him. Either way, at least we tried, right?

I stretched out on the bed and tuned Davis out. It wasn't until the rain started that his enthusiasm for his own voice seemed to waver at all. That was when he stopped talking—Finally, I thought—and picked up the remote control.

"Do we have to?" I asked.

"It relaxes me," he said, lingering over a mail-order catheter commercial. "Wow," he muttered, and changed the channel.

A few minutes later, my phone rang. This was a lot sooner than I'd been expecting. Just relax—maybe the rain ruined their plans for the day, I thought. Well. This was it. I took a deep breath and answered the phone.

"Hello, Alton."

"I think—I think it's time," he said. "If you're ready, I can head over there now."

"That's fine," I said. "If that works best for you."

"You said room thirty-five, right?" he asked.

"That's right."

"Okay. We'll be there soon," he said, and he hung up. Davis loomed over me.

"Well? Is he on his way? Should I get ready?"

I opened my mouth, all prepared to tell Davis to get ready for whatever he was going to do because Alton would be here in a couple of minutes. But for some reason—maybe it was the gratitude I suddenly felt, of all things, this completely illogical gratitude toward Alton for bringing my own daughter back to me—I hesitated. He didn't have to do this. He could have gone ahead and taken her to wherever he was planning to go, and I never would have seen my sweet daughter again. But he didn't. Maybe, just maybe, that earned him some consideration here.

So instead I said, "No, he's not going to be here until after dinner. The rain screwed up their plans, and I guess they're all the way on the other side of town or something. So they're gonna go do whatever for the afternoon and he'll bring her over after they have dinner."

"And that was okay with you?"

"I figured," I said, "if we're gonna take all his money, it's really the least we can do," and at that Davis broke into a wide grin.

"See," he said. "This is why I love you, babe."

I smiled back at him, brushed his hand with my fingertips. "Look, since he's not going to be here for a while, I was wondering—"

"Uh-huh," he said, and leered at me.

"Not that," I said. "Would you mind going to pick up some lunch or something? I just realized I haven't eaten since dinner yesterday."

"Sure thing, babe," he said. "Any requests?"

"Whatever you bring back will be fine, I'm sure."

"Okay," he said, "back in a few," and he grabbed the car keys from the nightstand and left. That was the last time I saw him.

FORTY-SIX

Alton

The rain was starting to pick up, pelting my windshield with drops like sharp nails that broke into tiny shards on impact.

"We'll be there soon," I said into the phone, watching the door to room 35 of the Del Rio Inn at the same time. I'd been in the motel parking lot for the last ten minutes.

"It's really raining really hard," Clara said.

"Yes it is, honey." I turned the key and the car sputtered to life. I was going to drive right up to the building so that Clara could stay dry after she got out of the car and walked to Nicole's room by herself. There was no way I'd be going inside that hotel room. I didn't know what might be waiting for me there, and I wasn't going to find out.

And then, just as I was about to put the car into gear, the door to room 35 opened up. A man slipped out and scanned the lot, maybe just taking stock of the rain, but maybe—Wait a minute, I thought. I know that fucking guy. Jesus Christ. The car salesman. The goddamn car salesman is here.

What the hell is he doing here?

And then I knew. They were going to take my money. The money I worked so hard for, sacrificed so much for, the money that was meant to give everyone a fresh start in life, me, Nicole, Clara—she was going to steal it from me, steal it all, and she was going to use this empty-headed vessel to do it. There was no other reason for him to be here.

Well, I'd be damned if that was going to happen, and I'd be doubly damned if I was going to give Clara back to such a deceitful, lying, conniving excuse for a mother.

Montana it is, then. I yanked the steering wheel hard to the left and brought the Camry in a wide arc around the outside of the lot.

"Daddy," Clara said, her voice shot through with concern, "are we going to see Mommy now?"

"No," I said. "Mommy tricked us. She lied to us. She's not here after all."

"But you said," Clara started, and then began to cry.

"I guess Mommy doesn't want you to live with her anymore," I said. I struggled to control the car in the rain; its bald tires swerved on the slick blacktop. Then I looked up and saw that the hood was pointing directly at Davis Spaulding, who seemed to be having his own problems unlocking his car.

Without even thinking, I stomped my foot on the gas pedal. The tires spun lamely in the parking lot's shallow puddles before getting purchase on the asphalt, and then the car launched forward at the car salesman. He had only a fraction of a second to leap out of the way before we T-boned the rented Nissan. I threw the car into reverse, trying not to lose sight of the little worm scrambling away from me. I'd get him on the way back.

Clara was screaming in the backseat. "Daddy, we just had a car crash! Why did you do that?" I ignored her. I barely even heard her. Instead I lined up the Camry for another go at the car salesman, who was by now in open ground between the parking lot on one side and the motel on the other. Nowhere to go, I thought, and I gunned the accelerator again. Spaulding tried to dive to his right, back toward the parking lot, like he was timing it so that I wouldn't have time to adjust. But when he put his weight on his right leg and pushed off with his left, his footing gave out and he slipped, and there he was, sprawled out on the wet blacktop as the Camry bore down on him. He managed to get to his feet just as the car smashed into his leg and tossed him onto the roof of the car and then back onto the pavement.

I stepped on the brake pedal, but instead of stopping, the car fishtailed, spinning out of the parking lot and into the street where oh shit is that a bus or a—

The bus slammed into my trunk and spun the Camry around to face the opposite direction, dragging us along with it as it came to a stop. I was dazed, couldn't see, couldn't hear anything except my daughter screaming Daddy Daddy Daddy over and over again. There was something in my eyes; I smelled copper and realized I must be bleeding, must have hit my head on the steering wheel or something. And then I heard the sirens, slicing through my daughter's voice, and even through the thick fog in my head I knew they were police sirens, and they were wailing for me.

It was over. Everything lost. All of it for nothing. I was fucked.

But.

Wait.

The engine is still running.

How the hell was that even possible? I'd just been hit by a fucking bus, for Chrissakes. It spun the car completely around. How could any individual part of that Camry have still even been functional after a smashup like that? Let alone the engine.

But it was. And there was no point in asking myself how, or why, or anything else. It was a gift from the universe. All there was for me to do was accept it.

So I wiped the blood out of my eyes, pulled the steering wheel to the left, and put my foot on the gas. From the sound of the sirens, the cops were still a few blocks away when I turned right at the next corner, vanishing into the dark gray sheets of Texas rain.

<

FORTY-SEVEN
Nicole

I remember it seemed like he hung there in the air for a long time, like he was trying to break free of the Earth's gravity and almost, almost succeeding but not quite. It was like he refused to accept that he—his body, not him, just his body—had to fall back to Earth at all. It felt like it took a long time, maybe even over a minute.

Then the spell broke, and all at once the body of Davis Spaulding came crashing back to the asphalt of the parking lot in front of a dingy southeast Austin motel. I saw it. I heard it. I'll never forget it.

The sound of it was horrible, this loud wet and brittle sound, part snap and part slap, that could only be exactly what it was. I'd have known it instantly even if I hadn't actually seen it. But it still wasn't as bad as the sickening crunch sound of Alton's car slamming into him, tossing him into the air without any regard at all. That sound is something else about that day I will never forget. It haunts me, even now, all these months later. Sometimes it even wakes me up in the middle of the night. Not as much as it used to. But still sometimes.

FORTY-EIGHT
Alton

The rain just kept coming down harder with each passing minute, just sheets of needles raking across the landscape. That poor car. I'd put it through so much. I just hoped it would hold together long enough to get us, well, to wherever we were going now. I figured I could buy something else once we were out of immediate danger, something in better shape that could get us the rest of the way.

It was less than an hour after the bus accident and there was no denying it, we were lost, grinding out miles on a two-lane road that seemed to be going out of its way to avoid even brushing up against human civilization. With the storm and the adrenaline, I'd lost track of the turns I'd taken to get out of Austin, and by this point the only thing I could say for sure is that we were probably somewhere west of the city. The landscape was thick with heavy live oaks; the road rose and fell along the bulges of Texas Hill Country, pushing their way up from the bedrock and spilling out westward. And we were alone in it, completely alone, an insignificant metal box squeaking and clattering its way through the dark.

Clara hadn't spoken almost since the crash. Hadn't even made a sound. Every few minutes I checked on her in the rearview mirror, quickly, so she wouldn't notice if she happened to be looking. But she didn't move. Just stared out the window, her face shocked into a sort of slackness, a vacancy that scared me. No child's face should ever look like that.

Then the rain started to clear, just in time for Clara to spot a pair of golden arches in the distance, perched high upon a pole and glowing like a beacon of diabetes and heart disease.

"Daddy," she began. She sounded unsure of herself. "Can we please stop at McDonald's? Please?"

There's just no escaping it, is there? You just can't. Not if you have a kid. I pondered the odds that there weren't any McDonald's in Costa Rica.

"Yes," I said. "Fine. We can stop. Fine."

"Can I have chicken nuggets?"

"You can have chicken nuggets," I said, and sneaked another quick glance in the mirror. "But only if you take your finger out of your nose."

It wasn't late, but for some reason the McDonald's was mostly empty. The weather, probably. Only an old leathery cowboy and a rippling obese couple had braved the rain for dinner out tonight. The obese couple wore complementary Insane Clown Posse concert T-shirts.

"I don't give a fuck about none of that," she snapped at him. "It's all bullshit." She jabbed her index finger in the air, just a hair's width from his nose. He didn't flinch.

"Girl, come on now," he said. "Use your got-damn brain already."

I ordered a six-piece box of nuggets and a milk for Clara, and a large coffee for myself. We sat in a booth and I watched her eat, just picking apart that first processed chunk of some vaguely chickenlike substance. But she found her appetite by the time she got to the second one, and she popped the whole thing into her mouth.

"I have to go to the bathroom, Daddy," she announced after scarfing the fourth nugget of the box.

"Okay." I stood up.

"Noooooo," she said. "I wanna go by myself."

"Well, I wish you would have said so before I stood up," I said as she bounced past. "And wash your hands."

I watched her sprint to the back of the restaurant. But I didn't sit back down. I just stood there, watched Clara shove her way past the bathroom door, and waited for the door to completely close.

Waited to make sure nobody was watching me. To make sure nobody saw what I was about to do.

The obese couple were immersed in their conversation. The cashier's eyes were locked on her phone. The old cowboy looked asleep. Nobody was paying me the slightest bit of attention.

I started toward the exit.

I remember worrying about my speed. How fast I was moving toward the door. Too fast and you draw attention to yourself. People wonder what the hurry is. Too slow and you look suspicious, like you're trying to sneak into the night, unseen and unnoticed. Am I getting it right? No, no, it's all wrong. They all see right through me. Of course they do. They must.

Then I was there, at the way out, the door just inches in front of me. And all I had to do was open it.

My arm trembled as I lifted it, pushed the door open. I stepped outside and tendrils of humidity wrapped themselves around me, weighing me down. Was I really doing this? Each step took tremendous effort. My legs quivered with each one. I couldn't breathe.

It's better for her. Better for you. Better for everyone.

It is, though, isn't it? It's the best thing. In a couple hours she'll be back with her mother. She'll be fine. She'll have a normal, middle America, cul-de-sac childhood. She'll grow up happy, or at least thinking she's happy. She'll have everything she thinks she wants.

Then I was standing by the car.

Nobody called out. Nobody screamed. Nobody cried.

The night was silent, in that just-rained-for-three-hours kind of way. The low-frequency buzzing of the parking lot lights was the only sound.

Or maybe the buzzing was in my head. There was no way to know.

My fingers curled around the door handle. This is it, I thought. This is one of those moments that defines who you are. They come up, what, five or six times over the course of a lifetime? You spend your entire life trying to be something, or maybe just pretending to be something you hope you are, or maybe something you want people to think you are. And it's easy enough when there's nothing at stake, but sooner or later you have to decide whether you're going to walk the walk or not. What are you going to do, right now, in this moment? Who are you, I mean really who are you?

I took a breath and squeezed my hand. I felt the door latch click. And then I knew, I knew exactly who I was, who I'd always been, and I hated myself for it. But if I was being honest with myself, maybe I'd known it my whole life.

That's when I saw the lights, red and blue and flashing, reflecting off the window.

I let my hand fall to my side.

Then someone—several someones, I think—shouting something, overlapping voices washing over each other, words crashing into each other and shattering in my ears. There was a sudden flash of light inside my skull, my knees buckled, and then blackness. That's the last thing I remember.

FORTY-NINE
Nicole

And then Alton's car getting hit by that bus. It's funny, people told me that's what happened, and somehow it all sounds familiar to me. But I don't actually remember that part of it. I don't remember very much about the rest of that day, at least not clearly. I guess it's probably natural for a mother to repress the sight of a speeding city bus plowing into the car her baby girl is riding in. Or maybe my brain was just completely full up with traumatic memories of that day already. I mean, there's only so much room in there, you know?

And how does a man do that? I will never understand that. Abandon his own child at a McDonald's? Or any child? I can't even process it. The man I knew, the one I married, the one I loved for so long . . . well, that man would never do something like that. I don't know who this guy is. Maybe I never even did.

I didn't go see him at the hospital after. I went straight home instead. I knew I would have killed him myself if they'd left me alone with him. Injected him with something, maybe. Better yet, strangled him with my bare hands. Oh well. He could just rot in Texas for all I cared. I probably couldn't have gotten past the deputies anyway.

Every night he was in there, I wished for him to die before morning. I even started praying again. My mother was happy when I told her that, but I doubt she'd have approved of the fact that I came back to God because I wanted him to kill my husband and deliver unto me the insurance money I'd earned.

Then again, maybe she would. For all her faults, she's a pretty good judge of character.

257

I haven't talked to her for a while, though. Not since we moved up here. A clean break won't stick unless you break clean, you know? It's pretty nice here. Trees, mountains, nature. Clara likes it, and nobody recognizes me—or at least nobody's tacky enough to admit it if they do. Of course, the house isn't selling. Nobody's buying houses in Florida right now anyway, and nobody but weirdos wants to live in a crime scene. I imagine we'll end up losing it to the bank, which means I will just have to find some other way to pay all the goddamn lawyer bills.

Alton can pay his own, though. I hope for his sake he stashed some more cash away somewhere. And that he wasn't such a goddamn fool with that money too.

I should have seen what he was a long time ago. Empty. He is a disembodied mouth, a black bottomless pit of greed and narcissism. He loves himself so much that he wouldn't— he didn't—think twice about ruining my life, my daughter's life. His daughter's life. I swear, thinking about that, well, I can't let myself do it. I just want revenge, to ruin his life like he's ruined mine, to keep him from ever seeing his daughter again. But I can't do that to him because he's already done it to himself. He even stole my revenge from me. He got caught, and he stole my revenge away and gave it to the state of Texas and the federal government to bicker over instead.

Not blaming, though. Not blaming. I take full responsibility for my own choices.

So you asked me a question at the beginning of our sessions, all those weeks ago. But I want to know what you think. So why don't you tell me, Justine. Do you think I have an anger problem?

FIFTY

Alton

The first day or so after I woke up handcuffed to that hospital bed, that's still a blur. I was in and out for a while there; I guess I must have hit my head harder than I thought. Or, you know, the painkillers. Could have been them too, I guess. Either way, thinking about that first day now is like trying to remember a dream. Mostly what I remember is people's faces, people looming over me. I didn't recognize any of them except Nicole.

When my head cleared the next day I was surprised that she had been there. I was more surprised that she hadn't taken the opportunity to smother me with a pillow. I asked one of the nurses how long she had stayed and if she was still in the building.

"Nobody been here for you," the nurse said. She had brought a tray for me.

"Nobody?"

"Well, the police," she said. "They been waitin' on you to wake up. And the nurses and Dr. Cheng. That's it though."

"My wife?" My chest tightened, and I realized that I actually did want to see her.

The nurse pursed her lips. "Honey, I wouldn't hold my breath there."

I figured it out a few hours later. I saw a news story about my arrest on the TV mounted high along the opposite wall. The volume was off, so I have no idea what they were saying about me, but I recognized the footage of my boat right away. There was a shot of the smashed-up Camry in

259

the McDonald's parking lot. Then my driver's license photo, which was really unforgivable, because they'd had weeks
to get something better. Then a picture of Davis Spaulding.
And then Nicole, parrying the microphones thrust into her
face, elbowing through the thicket of cameramen as best she
could. I tried to guess where the footage had been shot, but I
didn't recognize the background at all. Probably somewhere
in Austin.

Then the story was over.

Davis Spaulding. I killed a man. I killed Davis Spaulding.
My lawyer made me promise not to say that to you. Under
no circumstances am I supposed to actually admit that out
loud, but you know, it's the truth. I did. I already told you the
story of how it happened, so I'm not sure what the point of
avoiding those four specific words could possibly be.

I didn't mean to kill him, though.

Well, maybe that's not exactly true. You don't try to run
someone over with your car unless you want to kill him. So I
guess I probably did mean to do it, at least in the moment.
Waking up handcuffed to a hospital bed makes a man take
stock of some things. What he's done. What he's capable of.
What he'll do to make up for those things.

Maybe that's what determines the true makeup of a man,
who he really is.

I wish I could have heard that news story, the one that
had put that image of Nicole into my drug-clouded subconscious. I knew it would be sensational—no, not sensational, exactly. More like sensationalistic. It would be very easy
to slap together a one-sided, hatchet-job-type story about a
greedy coward who abandoned his family and then put them
through hell just for a big payday.

But that's not me. That's not who I am.

You've been listening to me tell this story. You know
that's not how it was. But those producers, those parasites,
they haven't heard my story. They've heard Nicole's story.

They've heard the cops' story, the feds' story about me. They won't listen to me now. Why should they? They've got their narrative already, thanks to my backstabbing wife.

That's how it works. They settle on a storyline quickly, and then they run with it. Every new fact is squashed and molded to fit the storyline, whether it actually does or not. Anything I would tell them would contradict Nicole's version, the version they settled on, which would mean I must be lying.

I hope she makes a million bucks off this. And then I hope she fucking chokes on it.

I think . . . it may sound crazy, hell, it may be crazy, but I think Nicole will forgive me one day. I haven't spoken to her since I called her at the Del Rio that afternoon, so I haven't had the chance to tell her why I did what I did. Yes. What I did was wrong. I know this. Even though I did it for my family, for my daughter, it was still a crime. It was still wrong. I know this, okay? It turned a lot of people's lives upside down, at least for a little while. It was everything I was raised not to do. Someone even died because of me.

And you know what? I would do it again. In a heartbeat, honestly.

And I am sure that when the time comes for it, I will forgive her too. Forgiveness is in my nature. Almost to a fault.

But not yet. I can't yet.

I'm not ready. I need more time.

You know, I'm tired. I don't think I have anything more to say about this now.

Come back tomorrow. We can try again then.

ACKNOWLEDGEMENTS

Grechen Askins, Pricsilla Carver, Ken Eldridge, Amy Gawronski Zuccarro, Lynn Hurtak, and Jen O'Brian all delivered crucial early-stage critiques and notes, in which they identified the plot holes, awkward phrasing and uneven pacing issues that are the hallmark of early drafts, but that are often all but invisible to us authors.

Throughout the process, Ann Crossan Fleury, Brent Fleury, and Jen Hayes all offered unfailing encouragement and support, asking nothing in return.

Stephanie Hayes shared much advice and insight on how best to push this book out into the world.

And of course I cannot forget my parents, Robert and Ann Fleury, who worked so hard to teach me how to read and write in the first place. In the process, they instilled in me a persistent love of consuming and creating stories, which eventually led to the moment when you, the reader, first opened this novel.

Thanks to every one of you, and to anyone whose contributions I have inexcusably forgotten to mention. This book wouldn't exist without y'all.

ABOUT THE AUTHOR

Spencer Fleury has worked as a sailor, copywriter, economics professor, and record store clerk, among other disreputable professions. He was born in suburban Detroit, spent most of his life in Florida, and now lives in San Francisco. How I'm Spending My Afterlife is his first novel.

If you enjoyed this book, visit www.SpencerFleury.com to sign up for occasional email updates on future stories, books, and appearances by the author.